BRING FORTH YOUR DEAD

In darkness, a body is removed from a country cemetery: the body of a murdered man. It was apparent that Edmund Craven had been killed by one of those closest to him, and by a method both systematic and ruthless. The investigation represents a challenge for experienced Superintendent Lambert and his team. Never before had he investigated a murder perpetrated over a year earlier. Gradually he unearths a network of malice and deceit. Craven's son and daughter, his housekeeper and the American who was his friend for almost fifty years, all had reason to wish Craven dead – and the opportunity to kill him.

BRING FORTH YOUR DEAD

BRING FORTH YOUR DEAD

by

J. M. Gregson

Magna Large Print Books
Long Preston, North Yorkshire,
BD23 4ND, England.

British Library Cataloguing in Publication Data.

Gregson, J. M.
    Bring forth your dead.

    A catalogue record of this book is
    available from the British Library

    ISBN   0-7505-1957-6

First published in Great Britain in 1991 by
William Collins Sons & Co. Ltd.

Published in Large Print 2002 by arrangement with
J. M. Gregson, care of Juliet Burton Literary Agency

Magna Large Print is an imprint of Library Magna Books Ltd.

Printed and bound in Great Britain by
T.J. (International) Ltd., Cornwall, PL28 8RW

CHAPTER 1

They were subdued, all of them. Cast down by the place and the darkness. And perhaps by the weather, too: thin drizzle drifted through icy mist, as if the elements signalled their condemnation of what was happening.

They spoke in whispers, glancing behind them into the thick blackness in fear of discovery, keeping their torches resolutely hooded upon the ground where they trod. When they reached the place, the darkness was so thick that they trod upon each other's heels as they stopped; only the leaders of the uneven procession were aware that they had arrived.

While the two men with tools hammered in the poles and hung the arc lamps upon them, the others stood in uneasy silence, wondering what function they were to perform in the events to come. It was a relief when the lights were set up and connected to the batteries, so that the lower limbs of the bizarre tableau around the grave were suddenly and brilliantly illuminated. Instinctively, they moved a little closer to each other, as if the circle of amber light represented a protection against the spirits of the dead which lurked in the darkness around them.

As the two council workmen picked up their spades and set about their grisly assignment, the other four stood in pairs on either side of the grave, like parties opposing each other in this enterprise. Superintendent Lambert stood with the Coroner's Officer, Sergeant Jackson, their black shoes already liberally splashed with mud in the short journey from the cars.

The vicar who stood opposite them with the Coroner and the undertaker wore galoshes as a badge of his experience in this place: their wet rubber gleamed bright in the light of the lamps. Above them, he was all in black. Whether he had donned the cassock as a signal of his disapproval of what they were about or as a mark of formal respect to the corpse they were to disturb was not clear. His blackness seemed absolute; with the wide brim of his hat obscuring his face, he loomed on the edge of the grave like some mediæval visitant from a darker and more superstitious age.

He was flanked by two figures who stood still as statues as the spades rasped busily before them. The Coroner watched every move as closely and severely as a judge, conscious that he represented the law in this strange proceeding. The undertaker that the law required stood beside him, staring ahead with the outward calm his profession seemed to indicate, disguising the fact that this was the first exhumation he had ever been called upon to witness.

The workmen had been nervous at first, as if a consciousness of the irregularity of this business affected their physical movements. Their first diggings were jerky and puppet-like, so that small quantities of damp soil flew in unpredictable directions. Soon the rhythms of a familiar labour banished their nervousness; the pile of earth by the side of the grave grew steadily, the sounds of spades on soil and stone became more regular. Their silent audience watched and waited, each member trying to breathe evenly as the cavity grew in size and depth.

As the work went on, the first faint light crept into the scene: in this place, it had the effect at first of making the surroundings seem even more sinister. The mist drifted in thin, irregular swathes around them. The gravestones and monuments, gradually revealed in greater numbers and detail, stretched away like grim sentinels. A carved Victorian angel loomed suddenly unnaturally high from the greyness; for a moment, with the movement of the cloud, it seemed to bear down upon them like the figurehead of a ship. Slowly, the outline of the ancient church became visible, its tower appearing and disappearing with the density of the mist, as though in an early horror film. For everything in this dimness that passed for dawn was in shades of black and white.

Although it was what they had been waiting for, each participant in the macabre drama felt his blood chill with the sound of a spade scraping against the smoothness of polished oak. They glanced anew behind them to make sure they were not observed, as if they were modern Burkes and Hares instead of officials, sanctioned in their actions by the Home Secretary. With the noise, the two men digging began to work more cautiously, moving soil and gravel with a concern that was almost reverential as they gradually exposed the whole of the lid of the coffin.

Down there, five feet below the surface of the surrounding ground, Stygian darkness prevailed still over the grey December dawn. When the senior gravedigger stooped to brush the earth carefully from the chrome with his hand, the plate gleamed unnaturally bright in the gloom. Then the man shone a torch upon it, and Lambert read in letters that were still sharp EDMUND CRAVEN, AGED 73 YEARS. It was at least the right coffin: for an instant, *grand guignol* grotesqueries had flashed through his mind.

It took some time to lever the coffin from the grave. For here the expertise of the council diggers ceased; they had never before been called upon to retrieve a body they had committed to the earth. They struggled clumsily for a full ten minutes, their boots slipping on damp wood and mud, their tongues slipping into low obscenities of ecumenical frustration which the vicar sensibly left unheard. The Coroner's Officer, Sergeant Jackson, and the undertaker had to lend reluctant assistance before the coffin was set precariously upon the level which it had left thirteen months earlier. To the secret relief of all of them, they smelt no odour save that of fœtid earth.

The four men who had set down the coffin clustered round it, their breath snorting in long white funnels amid the universal greys. Then they coiled the ropes with which they had finally succeeded in extricating the coffin and gingerly took up their burden, trying hard to implement the directions of the undertaker, in deference to his expertise. Lambert, who had successfully counselled to himself the imperatives of age and rank against the impulse to leap Hamlet-like into the grave and offer his assistance, followed behind with the vicar and the Coroner. Perhaps it was the tardily increasing daylight and a growing familiarity with their charge that made the bearers of the coffin forget their initial reserve; it moved slowly towards the gates of the

11

churchyard to an accompaniment of muttered oaths and increasingly secular comment.

The lamps and torches were put out now, acknowledging a dim natural light which could scarcely be called day. There was no frost, but with the mist swirling still across the sodden ground, the porters slipped and slid and their charge rocked precariously. The coffin, which had covered this ground on the shoulders of four professionally steady and stone-faced men a little over a year ago, was removed in erratic and undignified fashion, by men only too anxious now to have this bizarre task concluded.

In life, Edmund Craven had never entered a Black Maria. Now his decaying mortal remains were stowed swiftly and without ceremony upon the floor of the police van. Lambert watched the vehicle move swiftly and quietly away. His too vivid imagination provoked speculation he had no wish to entertain upon the condition of the coffin's contents.

CHAPTER 2

Even three hours later, there was not a lot more light. Lambert decided this was going to be one of those depressing days when autumn deepened into winter and the days were scarcely more than intervals between nights. The thought did not improve his humour.

In his modern office there was no problem of illumination. The new CID centre had eliminated most of the obvious discomforts of the old one. Beneath the hard white fluorescent glow, he tried hard not to long illogically for the cramped and untidy room which long usage had hung about with nostalgia for him. Nor to lecture his immediate subordinate; the youthful and confident Detective-Inspector Rushton was an irritant as usual with his breezy certainties. Rushton was in court that morning; he was going through the motions of consulting his chief about a case he thought perfectly straightforward.

'We'll oppose bail, of course. Keep Charlie boy as uncomfortable as possible for as long as we can.' Perhaps Rushton took his Superintendent's silence for opposition, for he went on at length about the young ruffian who had been apprehended in the middle of an untidy mugging. 'Buggers should be birched, if you ask me – but no one will!' he concluded.

Lambert suppressed the unkindly thought that this was just as well. He knew better than most, for his experience was longer, that the invective was no more than a safety-valve for police frustration. Frustration against the twin enemies of a law which did not always seem designed to protect the innocent and slick defence counsels whose unashamed function was to protect the guilty with every resource at their command. He looked down at his own handwritten query on Rushton's typewritten report. 'You're still determined to go for GBH?' he said. Even in his own ears, it sounded like the criticism he had been trying to avoid.

'Should be open and shut, once we present the evidence,' said Rushton. Lambert thought the black mark he mentally awarded the younger man for this was fully justified. DIs should be beyond indulging in bravado, but Rushton's attitude represented little more than that. The woman had been dumped firmly on her backside in the shopping precinct and considerably shocked, but there was little evidence of damage on flesh that was plump enough to bruise quite readily. Lambert wanted this tearaway punished as harshly as the law permitted: for mugging the middle-aged and elderly was the most despicable of modern criminal developments. But if they went for too much, their quarry would slip through their fingers and they would get nothing.

But it wasn't his case: if there did not seem much evidence of violence around, that should be a decision for Rushton. He said mildly, 'The defence will say his father is in prison and the boy has been roaming the streets at night since he was twelve.' They could be safely united in their resentment of that.

'That won't matter. Nothing can excuse the way this scum has behaved. Surely they'll all see that.' Rushton was one of the few officers who did not look like a policeman when he was in plain clothes. Picking a tiny piece of cotton from his sleeve, he looked now like a dynamic sales manager about to enthuse his staff.

'One hopes so. No doubt our prosecuting counsel will express the sentiment to them in rather different words.' Lambert wondered why he usually seemed to be lecturing Rushton when they had these little exchanges. The man always seemed to rub him up the wrong way. For the first time ever, he wondered if the reverse might also be true.

Rushton had copies of the photographs of

the victim's bruises, which would be presented as evidence in court. The two of them studied them carefully, each wishing that they showed that their villain had done more than grip the woman roughly by the upper arm as he seized her bag. Eventually Rushton said reluctantly, 'We might have to be prepared to settle for robbery with the threat of violence. Should I have a word with our prosecutor beforehand?' He spoke as if he were making a concession to Lambert, not deferring to the evidence.

The Superintendent said no more than, 'I think it might be best. It would give him the chance to consult with his opposite number if he thinks it advisable.'

'Very well.' Rushton stood up. He had the air of a man giving way to a senior rank who has lost his nerve. When he went out, Lambert, who had tried to do no more than protect Rushton from himself, was left feeling irritated. He worked his way through the paperwork which normally bored him with an unusual gusto, glad to be free for a while of his subordinates and the problems they brought.

The phone call he had been waiting for came at just after eleven. 'John? You've made an old man very happy once again.' The pathologist relished dark deeds more than Dracula. Amid the hundreds of routine deaths the law required him to investigate, he looked to the CID, and Lambert in particular, to provide him with the drama he craved.

Lambert, who felt he knew what was coming, dropped into officialese to act as straight man for the bloodthirsty doctor. 'You think there is evidence of suspicious circumstances?'

'There is evidence, my dear Superintendent, of murder most foul.' Dr Burgess rolled the phrase with the sonorous delight of Hamlet's father coming from beyond the grave to announce such deeds. As, in a sense, he was, Lambert supposed.

'Good evidence?'

'Splendid evidence. Good enough to delight a policeman. Strong enough for me to swear to in a court of law. Get down here and I'll show you.' As usual, Burgess wanted to make the most of the revelations of science. And Lambert, watching twists of thin mist caress the roofs of the Sierras in the police car park, saw the November day brighten with a new interest.

'I'll be there in half an hour.'

When there is no wind in the Cotswolds, mist hangs all day in the winter valleys. Every rise of the road to the top of a slope seemed to take the car into real cloud, and Lambert drove the four miles with extreme caution. There was moisture everywhere. It covered his car, the hawthorn hedges on the lanes, the tiled roofs on the amber stone cottages. It weighed down the few dank roses which hung in the gardens as a remembrance of the departed summer. Yet Lambert sang, low and cheerful, relishing the privacy of the car. Not for the first time, he wondered about the psyche of a man who could be so cheered by the thought of a murder investigation. ''Tis no sin for a man to labour in his vocation,' he told himself firmly, as he invariably did on these occasions, ignoring the fact that the aging reprobate who had originated the phrase had been using the argument to justify armed robbery.

Burgess had acquired a new assistant since his last visit. He was a severe-looking young man, who wore his white coat like armour designed to keep an uninformed public at bay. He held a test-tube at arm's length against the light to examine it; Lambert did not care to speculate upon the nature of the red-black contents. He began to announce himself, but was saved from enlargement by the arrival of Burgess from his inner sanctum, where he had obviously been listening for the sound of his visitor's voice.

'Come and view the remains, Superintendent. You will find them of surpassing interest, I promise you.' He must have caught the disapproval of this unprofessional approach on his assistant's face, for he stopped

18

in full flight to make an introduction. 'This is Mr Webster, my new assistant. With a name like that, you would think he would revel in the gorier aspects of our trade, but he does not appear to.' To an uncomprehending Webster, who had scarcely heard of his Jacobean namesake, he intoned,

'I know death hath ten thousand several doors
'For men to take their exits.'

Then he swept Lambert from the scene, before he could even offer the ascetic Mr Webster the consolation of a sympathetic shrug.

Lambert had been bracing himself for confrontation with decomposing flesh. He remembered vividly previous occasions when Burgess had enlarged upon the peculiarities of kidneys and livers, which had quivered before him on stainless steel while his stomach had threatened to reveal its all too normal functioning. Mercifully, Burgess passed straight through the laboratory, which looked like an operating theatre, and went into his small office beyond. Lambert, studiously avoiding any contemplation of organs which had left this life thirteen months earlier, was fearful nevertheless of the odours which might assail him. He need not have worried: he fancied the all-pervading smell of formaldehyde was stronger than ever, but that was all his apprehensive nostrils caught.

The tiny room was almost filled by a desk and two filing cabinets, but there was just room for two swivel armchairs. Burgess gestured expansively towards the larger of these and sat down himself behind the desk.

'Murder, as you no doubt suspected. Do you know how?'

'I haven't even speculated on that.'

Burgess was not at all deflated by this world-weary approach to his melodramatic announcements. 'I can tell you. The late Edmund Craven was undoubtedly poisoned. Presumably by person or persons unknown. Or do you already have a culprit in mind?'

'None whatsoever.'

'Ah, you will be starting from scratch.' Cyril Burgess, grey eyes twinkling with mischief, seemed to find the idea wholly beguiling. *Cherchez la femme,* I suppose, Superintendent?'

For a moment Lambert was at a loss; then he understood the train of thought. He felt like an avuncular WEA lecturer as he said, 'The popular idea that poisoning is a woman's crime is very much an over-simplification. There are more men than women among convicted poisoners.'

'But the annals of crime also show that among female murderers, poisoners form

20

the greatest proportion.'

Lambert realised that a man as interested in violent death as Burgess would have read up on the subject. 'I'll bear that in mind, Cyril. Maybe I'll have a confession within twenty-four hours.'

'Oh, I do hope not, John. Not that I want to complicate your life, of course.' The pathologist's smile belied his words. Then he became suddenly brisk and professional. 'You'll want all the details for your file and the eventual court case, no doubt. Or will that sturdy English yeoman you trail behind you be collecting them later?'

'Someone will be along to collect exhibits and reports later. Quite possibly the admirable Sergeant Hook to whom I presume you refer.' Hook had made a good-humoured enemy of Burgess by confessing a contempt for golf, a game the doctor played erratically but enthusiastically. 'In the meantime, I have no doubt you can tell me what poison was involved.'

'Arsenic,' said Burgess with relish. 'None of your clever modern insecticides or ricin in this case. And in anticipation of your next question, no, there's no possibility that it was ingested accidentally by the victim. This murder was deliberate and systematic.'

'You can tell so much, even at this stage?' Lambert was aware that a little flattery could scarcely come amiss, but his curiosity was genuine.

'There is clear evidence of arsenic throughout what remains of the body.' Burgess pursed his lips and stood up, so that for a moment Lambert thought he was to be taken after all to see the grisly evidence. He tried not to think what a stomach would look like after over a year in the grave. Instead, the pathologist took a small polythene bag from the top of the filing cabinet and placed it carefully on the desk between them. Lambert did not touch it, but he examined it as carefully as a man offered an exploding cigar. It appeared to contain rather dirty grey fibres from an old sock. He said so, and Burgess was immensely gratified.

He picked up the polythene and looked at it fondly. It was his turn to lecture. 'That is human hair, John. Hair from the corpse of Edmund Craven. Hair is a tough and long-lasting material, being composed of keratin, the same protein that forms human fingernails. It is also a highly identifiable and highly revealing material.'

'And what does it reveal in this case?' Lambert was aware of playing the eager student to keep this exposition running, but he was also genuinely fascinated. In a long CID career, this was only his second poisoning.

'The examination of the organs of the

body showed us quickly enough that death had been promoted by arsenic. It is this hair which tells us much more about how that arsenic was administered. Arsenic is excreted from the body in the usual way, but also by means of the roots of the hair. As the hair lengthens, so arsenic grows out.' Burgess leaned back and studied the long-dead hair indulgently, like a man studying a favourite cat in repose. With his white coat cast aside, he looked in his immaculate navy suit like the consultant surgeon he might have been. 'What is in that bag is a kind of arsenic read-out. By applying a test called a Newton activation analysis, I can tell with certainty whether the poison was administered as a single large dose or in the form of several small doses over a period.'

'And what does this analysis tell you in this case?'

'Arsenic was administered in systematic small doses.'

'Over how long a period?'

'That is impossible to define with the precision that a court of law demands. But I would be prepared to swear to not less than six weeks and not more than twelve.'

For a few moments, Lambert found it difficult to take his eyes off the drab-looking package that had established the parameters of his murder investigation. He said slowly, 'Then someone planned this death in ad-

vance and murdered Craven quite cold-
bloodedly over a lengthy period.'

'With malice aforethought,' said Cyril
Burgess. He beamed delightedly.

CHAPTER 3

Even with Lambert's extensive experience, the murder of Edmund Craven represented a first. He had never before had to begin a murder investigation over a year after the victim's death.

After his surge of interest in the thought, the Superintendent decided it was a first he could well have done without. A murder discovered thirteen months too late, with the scents long gone dry, was not after all a challenge to be welcomed, as the dying year struggled towards Christmas and the warehouse break-ins accumulated.

The CID section looked to him to set up the machinery of detection, little realizing that many of the problems were as new to him as to the most junior detective-constable. Did they need a murder room as usual? Should they set up a scene of crime team, when all evidence of the crime had presumably long since been removed? Should murder take precedence as usual over lesser crimes, even though in this case it was an old murder? Lambert decided eventually that the answer was yes to all these questions, but he did so with a lack of

25

conviction, which he hoped was not obvious to his colleagues.

He spent the afternoon setting up this framework of investigation. He rang Craven's doctor and solicitor and made arrangements to see both of them on the morrow. He called the Detective-Sergeant Bert Hook, and was cheered by the boyish eagerness for the hunt evinced so incongruously by that rubicund village-bobby figure. When he went home that evening, eleven hours after he had presided over the exhumation of Edmund Craven's body, he had begun the process of finding out what kind of man the victim had been, the first necessity in all but the most straightforward of murder inquiries.

It was an altogether more acceptable late autumn morning when he turned the big Vauxhall into the spacious avenue where the late Edmund Craven had spent his last days. The front gardens here were long enough to have forest trees at their limits. The leaves had clung late through a mild autumn, so that even now the last ones drifted in a golden curtain against the soft morning sun, covering the unpaved road with a carpet that would be transformed to slime with the first hard frost. Lambert, easing the car reverently through the postcard scene, indulged himself with 'Thick as autumnal leaves in Vallombrosa'. Hook's assumption that he was quoting an advert for condensed milk was as straight-faced as ever: Lambert felt back in a world which he could understand, however much it was one of his own creation.

Tall Timbers, Craven's house, was a spacious Edwardian residence at the end of this opulent cul-de-sac. The detectives studied its ivy-clad elevations for a moment before they left the car, assessing the atmosphere, trying to feel what this place had to tell them about the man who had owned and controlled it for over thirty years. Sixteen hundred weeks, eleven thousand days, surely the place could offer some clues about the occupant and the manner of his death? Except, of course, that a murderer cool and ruthless enough to carry through a poisoning stretching over many of those weeks had had over a year to remove anything which might be even mildly helpful to them.

As if to echo that gloomy thought, there stood before them a tangible sign that the remaining connection of Edmund Craven with this place was about to be formally severed. An estate agent's board, with its bold red and white lettering standing out starkly against the blue background, contrasted sharply with the autumn shades all around. It proclaimed that this desirable site was now for sale.

Despite much folklore about policemen's feet, big men tread softly as a rule. But as Lambert and Hook walked carefully up the wide drive, their feet crunched on crisp gravel beneath the leaves, recalling the days of the house's infancy, when ponies and traps had moved briskly over this area to the stables at the rear. They pressed the ceramic bell push and heard the distant sound of the bell in the silent house.

Lambert realized afterwards that his expectations of housekeepers derived solely from a vividly remembered Mrs Danvers in *Rebecca*. The woman who opened the heavy oak door was no more than forty-five. She had ash-blond hair which owed nothing to a bottle, bright blue eyes, and features whose attractiveness was clouded by caution as she sized up the two large men on the wide stone step. She said firmly, 'I'm afraid viewing of the house is by appointment only; it says so clearly on the board.'

'We're police officers,' said Lambert. He fumbled for his warrant, but she said with a curt nod, 'You'd better come inside,' and turned to lead the way. So she had been expecting them. They had made no appointment to see her; he wondered who had spoken to her.

They passed through a high hall with a decorative plaster cornice. A blue stair-carpet ran away to the upper parts of the house beneath what looked like the original brass stair-rods. They gleamed brightly in the relative gloom of the north-facing hall, setting the note of care that ran through the house. The drawing-room to which she took them looked as if it was ready to receive guests. There was not a speck to be seen on the huge Turkish carpet, and the parquet gleamed brightly at its edges from much polishing. The huge leather armchairs received them as though eager to cosset their ample frames, the long velvet curtains were neatly held in their containing ropes. The room was generously heated. Lambert half-expected a genial host to appear and offer them sherry or coffee.

Instead the woman who had led them here perched herself on the edge of one of the big armchairs opposite them, as if to emphasize that she was here only on sufferance. She pulled the tweed skirt demurely over her knees and checked the buttoning of the green mohair cardigan over the immaculate white blouse. It was a gesture only: she was not the kind of woman who found herself with buttons undone.

'You are Mrs Margaret Lewis?' said Lambert. He had expected this opening exchange to take place on the doorstep; it was curious how its delay had thrown him momentarily out of his stride.

She nodded, then listened carefully as he introduced himself and Sergeant Hook. She crossed slim, nylon-clad ankles; he noticed leather shoes, with a heel high enough to be elegant without sacrificing comfort. She was clothed both fashionably and expensively. He wondered if she had dressed herself specifically for this meeting. He said, 'I see the house is for sale.'

It was not quite the conversational small-talk it appeared: he was looking for any sign of resentment in the blue eyes. He detected none. She said, 'Yes. It went on the market two months ago. Probate took time, but the planning permission took longer still.' She might have been a businesswoman explaining the situation to a naïve inquirer: there was no hint of bitterness at the prospect of losing the roof which had sheltered her for the last fourteen years. Yet all around them was evidence of her pride in this place.

He moved on with any attempt at briskness. 'Do you know why we are here, Mrs Lewis?'

'I know about the exhumation.' There was the first hint now of a tautness disturbing her composure, the first sign that her demeanour might just have been a carefully assumed disguise. But if she had liked her employer, as it was reasonable to project from her length of time in his service, the disturbance of that quiet grave would have

30

upset her a little anyway. And the deduction that any intelligent woman would make that his death had not been as straightforward as she had previously assumed would be more distressing still. It was time to turn the screw a little.

'I have to tell you now that the examination of the remains of Edmund Craven by medical experts reveals that he quite certainly did not die from natural causes.' The formal recitation enabled him to protract the inevitable announcement, to study his listener's reaction as it were in slow motion. He elicited nothing more here than a slow nod and a slight lift of the chin in anticipation. With the irritating lack of timing which makes the human brain a disconcerting instrument, he noticed at this moment that Margaret Lewis had a neck that was almost unlined and which offered no sign of the incipient double chin that her pleasantly curved form might have suggested in one of her years. He went on almost hastily, 'I have to tell you, indeed, that we are now at the beginning of a murder inquiry.'

There was, at last, a small involuntary gasp from the woman opposite him. Probably it was no more than the reaction which the first mention of that word always brought. Lambert said, 'The news is a surprise to you?'

She took her time before answering. Then she said coolly, 'No. I don't suppose it is.' For a moment, he thought she was not going to elaborate without further prompting. Then she said, 'I'd heard, you see, that there was to be an exhumation, so I presumed something serious was wrong.'

'Who told you about the exhumation?'

'Mr Craven's daughter, Angela Harrison, told me. Otherwise I should not have known.' The terse statement became an accusation.

'I'm sorry about that, Mrs Lewis. The regulations require that we inform only the next of kin about an exhumation when the permission comes through from the Home Secretary's Office. You would understand, I am sure, that it is in the interests of all that these things should be kept as private as possible until we know that there is a crime involved. If the death had been after all from natural causes, the fewer people who knew about the exhumation the better. I hope you see that.'

She nodded, almost impatiently, with the air of one who has already put these arguments to herself repeatedly. 'Apart from two weeks holiday a year when I was away from here, I saw Edmund Craven every day during the last thirteen years of his life. No one else could claim that.' Lambert noted that for the first time she had dropped the title;

his mind speculated for the instant before he controlled it on the possibilities of a sexual relationship between the personable Margaret Lewis and her elderly employer. There would be time enough for the investigation of such possibilities later. No doubt other people would be ready enough to tell him of any such liaison – it was always easier to collect salacious detail from those who observed than from those who were involved.

He said stiffly, 'We have to go by the rules, Mrs Lewis, even though we may sometimes feel privately that they do not operate fairly. Blood ties may not always be close, but they are usually all that the law recognizes.'

She gave him a small, grateful smile for the fact that he had bothered to explain, and said, 'I acknowledge that it must be so. The role of housekeeper may involve all manner of things, but it has few rights or privileges attached to it, once people have to reach for the rule books. I was – still am, I suppose – a paid employee. No doubt it is good for me to be reminded of that from time to time.'

Lambert chose to pick up the fact she had hinted at rather than the resentment. 'You are still paid to be here, Mrs Lewis?'

'I have been paid my full salary without a break since Mr Craven's death. I have stayed on in the house and made sure to the best of my ability that it has been kept in good order.' She gave an involuntary glance of pride around the comfortable room, caught Bert Hook's unblinking eye, and desisted immediately from such a weakness. 'The family have been most generous.' It was impossible to tell from her pronunciation of the word whether any irony was intended. 'I have tried to repay them by getting the house ready to sell.' This time he was sure there was a little bitterness in the simple statement: he stored the thought away for future clarification.

'You have lived here alone since the death of Edmund Craven?'

'Quite alone, Superintendent.' He wondered why she seemed anxious to assert this so definitely. He left a pause, hoping she would elaborate on her situation, but she said only, 'If this is going to take a little time, perhaps you would care for a cup of tea or coffee.'

To Hook's consternation, Lambert refused the offer, on the grounds that it was not long since breakfast and that they had a crowded schedule to observe. He was obscurely aware that this interview was causing her more concern than she cared to reveal; he did not want to break its thread here. Margaret Lewis said abruptly, 'How was Mr Craven killed?'

Lambert had expected the question, but not quite so quickly. Normally he would have withheld the information. But she would know soon enough: his decision to employ a scene of crime team meant that there would be police officers swarming all over the house later in the day, looking for any evidence of arsenic and where it might have been kept over a period of months. And he wanted to study her reaction to the news – if news it was, he reminded himself automatically.

'Edmund Craven was poisoned, Mrs Lewis. I'd be obliged if you'd keep that information to yourself for the time being.'

The clear blue eyes widened, the full lips parted a little. She looked at the tall man opposite her, wondering what was going on beneath the dark hair with its flecks of grey. Perched on the very edge of the big armchair, she looked even more as if she was in the room on sufferance. But there was no revelatory outburst of the kind Lambert had hoped for. Indeed, she said nothing for a long moment, during which Hook chose to heighten the tension by switching to a new page of his notebook for the information he knew from experience he would be recording in the next few minutes. Then she said, in a voice low enough for them to have to strain after it in the quiet room, 'Why wasn't this discovered at the time?'

'That, among other things, is what we shall have to find out in the course of our inquiries,' said Lambert, almost as quietly.

'Dr Carroll certified death was due to natural causes,' she said dully.

'I know. I shall be seeing him this afternoon. In the meantime, can you suggest any reason why he should have missed the real reason for death?'

There was a small shrug of the slim shoulders under the mohair. 'Edmund – Mr Craven – was a sick man. He'd had heart trouble for a number of years and been treated for it.'

'Did he have a pacemaker?'

'No. At the time, I thought that might have cost him his life. It had been discussed, you see, but he wasn't keen on the surgery.'

'When was it discussed? Can you remember?'

'I couldn't be certain; I think about six months before his death. Dr Carroll could tell you.'

'It wasn't raised again as his condition worsened?'

'Not that I'm aware of. He went downhill very rapidly at the end, you see.' Then her well-groomed hands suddenly clasped each other until the fingers shone white, and she said, 'Is that when–?'

Lambert let the unspoken horror hang between them for a moment, assessing the genuineness of her reaction, before he said, 'Yes. It seems that Mr Craven was poisoned systematically over a period of weeks or months, rather than with one fatal administration.' The formal jargon of the statement, which he had intended to mitigate its harshness, seemed to accentuate it. The listener, having to work out what the words meant in plain English, became more involved. It seemed a black parody of the subtle comedian who makes his audience work for their humour. He made a mental note of the technique he had applied unwittingly, so that he might use it deliberately on other occasions. It was no sin for a man to labour at his vocation, after all.

Margaret Lewis's face had turned quite grey. As usual in those with fair colouring, swiftly changing emotions were plainly revealed in the face. When she managed to speak, at the second attempt, it was only to say unhelpfully, 'It's a shock, you see.'

Lambert said with a sympathetic smile, 'It must be, of course.' Secretly, he wondered as he studied her reaction whether the shock was in the discovery that Craven had died like this or in the realization that the police now knew so much about a death that had almost escaped them. 'No doubt it helps to explain why the death was recorded as being a natural one at the time. That, of course, is exactly what the killer planned when he or she operated in this way.'

There was the kind of reaction he was expecting on his slightly stressed 'or she': a sudden flash of those wary blue eyes as they were raised to his, a shaft of something that might have been fear in them before they fell again. But that would be as natural in the innocent as the guilty. Or those who shared guilt: it occurred to him suddenly that if there were an accessory involved in this crime, as seemed more than usually likely, the housekeeper would be the most useful one to have.

He decided to press on towards the others who must have surrounded Edmund Craven in his last days, while this woman who must have known them all was still shaken. 'What Sergeant Hook and I are anxious to do at this stage, Mrs Lewis, is to compile a list of the people who were in regular contact with Mr Craven over the last months of his life.'

'A list of suspects, you mean?' It came from her like an accusation, but he had no intention of defending himself.

'If you like, yes. If you look at it another way, it is the first step in protecting the innocent. We often find ourselves proceeding by eliminating innocent people from the suspicion of a crime. I don't think I need to remind you that it is your duty to give us all the help you can in this respect: it would be most unwise to withhold information which we shall extract from other people in due course.'

Bert Hook, eyes committed firmly to the blank sheet in front of him, thought his chief was being unusually hard and formal with a woman who had given no sign of resisting their inquiries. Perhaps it was the perverse reaction to an attractive woman he thought to have seen in him before.

The housekeeper said dully, 'All of us had a motive, I suppose. You'll no doubt be interested in those.'

Lambert was suddenly at his most urbane and reassuring. 'They will perhaps emerge in due course. For the moment, I am more concerned with the simple facts of who had access to the deceased in the period before his death. It's no use pinning a huge motive on a person who had no opportunity to commit a crime. Now, what we need to know is exactly who was in regular contact with Mr Craven in the three months before his death.' Privately, he was already speculating about what she considered to be her own motive, but he preferred to delay such consideration until after his visits to doctor and solicitor later in the day.

She said bleakly, 'I've already told you that I was the only one who saw him every day.'

'And we've already recorded your name and your function, Mrs Lewis. We shall return to you in due course, I assure you. But unless you are going to offer us a confession to homicide, we had better begin a list of other possibilities. Perhaps I should tell you that our information is that a killer would not have needed to be in daily contact with the victim in this case. Once a week, perhaps even a little less than that, would have sufficed.'

She took a deep, contemplative breath and said reluctantly. 'There's the family, of course.' She spoke like one who assumed they were already intimately acquainted with the details of Craven's relatives. It was a reaction they were used to meeting; perhaps in this case it owed something to shock.

Hook, who was anxious to continue the list he had already surreptitiously begun with the housekeeper, said, 'Are we right in assuming that there is no Mrs Craven?'

'She has been dead for many years.' Was the obvious surprise which infused the statement that of an outraged mistress? Edmund Craven had been a quarter of a century older than this attractive woman, but policemen see too much of the world to be other than cynical about the attractions of money to those without easy access to it.

'But there are children?' This much Lambert already knew: the next of kin have to be informed when an exhumation is to be conducted. But he knew none of the detail of their access to the dead man. It would be interesting to learn how the housekeeper assessed their comings and goings. In due course he would ask the children themselves, probing for the divergences which were often the avenues to the truth in a murder inquiry.

'There are two children. Both married; both still living in the area.'

'And both on good terms with their father in his last days?'

Although Lambert prompted gently, they were all aware of the implications of the question in this context.

'Both of them loved their father.' It came so quickly that it was obvious she had already been asking herself these questions.

'And did both of them show this by visiting him regularly?'

'Yes. Angela came in every couple of days – probably almost every day as he weakened towards the end.' She stopped abruptly as she realized the possibilities she was opening up. Until this business was cleared up, every affectionate visit from family or friend would be clouded like this.

Lambert watched Hook compiling his record in his round, slow hand, his tongue poking from the corner of his mouth like that of a diligent small child. Then he said quietly, 'And Mr Craven's son?'

'David. He came in once a week. Still does. He pays me my wages, though he does that by cheque at the end of each month.'

Lambert thought he caught the faintest edge of hostility beneath the neutral statements, but he could not be sure. When she did not enlarge upon them, he said, 'Was this on the same day each week?'

'No. His business means that he travels about the country quite a lot.'

'That business being–?'

'David Craven runs what I believe is called a property company.' This time her distaste came out clearly in the phrase. He looked at her interrogatively, but she was too shrewd to be drawn further.

'But managed to come to this house at least once a week.'

She nodded. 'Probably a little more frequently than that as his father's condition worsened over the last few months.' It was said a little defiantly, as if she was pleased to be able to balance what she had said about Craven's daughter a moment earlier. But he had little doubt that her recollection was accurate.

Lambert said, 'Think carefully about this, Mrs Lewis, and if you can't be certain don't be afraid to say so. Was there any longer period – say, two or three weeks – when David Craven was not able to visit his father in those last months?'

It was an opportunity to give the son an alibi of sorts, and he thought she was intelligent enough to realize it. She thought carefully before she replied, as he had directed, but there was an air of satisfaction as her brow cleared and she said, 'No, I'm sure that there was nothing that kept him away for that length of time. In fact, I'm sure that in those last months a week would be the longest interval between any two of David's visits.'

Again the effect of murder was to invert the normal moral canons, so that what should have been a proper filial concern now laid a suspicion of the worst of evils upon the bereaved. Lambert saw Margaret Lewis's blue eyes watching as if hypnotized Hook's deliberate recording of these facts. To break the spell he said, 'And who else came regularly into the house in the months before Mr Craven died?'

She paused to think again. He thought what a good witness she would make in court: calm, intelligent, giving a proper attention to counsel's questions, not straying into irrelevancies in her replies. And it never came amiss in a good-looking woman to arrive smartly but not gaudily dressed. Eventually she said, 'Edmund did not have a hectic social life in the last years. Various friends came in to see him from time to time, but not as frequently as you are suggesting is significant.'

She stopped for a moment at the end of what sounded like a formal introduction to something of importance; probably that was what made both policemen aware that the real matter was yet to come. 'There was one visitor you will wish to add to your list, though I am quite sure he had nothing to do with the death. Walter Miller visited Edmund each week to play chess with him. They had known each other for almost fifty years, I think.'

'Mr Miller was a contemporary of Mr Craven's?'

'Indeed, yes. Sometimes I thought that was the chief thing they had in common. But you must understand that they had been friends for many years before I came on the scene.'

Her manner had become suddenly stiff and formal again, as it had been at the start of the interview. Her words about the mysterious Mr Miller had the ring of a prepared statement. He decided not to press her: this was the beginning of an investigation and it might be better to probe specific areas after he had seen Miller himself. Hook took details of the elderly man's full name and address, which she was able to give them from memory.

She gave them details of the medical visitors who come to the chronically sick: doctor, chiropodist and district nurse. It was the last of these who had set running the hare which had led them to the exhumation, when she had eventually reported to the pathology people at the hospital the suspicions of a poisoning that had nagged at her insomniac mind for months. Lambert had interviewed the district nurse before the exhumation. He had cleared her as a suspect: though she had had ample opportunity, it was obviously highly unlikely that she would wish to draw attention to a crime successfully completed had she been involved herself. She was an intelligent woman; it was a conversation with the pathology staff about another poisoning which had set her mind racing about the death of Edmund Craven. There was no sign that Margaret Lewis was aware of this as she watched Hook dutifully lengthening his list of those with access to the deceased.

Lambert said, 'Was there anyone else, Mrs Lewis, who came regularly into the house in the period which concerns us?'

'No. Not that I can remember. It's over a year ago now, you know.' She was suddenly defensive. They waited for her to elaborate, but she looked resolutely down at those elegant shoes and said nothing. This time Lambert was sure that she was concealing something, but equally sure that she would not be drawn into admission at this moment if he pressed her.

'All right, Mrs Lewis.' She looked up at him quickly, and gave herself away in the relief which flashed briefly across her face. She had expected to be questioned harder; that only convinced him that she had been determined to reveal nothing more. 'Thank you for helping us to begin compiling our list of facts. We shall be back, of course, as the investigation develops and we become more interested in certain areas.' It sounded like the threat he realized he had half-intended. 'In the meantime, if you remember anything else that you think might be of interest to us, please contact us immediately.'

She stood up quickly then, and saw them to the door, as no doubt she had seen thousands of other visitors over fourteen years. She was polite but relaxed; they wondered how far her relief was a perfectly normal reaction to the end of an interview with a Superintendent pursuing a homicide inquiry.

Margaret Lewis watched the big Vauxhall all the way to the end of the avenue before she shut the heavy oak door and went back into the big, silent house. She looked at the telephone for a full minute before she picked it up. When the young man's voice answered her, she did not trouble to introduce herself.

She took a long breath and said only, 'The police have just left here. They know now that Edmund was murdered. You'd better keep away.'

46

CHAPTER 4

There are not many deaths like that of Edmund Craven, where a poisoner so nearly gets away with murder. When they do occur, the first person to fall under suspicion is the patient's doctor. In a few cases, he may be the deliberate agent of death: he is the person in the best position to administer poison without detection. In other, fortunately even fewer, cases, he may be an accessory after the fact, deliberately concealing evidence to protect someone, usually a lover. The law has dealt harshly with the small number of medical men known to have gone astray in this way – there are few women doctors who have been detected in such actions. Equality will no doubt in time bring its inevitable side-effects, here as elsewhere.

In a much larger proportion of these cases, it is possible to detect a degree of negligence in medical practice, where the doctor in question has failed to spot that death did not occur from the natural causes he specified and signed for on the death certificate. Such omissions are not always publicized, medical men being more than usually charitable towards their fellow practitioners. All professions are conspiracies against the laity, Lambert reminded Hook, as the big car moved smoothly towards the house of Dr Carroll; he was sure Bert would have been a wholehearted supporter of Shaw's Fabianism had he been given the opportunity.

Carroll lived in a box-like modern house with a trim front garden, modest and characterless after the Edwardian confidence of Craven's house, but no doubt much more convenient to live in and to run. Mrs Carroll, who was at the door before they had time to ring, was as trim and well-organized as her house. It was still quite early in the afternoon, but she brought in the tea-tray without asking if they required it, to Bert Hook's undisguised approval. Then, having poured the tea, she left them alone with her husband.

Dr James Carroll was scarcely the best advert for the efficacy of his own profession. He was probably not more than two years older than his wife, but he looked ten and behaved more. His hand shook as he offered them the cups and saucers, so that Hook sprang forward to take over the duty. His wife had fussed over him maternally in arranging the seating arrangements; where her movements had been those of an alert and active senior citizen, her husband's had the careful but uncontrolled energy of the aging arthritic. Having manœuvred himself carefully into position over his armchair, he began a slow descent, which was transformed into a collapse in its latter stages. Despite the sun outside and the central heating within, his voice had the wheezing hint of bronchitis when he spoke, and his breathing was shallow and quick.

He said, 'I believe you told my wife when you made the appointment that you were inquiring into the death of my old friend Edmund Craven.' His fingers twisted nervously in and out of the bottom buttonhole of his cardigan. Lambert was reminded of those occasions long ago when he had sat as a young constable at the bedside of hospital patients, with only a brief period allowed to him to extract statements from them. It was perhaps that image that made him determined to be brisk here.

'It is now established that Mr Craven was murdered, Dr Carroll.'

'And I signed a death certificate to say that death was from natural causes. That is, of course, the purpose of your visit here.' He gave them a small, grim smile over his rimless spectacles, as if to remind them that the brain could remain sharp when the body declined. 'May I ask what is the cause of death you have now established?'

'He was poisoned with arsenic. Systematically, by small but regular doses over a period.'

Carroll's rheumy, old man's eyes widened; Lambert thought it was with surprise rather than horror at the thought: medical men, like policemen, saw plenty of the viler things of which humanity is capable. 'So your murderer is someone who had regular access to the deceased. It seems scarcely credible, but of course I have to accept what you now tell me.'

Lambert was irritated by Carroll's refusal to confirm his own deficiencies in the business. He said, 'Can you tell me what medical condition you were treating in Edmund Craven?'

'Have I any excuse for slipping up as I did, you mean?' Carroll had the air of childish irresponsibility Lambert had met before only in the very old, who seem to become aware in their last days that life and its rule-makers have very few sanctions left with which to punish their transgressions. Carroll was not much over seventy, but perhaps he did not have much longer to live. 'Edmund had had a serious heart attack ten years before he died. He had two more minor flutters about three years before the end. He had quite a bit of pain with angina pectoris and took tablets for that. I attended him regularly, about once a month in the year before he died. It wasn't really necessary, but he was a rich man and seemed to enjoy the sense of being pampered that he got from my visits. And I had the time to indulge him: I've been retired, apart from a few private patients, for the last six years.'

'Did you notice any marked deterioration in the last few months of this patient's life?' It sounded like a criticism of his carelessness, but Lambert saw no point in treading carefully with a man who seemed to be almost enjoying the examination, as if it were a puzzle worthy of his professional attention.

'Yes. Over about the last three months. I can be so precise since I have naturally given the matter some thought since I heard about the exhumation.' The damp grey eyes pleaded their case to be taken seriously. 'I imagine you are going to tell me that it was during that time that Craven was being poisoned.'

Lambert nodded. 'So Dr Burgess informs us. Apparently he could tell this from an examination of the corpse's hair.'

'Good man, Burgess. That would be the Newton activation analysis.' With this unexpected piece of technical knowledge, the old doctor's face twinkled like that of a mischievous schoolboy giving hitherto unsuspected evidence of preparation. 'Well, Inspector, I suppose I should apologize for my shortcomings.' He seemed to be so evidently enjoying himself that Lambert wondered if his own demotion was deliberate rather than the accidental slip he was used to. 'But really, unless one was suspicious of what I believe you call foul play, there was honestly not much reason to apply other tests. The pattern of decline accelerated rapidly, but that is not so unusual when a man with a medical history like his gets over seventy.'

Carroll paused, studying the bookcase behind the busily writing Sergeant with an ironic smile as he confronted his own mortality head on. 'The symptoms of a heart which is ceasing to function properly are not very different from those of arsenic poisoning. Perhaps if I had thought of that at the time, I might have become suspicious, but I doubt it. Of course, as soon as the hospital contacted me to ask about the death, I could see the possibilities of arsenic. But you see, I've never seen anyone die from deliberate poisoning before. Perhaps, in view of your visit here this afternoon, I should say not to my knowledge at least.' It was the nearest he would come to an apology or an admission of carelessness; even here, his bitterness seemed rather against a dishonest world that presumed to deceive him rather than at his own omissions.

'You were the only doctor involved?'

'Yes, to my present regret. There was no

legal requirement for a post-mortem because I had been in regular attendance: I saw Edmund three days before his death. And I am sure you are aware that with a burial, only one doctor's signature is needed on the death certificate. The modern trend for cremation is a splendid thing: it brings extra income to chaps like us from the second signature required before you can burn a corpse.' His levity seemed quite incorrigible, though he looked tired now. He had forgotten all about his tea, which was almost cold as he found it belatedly beside him. He spilled a little of it in the saucer; then his face creased with distaste as he sipped the tepid liquid. The contrast between his crisp speech and the aging shell from which it emerged was more marked than ever.

'So you never considered the possibility that there might be more than a damaged heart involved in Craven's rapid decline?' Lambert pressed because he was anxious to know if Carroll had even suspected otherwise, but he was aware also that he was piqued by the man's cheerful abnegation of all responsibility; surely he should have at least shown a decent sense of guilt.

'Never, Inspector. Perhaps I should reiterate that the symptoms of decline stemming from a malfunctioning heart are not dissimilar to those of arsenic poisoning, when that is conducted over a period of time. And arsenic eventually causes heart failure. Technically, I think you would find that what I entered on the certificate as the cause of death was correct.' He leaned back in the chair and hugged himself at the thought, his tea finally abandoned. His shrunken figure was shaken for an instant with unseemly mirth.

Lambert realized that he would get no further with this line of questioning. He said, 'Dr Carroll, you were in regular attendance upon a patient we now know to have been systematically murdered over a period of months. As an outsider entering each week into that household, you may have become aware of undercurrents of feeling. I should like to know if you noted any incident or relationship which might now seem significant. Think carefully, please. Those with regular access to Mr Craven's food – which means once a week or thereabouts – appear to be Mrs Lewis, his housekeeper, his daughter Angela Harrison, his son David Craven, and his old friend Walter Miller, who went in to play chess with him once a week.'

'There are other methods of disguising arsenic than food, of course. For instance, you could inject a solution directly into the bloodstream. However, let us agree for the moment that food is the most likely method of ingestion.' Carroll's pedantry was such that for a moment Lambert had the unworthy desire to shake the frail old shoulders. Yet he knew that he was annoyed less by the old man's omission than by his failure to show a seemly remorse: had he been properly cowed, he might have met a Superintendent full of sympathy. Lambert forced a smile at himself as the doctor went on, 'Well, the person with the best opportunity was me.' He cackled outright at the ridiculous thought; Lambert's experience told him not to dismiss it so lightly. He would investigate the possibilities of the idea in due course, though he fancied that here motive, which he had dismissed so lightly when questioning Margaret Lewis, might be important by its very absence.

James Carroll was studying him intently, with his head on one side, like a child who teases a small animal and awaits a reaction. Lambert and Hook stared back at him stolidly, refusing to feed him further material. Denied such stimulus, Carroll lost his intensity and suddenly looked very tired. He said petulantly, 'Any of the people you mention could have done it, in theory. Assuming one of them did, you'd better keep your eye on young David Craven.'

They got nothing more out of the enigmatic Dr Carroll. If there was anything more than a personal preference in him for David Craven as a murderer, they failed to elicit it. Twenty minutes later they stood outside the original Georgian windows of the offices of Arkwright and Company, Solicitors, in the middle of Oldford, and Lambert contemplated the prospect of another interview with a professional man without enthusiasm.

Alfred Arkwright gave the impression that his firm had been here as long as the wool on which the original wealth of the Cotswold town had been built, instead of the mere two hundred years which were the fact. He received Lambert and Hook at the appointed time with the air of an aristocrat doing trade an immense favour in granting it an audience. 'Sit down, please,' he said, waving a lordly arm at the only two chairs available in his small office, as though inviting them to select from hundreds. 'I am at your service. Just let me know how I can be of assistance.' He knew perfectly well, of course: Hook had explained things painstakingly in arranging this visit. But the forms – Alfred Arkwright's forms – must be observed.

Lambert, who had long considered Arkwright his ideal Polonius, very nearly demanded more matter with less art. Instead, he had to content himself with stressing his opening phrase as he said, 'As you know, we are here in connection with the death thirteen months ago of a certain Edmund Craven.' He noticed himself being drawn into Arkwright's formalities of language; the solicitor tapped a perfectly manicured finger on the file in front of him and permitted himself a deprecating smile of acknowledgment. 'Perhaps you would also like to be told officially that we are now in the early stages of a murder inquiry. Which makes Mr Craven's legal arrangements of special interest to us.' Arkwright nodded an urbane acknowledgment of the inevitable centrality of the law in all important concerns of men. 'It will therefore be necessary that you reveal to us not merely legal documents, but everything you know about his thoughts in the last year or so of his life.'

Alfred Arkwright's brow contracted for a moment beneath the line of his still plentiful silver hair at the crudity of this approach. 'There is little I can tell you that has not already been made public. As you know, the peculiarities of the law compel us to reveal the details of wills to the fourth estate. When there is an absence of violent crimes or scandal in the locality, which surprisingly enough is still the case in some weeks, our local press fills its columns with the raw detail of the estates of people who can no longer defend their privacy. The details of Edmund Craven's arrangements appeared there some time ago.'

'So remind me of them, please,' said Lambert. He had dealt with Arkwright before; it was like a complex eighteenth-century dance in which each knew the conclusion, but had to go through the elaborate steps to arrive there. Lambert's brisk injunction here broke the sequence: as if in response. Arkwright rose unhurriedly from his chair and left the office with a muttered excuse. '"Thou wretched, rash, intruding fool, farewell,"' intoned Lambert moodily as the solicitor passed from earshot. He knew he was indulging himself: Arkwright was unfortunately neither wretched nor rash. When Hook gave him the required interrogative look, he said, 'Don't worry, he gets stabbed through the arras in the fourth act.'

'How very painful,' said Bert. 'Still, I do think a bit of police brutality is called for in cases like this.' He made an elaborate mime out of his preparations to write as Arkwright came back with a thin cardboard file.

'I have here details of all our correspondence with Edmund Craven. The will, as a legal document, is kept in our strongroom: I had already extracted it in preparation for your visit. It was returned here by Mr Craven's daughter after probate arrangements had been completed.'

'Angela Harrison was named in the will as executor?'

'Indeed, yes.' There was no need to aplogize to Arkwright for surprise at a female being thus entrusted: his tone announced that he found it most surprising and probably ill-advised. So much so that for once he did not need prompting to say, 'The son is the elder child by several years; I pointed out to Craven that this would be the more usual person to name as executor, but he was adamant that Angela should be so named. It is unusual, but by no means unique in these times.' His tone indicated that it was one more proof of decadence in the times in question.

'Do you know of any reason why David Craven should be excluded from the duties of executor?'

'None whatsoever. As I say, I commented to Craven at the time that it seemed unusual to exclude his only son, but he merely confirmed what he had already instructed me to do in writing. Perhaps we should not read too much into it: the will itself shows no bias against David. Rather the reverse, as things have turned out.'

'Meaning?' said Lambert. He was suddenly tired of observing the forms Arkwright seemed to require of him.

The solicitor looked professional surprise over his gold-rimmed glasses. It was a gesture he often practised and rather enjoyed. Lambert thought suddenly that he could be only a few years younger than Dr Carroll; yet the solicitor seemed at this moment unchanging and immortal, as though invested with such qualities by long service in a profession that deplored change. Arkwright said heavily, 'I understand that young Mr Craven has obtained planning permission for the site of Tall Timbers. The old house is apparently to be demolished and a block of flats erected in its place. No doubt it is now being sold for a considerable amount.'

Lambert suspected that Arkwright knew exactly how much that considerable amount was, but he did not offer him the satisfaction of the series of questions which would be necessary to reveal it. The fact was enough for the moment: it provided room for considerable detective thought. He said after a pause, 'We need the details of the will, Mr Arkwright.'

'That is fairly straightforward, but I prefer not to rely on memory,' he opened the will and adjusted his glasses. 'Craven was a rich man, even by today's standards. His estate was eventually valued for probate purposes at nine hundred and forty-two thousand pounds.' He looked from Lambert to Sergeant Hook in search of a reaction. Lambert was proud of Bert's determined inscrutability, which could not have come easily to a Barnardo's boy. 'The main beneficiaries, as you might expect, were David Craven and Angela Harrison. They received items to the value of approximately four hundred thousand pounds each, if we take the value agreed by the probate office. David received the house, plus an insurance policy realizing just over a hundred thousand; Angela was left shares and bonds worth the full four hundred thousand.'

'Was there a reason for dividing the inheritance in this way?'

'Edmund Craven originally thought in terms of leaving the house jointly between his children, with the rest of his money after other bequests divided equally between the two. Angela was worried about the joint bequest of the house, and I had to advise that leaving a house jointly can cause difficulties where one partner wishes to sell and the other one to retain the property. Edmund Craven saw the point immediately. I think he hoped that his son would move into Tall Timbers after his death: he was fond of the house, I believe.'

'David, however, chose not to implement his father's wish in this. Was it a surprise when he did not do so?'

Lambert did not expect an answer to such a speculative sally. But it produced an unexpected effect. For a moment the gossip that lay somewhere deep within Alfred Arkwright's polished legal shell struggled with the reticence his professional image demanded. His profession won, of course, as it always would within his chambers. He said, 'You will no doubt be seeing David Craven in the course of your inquiries. You will form your own impression of his character and actions then, I am sure.' But for a moment the corners of his mouth had crinkled with distaste. Plainly, like Dr Carroll, he did not like the surviving Mr Craven. In his present irritation, Lambert found it hard not to account that a mark in the young man's favour.

'All parties were happy with this arrangement, though, at the time when the will was made?'

'Superintendent, you must understand that it is my duty to execute the wishes of my client, not to make sure that other parties are happy or otherwise with the details.' Arkwright smiled at Lambert's naïvety and adjusted the lapels of a suit that was impeccably cut in the fashion of a previous decade. 'But I gathered from Edmund Craven at the time that the will seemed to accord with the wishes of the main beneficiaries.'

Lambert sighed: it took a long time to extract a yes. 'Would you please list the other provisions of the will for us as succinctly as possible?'

Perhaps Arkwright noticed Lambert's

patience wearing thin; more likely even he was beginning to tire of the game of circumlocutions. He glanced at his watch and looked surprised, indicating that his next appointment was now pressing and the policemen were taking up far too much of his valuable time. 'The only other bequest of any substance was to Mrs Margaret Lewis. She was left a cottage in Burnham-on-Sea, and ten thousand pounds. Mr Craven had owned the cottage for thirty-six years; in his younger days, I believe the family used it as a holiday home. Mrs Craven was alive then, of course.'

'When did she die, Mr Arkwright?'

'About fourteen years ago.'

'So that means that Mrs Lewis was his housekeeper for about thirteen years.'

'Yes. A little less, I think. I believe there were two previous incumbents who held the post for short periods without giving satisfaction.' If Alfred Arkwright was aware that his phrasing was open to any but the most straightforward of interpretations, he gave no sign as his eyes studied the file in front of him, which Lambert was sure did not contain this information.

'What was the probate value of the cottage?'

'Exactly one hundred thousand pounds. It had been well maintained and modernized by Craven over the years, though it was leased on long lets in later times.' So Margaret Lewis was right when she said that all those close to the dead man had motives. Bert Hook, recording the value of her bequest carefully, reflected that he had known several people who had killed for much less than this.

Arkwright must have been genuinely conscious of the passing minutes: he went on without further prompting. 'There were bequests of ten thousand pounds to the local Anglican church, St Gabriel's and five thousand pounds to a nephew in Australia, whom I understand Mr Craven had not seen for thirty years. Finally Mr Craven left a thousand pounds and his small collection of Second World War memorabilia to Walter John Miller, whom he calls "my old friend of many years with whom I have shared so much".' Arkwright closed the will with the air of finality that he had perfected over the years to remind his clients of their mortality.

It seemed straightforward enough. Lambert, looking in the document for clues about the actions of those it named, reminded himself that omissions could sometimes be as significant as bequests. 'Were there any grandchildren?'

'Not at the time this will was made. Angela now has two children, but David remains without issue.' Arkwright rolled off the legal phrase with the air of a man who has concluded a routine voyage with a safe berthing.

'And when was this will made?'

Arkwright reopened the document reluctantly at the first page. 'It was signed and attested exactly nine years and three months ago today.' He stared across the desk expectantly.

Suddenly, Lambert knew exactly the question that was now required of him. And this time he offered it readily, trying not to reveal the first moment of real excitement he had felt in the case. 'Is there any possibility that Craven was planning to change the provisions?'

Arkwright had been fed his cue. He leaned slightly forward, so that he could steeple his spotless fingers with his elbows upon the desk. 'We do not advise changes and codicils to wills: they can cause great confusion. It is far better to make a completely new will. That is what I advised and what Edmund Craven said he proposed to do. But after he had indicated this intention, he never came back to me, and it would have been unprofessional of me to press him upon it. I should point out, perhaps, that I had no idea that his condition was worsening: his death came as a shock to me.'

Lambert said slowly, 'This is very important, as I think you appreciate. Have you any idea at all of what kind of change in his arrangements Mr Craven was proposing to make.'

'Regrettably, Superintendent, none whatsoever.'

'Did he tell you whether other people knew about his proposed changes?'

'No, Superintendent. It would be unusual, though, if he had not talked to the interested parties about them.'

Lambert sensed the answer to his last question even as he framed it. 'When did Craven indicate to you that he proposed to make a new will?

Arkwright looked him full in the eyes for the first time in their exchanges. 'I have a note here of the date of our phone conversation. It took place four months before his death.'

CHAPTER 5

David Craven watched the two dark shapes on the other side of the frosted glass as he spoke into the telephone. 'Surely another month now would be in everyone's interest? I can certainly now assure you that–' His face hardened at the interruption from the other end of the line. 'If we're talking about credit ratings, you're obviously not up to date. I suggest you make sure of your facts in that respect before we talk any further!'

Behind the glass, the shapes were following the smaller and lighter one of his secretary towards his door. He banged the phone roughly back into its cradle and pulled on the wide smile of greeting which felt daily more like a rubber mask. As the door opened and the shapes became people, he rose and moved to the side of his desk.

'Ah, Superintendent. Welcome to the humble centre of our activities. Do come and sit down. Tea, June, I think. And perhaps the odd custard cream.'

Lambert introduced Bert Hook and saw from the corner of his eye the Sergeant making his usual elaborate opening mime with his notebook. His main attention was on David Craven, who was working hard to seem at ease. There was nothing odd about that: almost everyone who is drawn into a murder inquiry feels a need to demonstrate his or her innocence. As they usually regard the adoption of a carefree manner as integral to this, and as very few of them are trained actors, the impression left is usually of ineffective artifice. That was certainly the case here.

David Craven was tall, as tall as Lambert, with a tanned face and iron grey hair. In his lightweight grey suit, white shirt and dark red tie, he was what romantic fiction would describe as 'distinguished'. Lambert thought that from the photographs he had seen of the dead man he might have looked much like this thirty years or so ago; his preliminary researches told him that the son was now forty-six. Craven's smile spread into a general affability as the introductions were completed and he retired behind the modern desk with its panelled leather top and executive trimmings. Only the dark blue eyes failed to catch the smile: they were cool and wary, as though run by a different motor from the one which painted the smile and drove the movements of the hands.

Lambert wondered whether the wariness was for them alone, or whether it was habitual in the man. He said, 'Sergeant Hook explained the reason for our visit when he made this appointment, so I won't waste time with preliminaries.'

Craven said, 'I knew about the exhumation, of course. The Coroner informed me, as next of kin. I must say I was shocked that it should be necessary.'

He had the air of a man who had prepared these comments and was determined to deliver them, despite the Superintendent's attempt at directness. Lambert said, 'In view of that, I should tell you at once that we are now engaged upon a full-scale murder inquiry. We have already contacted your father's doctor and solicitor. That is routine practice in these cases.' Lambert wondered wryly if Craven knew how little this was a routine case for him.

'I suppose there can be no doubt that it was murder? It seems quite incredible to me.'

Again Lambert had the impression of a man determined to go over ground that he had prepared, presumably in the hope that this would be a preliminary step to controlling the path of the whole interview. It was reaction to that thought which made him say abruptly, 'these cases.' Lambert wondered wryly if Craven knew how little this was a routine case for him.

Craven gasped, whether at the news itself or at the sharpness of its delivery it was impossible to tell. Both detectives studied him openly for a moment. He could be an affectionate only son distressed by the news that his father had been brutally despatched, or a murderer who knew all this and more and had to simulate his innocence. Eventually he said, 'You saw Mrs Lewis too, I believe.' It was a tiny attempt to retain the initiative, by reminding them that he knew about actions they had not so far revealed to him. Lambert liked nettling his witnesses; it caused them to reveal things they might otherwise have concealed. In this case, that Craven was in touch with Margaret Lewis, or some third party who knew them both. Collusion, always likely when death was contrived over a protracted period, seemed more than ever a possibility.

'We did indeed. Even after so long a period, one likes to begin at the scene of the crime.'

'And no doubt the splendid Margaret gave you her estimation of the possibilities of all the suspects.' Perhaps he was rattled by Lambert's cool resilience: he was giving away far more than he thought.

The Superintendent raised his eyebrows a little and decided to stonewall. 'Mrs Lewis assisted us in compiling a list of those close to your father in his last months. As they were the people with the most obvious opportunities to administer poison, I wouldn't dispute your description of them as suspects.'

Craven wanted to know what she had said about them, and presumably in particular about him. He would not know that she had neither offered nor been pressed for opinions about the people she had mentioned. Craven drummed his fingers on the desk and said, 'Not a great admirer of yours truly, the admirable Mrs Lewis. I thought she had too much influence over Dad, and said so. Someone had to.' So no one else had felt so strongly; it began to look as though the housekeeper had been rather charitable in her reticence about her employer's son. Lambert remembered her faint air of satisfaction when she had been unable to give David Craven an alibi. While he deliberately refused to react to this comment about Mrs Lewis, the Superintendent considered a second interview with her with renewed interest.

He said, 'I understand you inherited your father's house.'

Craven laughed, bitterly and theatrically. 'I expect she gave you the full benefit of her views on that. Well, all I'm doing is taking advantage of circumstances. Dad isn't here any more, unfortunately, and what he would have wanted is no more than sentimental supposition. We live in today's world and no one pays you a single quid for sentiment. That site is worth far more for development than as a single house, and even toffee-nosed Margaret knows it.'

Lambert let him run on with the indignant clichés until they petered out. Then he said, 'Actually, Mrs Lewis said nothing about this. Our sole source of information was your father's solicitor. He gave us all the details of the will, as the law requires him to do. If you know Mr Arkwright, you will hardly need me to tell you that he made no comment on the ethics of the development of the site.'

Craven was left looking rather crestfallen. Foolishly, he tried to justify himself. 'That's just what it is: development. Progress. People in Oldford don't understand that. Most of them think it's a sin to make a profit.'

That seemed extremely unlikely in an area where the Conservative MP held a huge majority, but Lambert forbore to say so. It was Bert Hook, predictably irritated by Craven's public school manner and capitalist blusterings, who said unexpectedly, 'There is profit in the development then, sir?'

It was spoken with the air of peaceful naïvety which Hook managed very well, and it took Craven completely by surprise. He had been concentrating on Lambert; he looked now to the Superintendent for support in checking this impertinent underling. Lambert not only did not rebuke his

Sergeant, but waited impassively for a reaction. Craven said roughly, 'I don't see that what I make on Tall Timbers is any business of yours.'

Hook spoke even more quietly this time. 'No, sir. Except, you see, that a large financial gain provides an excellent motive for murder.'

Craven flushed so deeply that his tan suddenly looked artificial. He said, 'This is ridiculous. I invite you here to be as helpful as I can in a situation I naturally find distressing, and within ten minutes I'm being accused of murdering my own father! I want a lawyer before this goes any further.'

Lambert's voice cut through the air of the overheated room like cold steel. 'First of all, Mr Craven, you did not invite us here. We made an appointment in pursuance of a murder inquiry. Secondly, no one has accused you of anything, let alone murder. Sergeant Hook replied to a comment of yours about the irrelevance of wealth with the observation that it frequently provides a motive for murder. That is a fact that is manifest in crime statistics throughout Europe. If you wish to be questioned in the presence of a lawyer, that can be arranged. I should prefer that we conduct what I must stress are preliminary inquiries in a more informal atmosphere, if that is possible.'

Craven was saved from an impulsive

reaction by the arrival of the tea. The young secretary deposited the tray and bustled out again as quickly as she could; perhaps she was used to her employer's conferences coming to an abrupt halt when she entered. As the door shut behind her, Lambert said, 'We are now familiar, as I indicated, with the full terms of the will. Have you any comment you would like to make on those terms?'

It was an irregular question, but he was already sure that Craven was not going to carry his threats through into any formal complaint. He looked up defiantly and said, 'No. Why should I? I saw the potential of the site as you would expect me to do–'

'Forgive me interrupting, Mr Craven, but people usually assume we know far more than we do, I find. Are you an architect?'

Lambert was back to his silkiest tone. Craven looked at him suspiciously before he said, 'I am an architect by training, yes. I realized a few years ago that there was far more money in property development than in drawing plans.' His attitude made Lambert wonder where he had argued thus before. With his father perhaps? Or his sister? And what had the reception been then? 'Everyone was happy with the will when it was made. When Dad eventually died, I considered the possibilities of the site. I am a businessman, Superintendent, and I could see immediately that if we could get permission for flats, Tall Timbers would have to go.'

'I see. I appreciate that this would imply no legal condition, and indeed that you may not wish to answer, but I would remind you that anything which would throw light on the attitudes of others close to your father is bound to be of interest to us. Can you tell us if your actions have caused resentment among the other legatees?'

Craven did not explode into rage, but looked at him carefully before he answered. 'None of them like it, I'm sure. I think they all assumed as Dad did that I'd be making Tall Timbers my own home. That would not have been possible in any case.' For a moment Lambert thought he was going to enlarge upon this, but he thought better of it and went on, 'Once we got planning permission, there was no decision to make. Much as I had always liked Tall Timbers, there was no question of me moving in. The old place had to come down.'

'I suppose Mrs Lewis had always expected to move out after your father's death?'

Craven smiled at the thought. 'I cannot think that Margaret would expect to stay on with the house in my ownership, whatever the circumstances. It must have been quite a windfall for her to be there this long – at her old wages, too.'

'Presumably, though, you thought Mrs Lewis could offer you a useful service by being in residence.'

'I wasn't merely being charitable to Margaret, if that's what you mean. I don't suppose she'd have accepted the situation if she'd thought that. There is a lot of valuable stuff in Tall Timbers and it suited me to have the house occupied while we were applying for planning. Now that it's being sold with planning permission for the flats, that's less important, but I'm happy to have someone on the spot to make sure nothing disappears from the place. I can afford it; the asking price for the site is one million pounds.'

There was silence at this revelation. Craven looked quite pleased, as though this was the proper homage journeymen should pay to great wealth. Then Bert Hook said, 'When did you first explore the possibility of building flats on the site, Mr Craven?'

Craven's blue eyes flashed a look at the Sergeant which demanded to know whether the question was as innocent as his tone. He discovered nothing, for Hook's attention was determinedly on his notebook; the poised ball-pen left the murder victim's son in no doubt that his replies would be recorded. Craven took his time, giving his attention to the manner rather than the substance of his reply. He stood and walked over to the bookcase on the other side of the room, fingering a heavy marble statue on top of it.

He contrived to sound unruffled as he said, 'Oh, I couldn't be precise, but these things certainly take time. The local authority's Planning Officer has to report. If the application is turned down at the Planning Committee meeting, or even held in suspension until the whole Committee has a look at the site, one has to go back in the queue and wait for another meeting. Patience is not only a virtue but a requisite when dealing with planning applications.' His delivery became smoother as he moved towards a well-worn theme and sentiments he had delivered many times before to clients. 'Of course, it pays to know one's way around and whom one is dealing with–'

'Quite,' said Lambert. 'And when did the whole process begin in this case?'

'Well, as I say, it takes a long time. I didn't wait for probate to be granted before I began the process, I seem to remember.' It sounded evasive, even in his own ears: he felt himself a victim of a pincer movement by these calm, experienced men.

Hook, without even looking up, said, 'I think it was in fact much earlier than that, Mr Craven.' The Sergeant found himself using the technique of slow revelation he found effective when he caught the young tearaways of the district in a lie. This time he positively enjoyed watching his forty-six-year-old victim squirm.

Craven said, 'Perhaps it was. I could check my files if you think it's important, but–'

'It could be very important, Mr Craven.' Lambert looked him boldly in the eye when he interrupted, studying his reactions without any attempt at concealment. 'But you needn't bother with your files. Our information is that the Planning Committee received your preliminary application for outline planning permission over eighteen months ago.'

Beyond several walls, a phone rang, faint and unanswered, its note clearly audible here because the comfortable office was so unnaturally silent. Hook thought of the noisy ebullience of their reception, while they waited for a reaction from the man who had thought to deceive them. They had caught him out, in what might be no more than a rather shameful commercial contrivance, but they would behave as though it were crucial to their investigation, in case the man by his reaction proved it to be so. They had trapped him by one of the few facts they had been able to check before they came here, and he had closed the trap himself by his shoddy attempts at evasion.

All this the three of them knew and weighed, while the silence hung unbroken for a long moment. When Craven eventually spoke, he stared fixedly at the top of his desk; he might have been one of those adolescents Bert Hook grilled in the tiny CID interview rooms, who stared at the scratched table which separated them from their tormentor as they lost all their surface arrogance and confessed their tawdry misdemeanours. 'I needed the money. The property slump caught us rather overstretched. There seemed no harm in making preliminary inquiries...' His words petered out and he made a small, hopeless gesture of the hands. For an instant as he turned them upwards, they seemed like those of a black man, so strong was the contrast between the deep brown of the backs and the pallor of the palms.

The fish was landed now. Hook admired as he had done so many times before the skill with which Lambert gutted it. With an admission made, the Superintendent became understanding, almost conciliatory: the trick, he knew, was to keep the man talking, rather than recalcitrant or dumb with shame. As long as he communicated, they might learn more yet. 'Obviously, Mr Craven, you understand the significance of the timing for us, just as we can appreciate the importance for you of checking out planning possibilities at that particular moment. The importance for us stems from the fact I have indicated, that it was about eighteen months ago or a little later that one or more persons began to implement plans to kill your father. What we have now to determine is whether those two events might be connected.'

'I don't think they are,' Craven still did not look up. His words carried no certainty: they had the automatic, illogical defiance of an adolescent losing an argument.

'They may not be. It is part of our business to seek connections between facts. The solutions to murder inquiries normally emerge when we find the connections which bear on the particular death. Working as we are in this case so long after the murder, it is more than usually difficult to unearth those facts which are likely to be significant.' He spoke like a tutor taking an undergraduate through an intricate point of theory. 'Who else in the group of people around your father knew that you were exploring the possibilities of the site of Tall Timbers?'

Now at last Craven looked up. It was a quick, fearful glance into his questioner's eyes, where he discovered nothing. He had no idea how much Lambert knew; having been caught out once, he opted for honesty. 'I didn't tell them, but they found out.'

'All of them?'

'Yes. Planning applications are published in the small print of the local rag. I don't know who told whom, but someone spotted it and told the others.'

'And it wasn't popular?'

Craven gave a smile in which there was no mirth. 'That's an understatement. When I came into the house for my weekly visit, all hell broke loose around me.'

'What was your father's reaction?'

'Does that really matter? The old man's dead; can't we let him rest in peace?' The ludicrousness of that conventional sentiment in the face of an exhumation struck him too late; he signified with a small, hopeless shrug of the shoulders that his rhetoric needed no answer. 'Dad hated the idea that I wouldn't take over Tall Timbers when he was gone, though I think he knew enough to suspect I never would. The thought that it might actually be demolished to make way for new building hadn't even occurred to him. He took it badly.'

In his misery, David Craven felt a need to explain, when he might have been better to say no more. 'Dad came from humble origins. His father was a professional cricketer – like H.G. Wells's father,' he added inconsequentially. 'I believe Grandad, who was dead before I was born, played with Jack Hobbs and Frank Woolley.' For a moment, Bert Hook, a sterling club seamer himself for many a year, saw David Craven as a boy on the playing fields of some Greyfriars replica, pleading for a little vicarious glory among his peers, recounting this accident of antecedence which surfaced even now as he strove for sympathy. 'He worked hard to educate Dad as a surveyor. Dad grew up in a terraced Victorian cottage in Bristol: his mother took in washing when times were hard during the winter. To him, Tall Timbers was a proof that he had made it in life, a guarantee of prosperity. He lived in the house long enough to grow to love it; he couldn't understand that his son should not feel that way about it.'

'So he was annoyed.' Lambert pulled him gently back to the present. 'Did he threaten to do anything about his annoyance?'

'What do you mean?'

'Our information from Alfred Arkwright is that he planned to change his will.'

'He did. And not in my favour. Under the terms of the new will, I believe Tall Timbers would no longer have come to me.'

It was so open an admission, and the speaker looked so wretched, that it sounded for a moment like the prelude to a full confession. But Craven said no more. He had about him now the sort of relief that sits eventually upon people who have been discovered in deceit and forced to abandon it.

If he was indeed guilty of that ancient, primitive horror, the murder of a father by his firstborn son, they were not going to hear it from his own lips.

CHAPTER 6

It was a relief to leave Craven's office and the raw red building which held it. It was not a persuasive advertisement for the architecture of the nineteen-nineties, being essentially a large brick box with a series of identical smaller boxes within it. Unless the sun illuminated its south face, it was difficult to know from the outside which side of the building confronted you; within it, only memory could determine for you which floor you were on. The net effect was to make you long for the ornamental excesses of those other and naughtier 'nineties of a hundred years earlier. Lambert and Hook breathed deeply of the warm autumn air, looking with unconscious relief towards the beeches the planners had decreed should be left standing at the edge of the car park to preside over two thousand square metres of tarmac.

'Do you think he did it?' said Lambert when they were safely cocooned in the Vauxhall.

'He couldn't have. His grandfather was a county cricketer,' said Bert Hook resolutely.

'You think the genes are that strong? It's a

long time ago.'

Bert, having set up his chief, launched into the only verse he had ever willingly learnt by heart:

> For the field is full of shades as I near the
> shadowy coast,
> And a ghostly batsman plays to the
> bowling of a ghost,
> And I look through my tears on a
> soundless-clapping host,
> As the run-stealers flicker to and fro, to
> and fro: –
> O my Hornby and my Barlow long ago!

'Written when even Jack Hobbs was a young lad. Somehow, I doubt whether in these insensitive times even clear documentary evidence of a grandfather at Lord's would be accepted as irrefutable proof of innocence. Still, this is at least proof of sensitivity in my Sergeant, which I shall release to the tabloids in its full glory when the next bent copper hits the headlines.'

He was cheerful as he shaded his eyes against the sun. The case was beginning to acquire shape: a more appealing shape than he had anticipated it showing at this stage. He reserved judgment yet on whether David Craven was their murderer, but he had told them much – even more than he realized he had. It promised to be an intriguing case, and at this moment he had no doubt that he would meet its challenge. He hummed a little as he shaded his eyes against the low sun, which at this time of the day gilded even the most mundane Cotswold buildings with a brief glory. He had at that moment nothing but satisfaction in the thought of locking someone away for life.

It was well after five o'clock when they parked outside Oldford's National Westminster Bank. Bank staff do not depart for home when the doors close to the public at half past three, as many uncharitable citizens still fondly believe, but at this hour only the manager was waiting to receive them. Privacy of this kind is an encouragement towards confidences; bank managers even more than solicitors choose sometimes to regard their customers' secrets as though they were those of the confessional. But on this occasion there could be no reticence; this like other barricades must fall to murder.

George Taylor, the manager, knew it. He had given them difficulties on other occasions, even in cases of suspected fraud, but he had his records waiting for them now. Sober and a little nervous, he showed the frisson of excitement which contact with even the periphery of a murder inquiry brought to the honest citizen. 'Both Craven's children bank with us,' he said. 'So does Walter Miller, though I can't see the relevance of his account to your investigation.'

'Neither do I,' at the moment,' said Lambert patiently. He had almost forgotten about Edmund Craven's old friend. 'It may be that none of the accounts will throw up anything of great interest to us. But we are assembling all the facts we can in the early stages of an inquiry, and the financial ones may well be important. Don't underestimate your importance in the world, George: it grows all the time.' Lambert knew they were going through the preliminaries of salving Taylor's conscience about the disclosure of information about his clients: his reluctance was no more than a banker's Pavlovian reaction, but Lambert would play out the little ritual if it did not take too long.

He played golf occasionally with George Taylor: it was one of the benefits of a small community that one had a passing or better acquaintance with many of the people one met in the course of duty. It led to a kind of trust, never mentioned and rarely betrayed. And as Oldford was not big enough to support more than two banks, he could get what DI Rushton called the financial profile of three of his four present suspects from Taylor. Unless Margaret Lewis confined herself to a building society, she would be with Barclay's across the road; he had already set Rushton to check what he anticipated would be her unexceptional financial profile.

Taylor said, 'If you're agreeable, we'll dispense with Walter Miller first, since I don't think you'll find much of interest there.' He was right: the account could hardly have been more unexceptional. They looked carefully at the months before and after the murder of Edmund Craven in the hope of finding large deposits or payments. There was nothing to excite them; it was a routine chart of a well-organized retirement, with the inflow of a small war pension and a larger insurance company pension, and the outgoings of community charges, water, electricity and telephone. They could even identify clearly the deposit of exactly one thousand pounds in the week after Craven's will was admitted to probate. Miller's small legacy had been neither urgently required nor quickly spent. Lambert had to remind himself that a careful murderer would present himself exactly thus; it would not do to dismiss from all consideration a man they had still to see on the morrow. There are other reasons for murder as well as avarice.

'Angela Harrison,' Taylor announced as he turned to his next file. After a moment's hesitation, Bert Hook wrote the name carefully at the top of a new page: he had forgotten the married name of Edmund

Craven's daughter. George Taylor was able to help them with the interpretation of a file that at first sight looked as unexceptional as Miller's. In his anxiety to help, to become even for a little while involved in the hunt for a murderer, he forgot all the scruples which normally guided his actions. Perhaps it flattered him that he was able to display his professional expertise in guiding them so easily through the maze of figures and pointing out the things which should intrigue them. 'The interesting thing overall is what a modest account this is before Angela's father died.' He did a few swift calculations from the pages of computer print-out. 'Until less than a year ago – to be precise, until Edmund Craven's will was admitted to probate – the Harrisons were living on nine thousand a year or thereabouts. Not much, these days, for a family of four. They went carefully, as they had to; sometimes they were just in the red at the end of a month, but never for very long.'

Lambert considered this picture of genteel, respectable poverty, fascinated that pictures of a family he had never seen could be so vividly presented by a few pages of dull-looking figures. 'What happens after she collects her legacy?'

'Nothing very dramatic, but more is spent, as you might expect. There was a fairly modest holiday abroad this year: the payment was made in one instalment in June. Expenditure generally shows a considerable rise, but only from the very low base we were talking about just now. Most of Angela's four hundred thousand pound legacy went into unit trusts and bonds; she came in to ask for advice as soon as the money was paid in to her account.'

Lambert thought of the relief years ago when he became an Inspector and they celebrated by buying shoes for all their three children at once. 'Edmund Craven made no direct provision for his grandchildren in the will. Was he not fond of them?'

'That I wouldn't know, John. Our dealings with the whole family have been entirely financial, and usually conducted at a distance. Edmund could have supported his grandchildren while he was alive, of course. Small disbursements wouldn't show up in the account. But none of the Cravens came in to see me much – except David, of course, as things grew worse.'

Lambert saw Hook look up involuntarily from his notes. He had not pressed David Craven on the details of this, since he knew he was coming straight on here. 'George, I must tell you in confidence that the detail of David's financial position two years to eighteen months ago might be quite vital to our inquiry.'

Taylor shrugged. 'There is not too much

to tell. Most bank managers could recount similar stories to you. David Craven saw some of the big boys in the City making fortunes from property. In the two years before 1988 even small builders were making a killing: the housing market was rising so fast that they were often able to add thirty thousand to the selling price on which they had costed by the time the houses were finished. One of our customers is now a millionaire on the strength of a single estate of twenty-eight houses he built and sold in that period. David Craven saw what was going on more clearly than most, as an architect. He decided to become a developer and land speculator himself.'

Bert Hook, who had not liked Craven, expected to be told of some dramatic dissipation or corruption when he asked, 'But the situation you describe sounds like a licence to print money for those in on it. How did Craven come unstuck?'

Taylor smiled the wry smile of a man who has seen much of the follies of men. 'As with any investment, timing is vital. Craven bought land at the high prices of 1988, much of it with borrowed money. Then he ran into the property slump of the years which followed. In those circumstances, the big national builders sit on their land banks and wait for things to recover. Building land has been a good investment ever since 1945, but not always as immediately as most people think. Craven's land wasn't always well-chosen: he tended to gamble on planning permission, which wasn't always forthcoming as people in the Cotswolds became more sensitive about conservation and more hostile to second homes. Anyway, he didn't have time to wait: he was operating on borrowed money and interest rates kept rising. As things got worse, he made investments that were more and more speculative, more and more dependent on the rapid recovery of the property market that did not materialize.'

Lambert nodded. The police saw plenty of the mentality involved, though the degree of disaster varied widely. The transition from investor to speculator to gambler could be very rapid, as most followers of the turf who thought they had found a system could testify. 'The important thing for us is the timing. Can you tell us what Craven's situation was about eighteen months ago?'

Taylor flicked open the file. 'In a word, desperate. His creditors were closing in. I got permission from head office to extend his overdraft, but only for a few months at most.' He paused. He was a humane man, whatever disgruntled loan-applicants might think, and he had never been in this situation before. 'I – I feel as though I'm slipping the noose around someone's neck!' he said.

Lambert smiled; he felt like a doctor applying his bedside manner. 'Unless that's just a metaphor, it's a bit out of date, you know. In any case, what you're going to tell us is probably circumstantial evidence, though it's a popular myth that no one is ever convicted on that alone. But certainly any conviction will not be made solely upon what you are about to tell us; we shall need to prepare a much fuller case before we even charge someone.'

Thus reassured, Taylor licked his lips and said quietly, 'Things came to a head about three months later. I had him in to see me in August with an ultimatum from head office. He wasn't even meeting the interest on his loans.'

He pushed across a copy of the letter he had signed himself to summon Craven to a meeting. It was no more than three sentences of terse, impersonal prose. Lambert took note only of the date: August 27th, six weeks before Edmund Craven's death. 'What happened at that meeting, George?'

Taylor took a deep breath in an unsuccessful attempt to steady his voice. 'I put the situation clearly before him. Things were out of my hands now. Unless he could reduce his overdraft substantially in the next two weeks, he would be facing bankruptcy proceedings. He told me, as he had told me before, that he had substantial expectations

92

from his father's will. I was a little impatient, I think, because I had heard the story before and he did not seem to appreciate the urgency of the situation. I told him it might be true, but it was an uncertain, long-term situation which was no solution to his present problems.'

'And what did he say to that?' Lambert would not have spoken if Taylor had not dried up again. He felt his question toll like a bell; felt that he knew what must be coming as the conclusion of this tale.

Taylor said, 'He told me that there would not be long to wait. That his father was dying. That he would be dead within weeks.'

CHAPTER 7

It is a myth beloved of the public that a murderer feels a compulsion to return to the scene of the crime. Life would be much easier for policemen if the myth were true. Occasionally, of course, criminals revisit the scene of their offence, but it is usually for some real purpose rather than from a psychological compulsion.

The killer of Edmund Craven saw such a reason to be present in Tall Timbers two days after the murder had finally been revealed for what it was. The killer moved about the house with lights on; there was no need to disguise a presence for which there was a ready explanation. Homicide had brought its own mistaken confidence, that peculiar feeling of superiority to the rest of humanity, which is often one of its bizarre concomitants. Better to be bold here than to slink about like a guilty thing.

There was no fear in going into the room where the old man had fought his last, doomed battle for breath. The murderer stood for a long moment contemplating the bed where the victim had died and been laid out, testing for the onset of remorse, feeling satisfaction when none came.

An executioner, then, who had done no more than despatch an old man who had grossly offended irrefutable moral canons. The executioner moved with relish through the familiar rooms, opening drawers unhurriedly, searching only to confirm that no copy of the document existed.

Having dwelt for a while in the room where David Craven had visited his father and Walter Miller had played his weekly game of chess with his old acquaintance, the killer passed unhurriedly through the rooms which had been used at the time of Craven's mortal illness by Margaret Lewis and Angela Harrison. What had to be done was done efficiently and unhurriedly.

That the crime had been identified as murder after all this time was a nuisance, no more. It necessitated certain precautions, for now that Edmund Craven's death was known to be not from natural causes, a culprit must be found. The exhumation had seemed a nuisance, even a threat.

Now it seemed no more than a new challenge, which would be overcome.

CHAPTER 8

'Caroline should get the results of her tests today.' Christine pushed the breakfast mug of tea determinedly between her husband and the cricket scores.

'Tests?' Lambert was aware that he was on dangerous ground, but unable to force his mind away from its professional pre-occupation. If even Gower's century had not registered there, there was small hope for his daughter's affairs. But it did not do to point out such things to a wife.

Christine regarded him with humorous irritation. Years ago, her annoyance would have been real, her resentment of his work and his concentration upon it bitter. Now she said with a resignedness that was near to affection, 'You've forgotten, haven't you? Already.'

Just too late for him to deny the accusation, it came back to him. 'Would I ever? You mean the pregnancy tests. You think she'll hear today?' He hadn't organized his thoughts enough to know what he wanted the outcome to be. He was not sure he was ready to be a grandfather yet, though he saw many of his contemporaries as perfectly suited to the role. He thought of Caroline upon his knee, earnestly watching a television serial at Sunday tea-time. So recently, it seemed. Could that happy child be now about to embark upon the long campaigns of parenthood?

'She'll give us a ring tonight, I'm sure, if there's any news. I'm off to set up my classroom for my thirty-four little darlings. Just remember you're a policeman and lock the doors, John. The French window was unlocked again when I came in yesterday.'

Lambert's carelessness about security was a running joke in the family. He watched Christine reverse expertly out of the garage and through the gates, pondering upon his family and the stretching of it into another generation.

Then the questions surrounding that other family, the Cravens, thrust themselves back into his thinking in a way that was all too familiar. He began to check through in his mind the timetable he had set himself for the day.

Outside its network of small towns, the Cotswolds can be a quiet place in November. There are few winter tourists; by nine-thirty the rural workers have long been at work and the office staff have poured sleepily into their various centres. The lanes which trace their way through the low hills and wooded valleys are then almost deserted.

It was unusual at that time of day to see two cars arrive almost simultaneously on one of the most remote of these roads, an ancient highway which had carried the precious woolpacks which made first the monks and then the merchants of this area into mediæval capitalists. A narrow road between hawthorn hedges, winding its way between the boundaries of farms which had guarded their independence jealously for centuries. The first car, a BMW, turned carefully off the lane into the cobbled area by a disused barn. Made superfluous by the spread of oil-seed rape over the English countryside in the 'eighties, the building would no doubt become a desirable residence for someone with no connection with the land when in due course it became a 'conversion' in the 'nineties. For the present, it made an ideal place for a meeting the participants wished to conceal. An aging Ford Cortina, arriving from the opposite direction, turned off the lane to join the BMW within two minutes.

An observer might have presumed a lovers' meeting. And indeed, the man who emerged from the first car and the woman from the second were obviously familiar with each other. Though they were muffled against the cold of a raw and sunless morning, it was not difficult to see that the woman was the younger of the two. They checked nervously to confirm they were not observed, then set off away from the cultivated land, on a path which ran, carpeted with leaves, through a wood which still held enough foliage to cut out the gloomy sky above them.

They did not hold hands, though, this pair, even when they were secure from human gaze. Their talk was desultory and troubled, with long pauses between the exchanges. Their agony of mind was manifest; and understandable, for their theme was the darkest and oldest of crimes. A murder; and the murder of a father they remembered to have loved, whatever disagreements his latter days had brought to them.

Angela Harrison said, 'Does the discovery of murder now invalidate the will?'

Her brother stole a sideways glance at the intense white face beside him. 'No. The will stands, unless anyone can produce clear evidence of other intentions in Father. Of course, no murderer would be allowed to benefit by the will.'

Emotion pares speech to its essentials, shearing away the niceties in which we choose to dress it in less stressful times. For a few moments, the woman watched her feet turning aside the dead leaves like tiny ploughs; then she said, 'Do you know who did it?'

This time David did not trouble to disguise his surprise as he looked directly at her: she did not raise her gaze from the leaves. Eventually he said, 'No. It seems incredible. Perhaps it's no one we know.'

She gave a weary smile, perhaps of contempt for his determined avoidance of reality. 'That hardly seems likely. One assumes these policemen know what they're about. What did they ask you?'

The words were spread over a hundred yards of their progress, but their directness again caught him off guard. But this time he made himself pause and think before he replied. 'A lot of embarrassing things about my financial situation before Dad died.'

'You must have expected that. Did you tell them about your row with Dad over the house?'

'Yes. I volunteered the information. It seemed best.' By this time, he had almost persuaded himself that he had offered freely the information which had been prised out of him. Through a gap in the trees, he watched a kestrel hang motionless for seconds on end over a neighbouring field, then drop like a stone on to some unseen prey. 'They asked me about Dad's plans to make a new will.'

'Naturally. That was bound to interest them.' Her calm, her cool detachment from anything other than her own thoughts, shocked him. For years she had been an indulgent sister, making excuses to others for his weaknesses, making small sacrifices of her own time and priorities to clear the paths he wished to tread. Now she seemed preoccupied with thoughts she did not trouble to reveal to him.

He said, 'Margaret Lewis saw to Dad's food in those last months.'

'She saw to most things in the house. It doesn't make her a murderer.' In the under-growth, some small animal fled unseen from their approach, the noise unnaturally loud in the stillness. There was no wind, but oak leaves drifted in a thin curtain before them as they reached a clearing. Angela said, 'I won't tell them the details of the new will Dad was planning. It might not do you any good with the police.'

Suddenly he felt the old rush of gratitude mingled with guilt, the feeling he had known in childhood when his young sister covered some small sin for him. She had said nothing to their parents when she had come upon him smoking with his friends, or when he had raided the decanter in the dining-room, or when she had found the first dubious book in his satchel. He had never had to ask or plead: she had simply kept silent, and he had known that she would. It had given her, he supposed now, a kind of hold over him, but she had never exploited it. He said, 'No, that might be as well.' He did not think of thanking her. He never had.

'I'll be vague about the terms of the new will Dad was planning. If they ask me.'

'Oh, they will. No doubt, as you said, the new terms would have cut me out. The Superintendent implied as much yesterday.' He had the spoilt child's tendency to turn routine practice into a personal attack upon himself.

If she noticed it, she gave no sign. Perhaps she had become too familiar with it over the years even to remark it now. He was too preoccupied with his own position to notice her nervousness. Her apparent calm was that of someone near to breaking-point. She kicked at the husk of a chestnut, revealing the rich, pristine shade of the kernel within which would be transformed so quickly to a dull russet now that it had been exposed. Everything around them seemed to her to be dead or dying. She said, 'What else did they ask you?'

'There wasn't a lot left by the time they'd finished implying what a bad lot I was. They asked about the people around Dad in those last months. Told me how he'd been poisoned systematically and cold-bloodedly by someone who must have planned the whole thing in advance.' He was too thoroughly back in the previous day's interview to notice her sudden intake of breath: it was the first time anyone had spoken to her about the details of the poisoning. Suddenly he was desperate, almost panicking in that quiet place. 'Angela, I think they've already made up their minds that I did it!'

If he hoped for reassurance, her response must have dismayed him. She looked at him for the first time since they had begun to walk. Her dark eyes were wide with trouble in the deep shade of the trees. 'And did you, David?' she said.

It was the first time since they were children that she had ever charged him with anything. Always in their youth, even when he was discovered in some obvious deceit, she had done no more than stand aside and let others offer the accusations and the retribution. He halted, stunned, but she walked on again, looking woodenly ahead of her after that one moment when she had stared him full in the face. Watching her rigid, hunched shoulders, he realized for the first time some of the strain she was under, some of the anxiety which had caused her to ask him to meet her out here. 'No, of course I didn't,' he said, almost running until he was alongside her again. 'I might be capable of a lot of things, but I could never have killed Dad. Surely you of all people believe that.'

This time it was she who stopped abruptly. 'Yes,' she said, with a little, secret half-smile.

'Yes, I believe you. If the police don't, I'll do everything I can to convince them you had nothing to do with it.'

The path followed different woods in a wide horseshoe, so that they were not far now from their starting point. They emerged from the cover of the woods and walked for two hundred yards along the road to the derelict barn from which they had started. After the deep shade, they felt suddenly exposed, though the sky's grey was still unbroken. Angela Harrison looked up at the low cloud and sniffed the dampness.

She looked for a moment like a wild animal as she said, 'I'm not going to tell the police. It might not be in our interests. But I think I know who did it.'

CHAPTER 9

At the very moment when Edmund Craven's children were agreeing to deceive them, Lambert and Hook were trying to give substance to the man who was as yet the most faceless of their suspects.

Walter Miller lived in a hamlet two miles outside Oldford. Even under the grey skies which seemed so menacing to that other pair in their remote assignation, Miller's small house looked attractive. It was constructed in Cotswold stone: not the sprayed-on imitation of today, but the solid amber stone of a century ago. The front faced south, and on this sheltered aspect the climbing rose around the door was still producing rich pink blooms, whose brightness was accentuated by the grey sky.

Almost before they could use the highly polished brass knocker, the door was opened by a trim, alert woman in a spotless skirt and blouse, who had obviously witnessed their approach up the long path which wound through cottage pinks along the edge of the narrow front garden. 'Superintendent Lambert?' It made a change to have the public initiate the introductions. 'And you must be

Sergeant Hook.' Bert found himself absurdly pleased to be so remembered and acknowledged; usually he was no more than an addendum to his leader. His gratification was increased when he found china crockery laid out on the low oak table in the lounge and caught the appealing scent of coffee from somewhere beyond. They sat carefully on the comfortable chintz-covered chairs, watched the reflected flames of the fire in the stone fireplace flickering in the brasses around it, and tried to resist the comfort which threatened to steal over their mental reflexes.

Mrs Miller brought her husband back with their coffee, then left them to their conference. He was less neat, more slow-moving, than his wife, but he fitted easily into the ambience of this most agreeable house. He was older than his wife: if he had fought alongside Craven in Hitler's war, he could scarcely be less than seventy, and Lambert recalled that Margaret Lewis had implied that he was an exact contemporary of the dead man. He was over six feet, with broad shoulders which had begun to stoop only a little with age. Though his hair was almost white, it was still thick and healthy. His brown eyes assessed his interlocutors shrewdly as he said, 'The news that Edmund's death was homicide was a hell of a shock to me, Superintendent.'

The village, the garden, the house, even the spouse of this man, were so English that his accent surprised them far more than it should have done. The words came in a pleasant North American drawl, which added to the relaxation which was all about them. With the perversity encouraged by his calling, Lambert wondered whether the pleasant snugness of it all was designed to conceal an anxiety in his subject. An unworthy thought, perhaps, but it was well to remind himself that for the present this man remained a suspect in a particularly ruthless murder case.

Lambert said, 'I can understand that, Mr Miller. You will appreciate from this delayed investigation that it was a surprise to the police too. And everyone I have seen so far has expressed the same sort of astonishment. Nevertheless, someone did murder Mr Craven, which means almost certainly that at least one of the people I have already seen, or will see before the end of today, is lying.'

Miller nodded, looked into the fire, stirred sugar slowly into his coffee. 'And have you come up with any ideas about who that person might be?'

Lambert afforded him the tiny, conspiratorial smile which acknowledges that this will be an exchange between intelligent men. 'You wouldn't expect me to reveal it if

107

I had, Mr Miller. Let's just say that I am beginning to get a slightly clearer picture of the victim and the people who surrounded him in his last few months.' The impressive head turned back to him, the brown eyes weighed the statement carefully, but the broad, thin lips framed no words. Yet Lambert knew as clearly as if they had spoken that Miller was speculating on what the others had said about him: it had been an effort of will for him not to ask. Lambert would not tell him that Margaret Lewis and David Craven had both seemed far too preoccupied with their own situations to tell him anything about the mysterious old friend of the dead man who came once a week to play chess: not even his country of birth, the Superintendent thought wryly. All the implications were that neither of them regarded Miller as a serious suspect; but there was no reason why he should be told this yet. Lambert said carefully, 'Do you know how Edmund Craven was killed, Mr Miller?'

The American shook his head slowly. 'No. No one has said anything to me about it. As I say, when your Sergeant here rang up about it, it was a hell of a shock.' It was the second time he had used exactly that phrase. A prepared reaction? Perhaps, but his surprise at the notion of murder might be no less genuine for that.

'Mr Craven was poisoned.'

It was impossible to deduce from Miller's face whether his slight surprise was feigned or not. He said very quietly, 'I guessed it had to be that.'

'I understand you knew him for many years.'

'Almost fifty of them. We go – went – back to the early years of the war. We first met at the end of 'forty-two when we were both flying Mustangs.'

'In this country, Mr Miller?'

Miller smiled: it was the first, oblique, reference to his origins. Even after all this time, he was used to the insular English making it their first query when he was introduced. 'In the States. Ed came over there on an eight-week training course. We were together on and off for the rest of the war. Most of that was in Europe. It was Ed who introduced me to Dorothy – my wife who let you in just now. After the war, I got a job in England and settled here. I went back to Philadelphia, every year until my parents died, but we haven't even been over there now for six or seven years.'

'So you and Craven remained friends throughout these years?'

'Indeed we did. I was up in Derbyshire for ten years, but we always kept in touch. I became a naturalized British citizen in 1960. When I began working in Gloucester, we moved here and we've seen each other weekly ever since.'

'This would be when Mr Craven's wife was still alive?' said Hook.

As often happened, a contribution from Bert seemed to throw the interviewee a little off balance for a moment. Perhaps it was no more than the surprise value of a question from that taciturn quarter, but Miller looked ruffled for the first time as he said, 'Yes. She and Dorothy were good friends.'

'And Craven knew both of them for even longer than you, I presume?' Lambert was wondering vaguely whether there was a possibility that he should add Dorothy Miller to his list of suspects. At the moment, she did not seem to have had the regular access to Craven which represented opportunity, but if she had worked with or through her husband...

'Yes. The four of us got on well together. I liked Ed's wife, Joan. It was a tragedy when she died and left him alone.' Miller's speech had become for the moment a series of terse statements. Hitherto, he had been expansive and leisured in his delivery, in what Lambert realized he regarded as a typical transatlantic manner. Now the manner of his delivery interested Lambert more than the unexceptional content. Had there been something in the relationship between the American and Craven's wife which could

110

now embarrass him?

He remembered that curious expression Alfred Arkwright had read from Craven's will, describing Miller as 'my old friend of many years, with whom I have shared so much'. Was there an ironic, posthumous barb embedded there? Then an old, half-forgotten phrase from his childhood came back to Lambert: 'Over-fed, over-sexed and over here,' was how the jaundiced, rationed British had described the influx of American servicemen in those war years. Miller was a handsome and striking figure still, in his well-cut blue airman's uniform, he must have been a glamorous figure in those spartan times. Suppose that his charisma had been carried into the postwar years, that the woman now long dead had found it difficult to resist, even after her marriage to Edmund Craven...

It was a beguiling scenario, but much too hypothetical yet for the taste of a grizzled detective. Far too much to build on to a passing embarrassment in his present subject; in any case, it was difficult to see why a possible conquest of Mrs Craven should be followed by the murder of her husband fourteen years after her death. Like a physician probing an area where he has discovered pain, Lambert asked, 'Did the four of you ever stay at Mr Craven's holiday home in Burnham-on-Sea?'

'Yes. I think we did. Angela came with us a little, but the other children were growing up by then.'

'You got on well with Mrs Craven?'

'Yes, I did. Ed didn't always treat her as well as he should have done, but she survived. Superintendent, are you sure this is relevant to your present inquiries?'

'Almost certainly it isn't, Mr Miller. But you must appreciate our position. We are trying to build up a picture of a dead man and a complex network of relationships, working over a year after his death. Murder is a unique crime, not just in its magnitude but in the fact that it is the only serious criminal offence where the victim is never available for questioning. If Craven were here, I expect he would have some interesting ideas on who might want to kill him. We have to try to find out those things without him, and in this particular case without much of the evidence that must have been around immediately after his death.'

Perhaps Miller took it as an apology. He said, 'I appreciate that. I don't envy you your task. It's just that it upsets me a little that we should seem to be disturbing the peace of a kind and generous lady who died of cancer fourteen years and more ago.'

Lambert noted the adjectives Miller chose; probably he meant them to be conventionally approving as far as his own admiration for the lady went, but sceptical detectives are always interested in the epithet 'generous' when it is applied to a lady's favours. He said, 'Good taste is one of the first casualties of our inquiries, I'm afraid. Let's move to the present then, and those who are still around us. I understand you visited Edmund Craven each week to play chess with him during those last fateful months.'

'Every Tuesday evening. We used to alternate between the houses: he came here once a fortnight. Tuesday was the day when Dorothy used to visit our daughter in Gloucester, so we had the house to ourselves. Once Edmund stopped driving, it was no longer easy for him to come here, so I went to him each time we played.' There was a satisfaction in the set of the mouth as he finished the sentence. Lambert wondered why it should give him more pleasure to visit Craven in his own home every time; had Tall Timbers associations with a long-dead affair for him? Or was a detective's imagination running riot in a case where there was too little material to exercise it more profitably? Miller brought him abruptly back to reality when he said, 'The last time I saw him was five days before his death. So you see, I can be of no real help: I wasn't there when the fatal poison was administered.'

For a moment, both detectives were puzzled. Then Lambert realized that they had given Miller no details of the method of murder beyond the bare fact that it was a poisoning. If Miller knew the full facts, and suspected they had been trying to trap him, he had stepped adroitly clear of the danger. Lambert looked into the brown, impassive eyes for a moment before he said with a little, acknowledging smile, 'We didn't give you the full facts, Mr Miller. I have to tell you that your friend was murdered by the systematic application of arsenic in relatively small doses over a period of months. That is why the death passed as being from natural causes at the time. The killer was very cool and totally ruthless.'

Miller looked suitably shaken. His hand was steady as he put his coffee cup back upon the low table, but he watched it with extreme care, as if wishing to assure himself of his control. Then he said softly, 'I guess I clung to the idea that somehow it might have been accidental, even when I knew it was poison.' He gazed out towards the thrush they could hear in the silence, innocent and uncaring, as the weak sun lightened the prevailing grey. For a moment he was far away from them, staring out in conjecture or nostalgia at a world they would never know. He looked now like a man of over seventy, saddened by the world.

But the mood passed quickly. His strong hands gripped the arms of the comfortable chair; above the comfortable green wool of his cardigan, his face was determined as he said, 'We must find out who killed him.'

Lambert did not comment on the banality of the statement, or the irony in its utterance to men who had already been trying for two days to do just that. He was merely pleased to see such earnest intent in the man before him. He was briskly businesslike as he said, 'Right. You were in and out of Edmund Craven's house every week in the three years before he died. Let us assume for the moment that you are not yourself a murderer. Did you see anyone among those around him who might be?'

Walter Miller took a long breath and looked from one to the other of his interlocutors. Hook suspected that he knew that it was irregular to ask him as directly as this about his fellow-suspects. But he showed no sign of resentment as he said, 'I've known David and Angela since they were children, so it's difficult for me to be objective. As you put me on the spot, I have to say that I can't see either of them as a murderer of any sort, let alone of their own father.'

Lambert, sensing that he was about to move on through the list of those around Craven, said, 'As you've known them for so long, you are perhaps in a better position than anyone to tell us about their relationship with their father in his last few months.' It was not true of course: Margaret Lewis was better qualified to observe the daily evolution of feelings in those fateful weeks because she was constantly in the house, observing all. But it rarely did any harm to stress to a witness his importance to the case, the necessity for him to recall with circumspection anything which might have bearing upon it.

And Miller did give his response much thought. He stood up, smiling a little at Bert Hook's earnest yeoman features and his ball-pen poised above the page. Then he walked across to the mullioned stone window and looked down the garden for a moment before he spoke. His face was grave with the responsibility of his evidence when he turned back to them. 'Both the children were affectionate towards their father before they were married. Angela resented the way Ed treated her mother when she was a teenager, but I've no doubt she got over that years ago. She was kindness itself to her Dad in his last months.

'I'm not quite as sure about Ed's son. David was married and divorced years ago. Nice girl; no children.' He sounded as though he were enunciating the priorities of his generation. 'I've no doubt Edmund was difficult at times in the last few years. But so was David – and how! Sometimes it seems children are just sent to try us.' He looked into the fire with a sad smile, so that they wondered for a moment what crosses his own children had heaped upon him.

Lambert, anxious to encourage this revelatory vein in their subject, said gently, 'We heard something of David's financial problems from his own lips. I believe his father was planning to revise his will.'

'So I understood from Edmund in those last days. I think it was more a matter of cutting someone out than making small amendments.'

'David?'

'So I assumed. You will understand that I didn't wish to get involved between father and children. I told him so. I said he should discuss his intentions with them.'

'And did he?'

Miller paused. 'I'm trying to recollect things from over a year ago: things that at the time I tried to dismiss as not being my concern. I think Edmund indicated without putting it in so many words that he had discussed it with the people affected.'

Lambert said, 'As you probably know, no new will was ever made, although we know that one was intended. We obviously have to investigate whether the person who murdered Edmund Craven was trying to forestall a new will. David has already admitted that his father found out about his plans for Tall Timbers and was distressed by them. It would be logical to reflect that in a new will.'

Miller looked troubled. 'David isn't my favourite man, by any means. But I don't want to see him locked up for life.'

Lambert said sternly, 'If he isn't guilty, he won't be. You must realize that it's your duty to reveal to us anything else that you know.'

Miller nodded miserably. 'All I know is that he was in trouble financially. He had been, on and off, for years: perhaps Ed indulged him too much when he was younger. The will came as a Godsend to him.'

'And you think a new will would have cut him out?'

'I don't know that.' His face set stubbornly on the sentiment.

'Neither do we, Mr Miller. We shall make it our business to find out if we possibly can.' Lambert waited, but there was as he expected no further reaction from the American. 'Can you tell us any more about old Mr Craven's relationship with his daughter?'

Walter Miller grimaced wryly. 'I was born in the year before "old Mr Craven", Superintendent.' Then he smiled more openly, in the relief of moving to a subject on which he could enthuse more happily. 'He liked

Angela, and she liked him, right up to the end. She made arrangements for someone to look after her children on quite a few days during the summer holidays, so that she could be with her father in that last summer.' Hook looked up sharply at his chief, more sharply than he had meant to do: this was the key period in the poisoning, some two months before Craven's death.

Perhaps Miller caught the look and divined their thinking, for his face filled with horror and he hastened on. 'They'd always been close, as father and daughter often are. I think David was closer to his mother – he certainly seemed to lose his way rather after Joan died. Anyway, Angela loved her father. She almost made herself ill by her concern for him and her determination to be near him as he weakened–' He broke off, aghast again at the implications of what he had intended as words to reinforce her innocence.

Lambert said gently, 'Until this business is cleared up, the best feelings and actions in all those around the deceased will be subject to this wretchedly warped interpretation. Murder has that effect, I'm afraid. Now, what can you tell me about Mr Craven's relationship with his grandchildren?'

Miller looked startled by the sudden shift of subject, which was quite deliberate on the part of his interlocutor. But he gave due thought to his reply; perhaps it was a relief to switch away from the children he had known for so many years to the next generation, with whom he was less involved. 'Ed was delighted when they were born, and very fond of them as toddlers. As he got older, he spoke of them to me less and less. He withdrew into himself in the last year or two, I'm afraid. He didn't mention them much.'

'Have you any idea why? Was there any family disagreement?'

'Not that I'm aware of. He just talked about them less, and I'm afraid I didn't press him.' Miller looked uncomfortable, but it seemed rather at his own social omissions that at anything he was concealing. Lambert thought that like most men he would be interested in his own grandchildren, but find those of his friends a bore. He had probably never thought to ask about the Craven grandchildren, never noticed their gradual disappearance from his friend's conversation. Now he felt guilty about this neglect of his stricken companion. 'They were at Ed's funeral. I remember them being quite upset. I suppose Angela thought Ed would have liked them to be there; she made all the funeral arrangements. I think David was too embarrassed – frightened of looking a hypocrite. His plans for the house were becoming more public, and there were those of us at the funeral who thought he had hastened his father's death.' Miller stopped aghast. 'I guess I didn't mean–'

'I know just what you meant, Mr Miller,' said Lambert with a grim smile. It was interesting to see how Walter Miller's transatlantic origins surfaced under stress among idioms which had for the most part become very English. 'What about Angela's husband. Did Mr Craven like his son-in-law?'

'No.' The response was surprisingly prompt and certain. 'I don't know exactly why. Ed tended to get annoyed if Michael was even mentioned, and he never raised him himself. I kept off the subject.'

'How long did this hostility between them go back?'

This time Miller did have to think. 'I don't think Ed was keen on him even before the marriage, but they were polite enough then. Michael Harrison is a Roman Catholic, of course, and Ed certainly didn't like that.' Miller looked up at the faces of the detectives and caught doubt there that this could be the source nowadays of any serious enmity. 'Religion meant more to my generation than yours. Especially to the British: Americans are used to being a mongrel race. Ed was a staunch Anglican of the old school and certainly not ecumenical. He stopped going to church in Oldford when there was a move towards joint services.

And he wouldn't have the vicar in to see him in those last years when he stopped going out much. He became more bigoted, I think, and those of us who might have felt differently from him just kept off the subject of religion. I'm afraid not many of us become more charitable in our views as we get older.' He stared into the fire, contemplating the increasing bleakness of the years which lay ahead.

Bert Hook thought that he would be protected as long as that trim, bright woman who had shown them in remained at his elbow. No woman who made such excellent gingerbread could be other than a benign and liberal influence. He said gently, preparing to turn to a new subject in his notes, 'You know of no other reason why there should be enmity between Michael Harrison and Edmund Craven?' He was thinking of the second circle of suspects they would have to move to if their first investigation proved fruitless. Perhaps it was no more than a demonstration to his chief of his alertness: he had already half-decided that their task was to find the necessary evidence to convict David Craven of the murder of his father.

'No. Ed used to do a little painting in the studio he made at the back of the garden of Tall Timbers. He asked Michael Harrison for his opinion and Michael was rather scathing; I think he might have been a little jealous that Ed had facilities as an amateur that were far better than those he enjoyed himself as a professional. Anyway, Ed took the criticism badly. But perhaps I've over-stressed the enmity between them. They didn't see each other much in the last few years, and for all I know Michael Harrison may not have borne any resentment – I'm afraid I hardly know him myself. And after all, his family has done well enough out of Ed's estate for him to be grateful now.'

It was an attempt to defend the memory of his old friend and Lambert liked him for it. He said, 'What about Mrs Lewis?'

'Margaret couldn't do enough for Ed as he got weaker.' Again he glanced at both of them quickly to see if they caught the unwittingly sinister implication of his words; this time they were both impassive. 'I'm glad Ed left her the house in Burnham-on-Sea. She deserves to be looked after. She kept house impeccably for Ed after Joan died, and she became more and more of a friend rather than an employee towards the end.'

Lambert was interested in this outsider's view of Margaret Lewis, as a counter-balance to the hostility David Craven had not troubled to conceal. He said gently. 'She looked after Mr Craven's food and medicines?'

The implication of the question was obvious. Miller said calmly, 'Yes. I've thought about that myself. But unless you are telling me that daily access was necessary, any of us had the opportunity to poison Ed. My money certainly wouldn't be on Margaret Lewis.'

'Thank you for being so frank with us, Mr Miller.' Lambert had risen. He was already impatiently anticipating their meeting with Angela Harrison. 'Needless to say, your views on the other three people who were close to Mr Craven in those last days will be kept strictly confidential.' He watched the thrush flitting swiftly from sight in the bushes, wondering if it could have caught his movement through the thick glass.

Miller said simply 'Four.' For a man dropping a bombshell, he seemed completely unaware of his effect. He reassembled the empty cups and plates carefully on the big tray and said, 'If you really asked me to put my money on someone, he would be the one I would choose. Unfortunately for Margaret.' Hook looked at him carefully to see if he knew he was talking in riddles, and decided that he did not.

Lambert felt very foolish as he said, 'We were not aware that there were more than four people with easy access to the deceased.' It at least had the virtue of honesty; he noticed how he lapsed into officialese in his uncertainty. His mind was working through a furious retrospect, he realized that he had taken Margaret Lewis's list of those who were residents or regular visitors to the house at the time without further check. David Craven had been too occupied with incriminating himself and then denying guilt to concern himself with others.

Walter Miller was genuinely puzzled. 'I didn't try to deceive you. I was expecting you to come to him.'

'No, Mr Miller. You didn't try to deceive us.' But someone had: Margaret Lewis. 'Who is the person we have so far omitted?'

'The one who had already shown he could be violent. The one who hated Ed and made no bones about it. The one whom I found with his hand in Ed's medicine cabinet in the bathroom five days before Ed died.'

He was not meaning to keep them in suspense. He had been waiting to tell them this. And they had apparently almost forgotten to ask him: it was inexplicable.

Lambert said heavily, insistently, 'Who, Mr Miller?'

'Why, Margaret Lewis's son, of course!'

CHAPTER 10

The PC was feeling aggressive. He had just had an almighty rollicking from the station sergeant and the injustice of it rankled. Policemen not being saints, his reaction was to take it out on the first suitably vulnerable member of the public it was his duty to police.

He got out of the Panda car and pulled his leather gloves on slowly as he strolled across the quiet suburban road. There was a raw breeze sweeping in from the sea, but the temperature had nothing to do with the gesture: he had seen older policemen smooth the leather over their knuckles in this way when they had been menacing groups of young toughs in the centre of Bristol. Here the gesture was wholly wasted as a token of menace because the subject of the constable's attention remained unconscious of his presence.

Though he made sure that his shoes rasped on the tarmac, the denim-clad legs did not react, the torso remained invisible beneath the long black bonnet. A Lotus, PC Davies noticed; envy did not make him more conciliatory. 'Out here, lad. And fast!' he said.

The boy was four inches shorter than the constable, even when he stood upright. There was a smear of oil across his cheek. More important, there was fear in his light blue eyes. And when he said, 'What do you want?' the fear sneaked into his voice.

Perhaps PC Davies mistook fear for guilt. If he was to bring him in for CID questioning, the boy was almost certainly suspected of some offence. 'I want *you*, lad. And I want you now. Get into the car.' He gestured with his head towards the white police Fiesta behind him, without turning his head. He was keeping his eye on the spanner in the boy's hand. If it moved at all, he would be in first: effecting an arrest in the face of an offensive weapon would look good on a record that was so far undistinguished.

'What for? I haven't done nothing.' The fear was there again in the voice as the boy put down the bonnet carefully, making no movement that could be construed as aggressive. Fear meant weakness, and the constable felt stronger all the time in this situation where he held all the real weapons. He thought that the boy had probably been in spots like this before, and lost.

'That's what you say. You might change your mind when the Super gets at you. You going to waste any more of my time?' He rubbed the palm of his left hand over his clenched right fist beneath the gloves. The youth was thin and pale: he must be the lighter of the two by three or four stones. From the corner of his eye, the constable watched the big, gleaming spanner.

'All right. Let me lock this car up.' The thin shoulders dropped, the spanner was placed on the floor of the car and PC Davies half-turned towards his own vehicle. He had won the little contest of *machismo* he had set up for himself. The youth leaned across the car towards the far door, with a gleam of contempt in the eyes PC Davies could no longer see. This policeman who had been so anxious to throw his weight about was not as clever as he pretended: he had not even realized that the modern Lotus was bound to have central locking.

The engine roared into life in the same instant that the driver's door slammed shut. By the time the constable realized what was happening, his prey had almost escaped. The throaty roar of the Lotus's sports engine jeered at his astonished face as the coupé leapt smoothly away. By the time his hasty, clumsy fingers had turned the key of the Fiesta, the low black shape had rounded the corner a hundred yards away. By the time he turned that corner himself, the Lotus was almost out of sight. His man was gone. Reluctantly, he radioed the news and turned back towards the station. Another bloody rollocking.

Not many drivers are foolish enough to take on the traffic police. They are among the best drivers in the land, in vehicles tuned and serviced to guarantee safe handling at high speeds. But fear makes people behave foolishly, and the young man in the Lotus was now filled with that rising, irrational fear which sharpens reflexes but makes the normal processes of reason cease to function. As the police Rover turned on its siren and eased on to the road behind him, he gunned the accelerator pedal and panicked. Very foolish.

He turned on to the coast road, where the black ribbon of tarmac ran straight for long patches and the turbo-charged 2.2 litres might tell in his favour. And for a time it did. His acceleration was superior to the Rover's; he wound it up quickly and watched the white car and its blue flashing light growing smaller in his mirror. It was a good thing he had finished servicing the car before his unwelcome visitor arrived. He wondered grimly if the owner would approve of the road test now in progress. He passed a middle-aged man in a red Sierra as if he were stationary, catching a sideways glimpse of the driver's face, vivid with astonished outrage.

The sergeant strapped firmly into the passenger seat of the police Rover watched their quarry as the needle crept past the hundred mark and their speed reached the point where the siren seemed to be behind rather than above them. 'That kid can drive,' he said, with the reluctant admiration of one expert for another. It was true, and it was a relief. Too many of the men they chased – it was always men, and often in stolen vehicles – drove like madmen once they knew they were pursued by the police. The constant nightmare was a chase ending in a crash in which innocent lives would be lost through the criminal negligence of the quarry. It was a nightmare which occasionally came true, resulting in official inquiries, where the implication could be that the police pursuers had harried the guilty driver into his reckless actions.

This pursuit did not seem likely to end like that. When the bends began to occur on this coastal road, which ran without hedges or fences along its undulating route, the youth used the full width of the road, often almost touching the verge on his right to minimize the degree of curve. But he did so only when the contours permitted him to see that there was no vehicle coming towards him in the other direction. And he used his gears like a champion rally driver, making sure that his speed never slackened more than it had to. The driver of the police vehicle had experience on his side, and all the advantages of a system with huge resources. So long as he kept the Lotus in sight, they would get him eventually. There was no need for heroics, with the risks they involved. He was twelve years older than PC Davies, and felt no need to prove himself. His companion radioed to his colleagues in the traffic police for help, while he strove only to keep within range of the flying Lotus.

The youth was a strange mixture of absolute concentration and blind terror. As always when he drove fast in a car like this, there was the feeling of man and machine operating as one, of moving in a more rarified world than the tawdry one he existed in for the rest of his life, of a misery of this better world and its rules. Yet he knew he should not have fled. The sight of the uniform, of the arrogance it gave to a face not much older than his own, had upset his judgement and made him forget the promises he had made to himself and others.

And he knew he would not succeed. He was not even sure what he was trying to do. His flight had been the reaction of a frightened animal. He had no idea of where he was going, no goal which would represent safety for him. And he was not stupid: he knew that the resources ranged against him would have to win in the end. Today would shatter the life he had been building. The human brain works with astonishing speed in a crisis, but inconsequently. As the youth's speed approached two miles a minute on the last long straight stretch of the road above the sea, he was wondering how to explain to the man who had trusted him to service this beautiful car exactly why he had used it as he had.

They were coming now to the outskirts of Weston-super-Mare. At this speed, the first houses leapt at them with startling speed, as if they had an independent motion of their own. The youth saw an identical police Rover coming out from the town with flashing lights to meet him, and knew in that moment that the pack would hunt him down in the labyrinth of streets they knew so much better than he. He swung away from the sea and the approaching car on a left fork in the road, the only way he could take. Already they were controlling his movements: the world of high speed, where he had felt in control, was behind him now. As if to reinforce the notion, the first red-circled 40 signs flashed past him and red brick walls closed out the sky.

The Rover which had followed him from the start closed up behind him on this road, its siren clearing a safe path for it through the thin traffic. The sergeant radioed the details of their position and movements to his colleagues; his eyes never left the tail of the black Lotus. Both he and the driver knew that the only way their prey could escape them now was to double back somehow on to the way he had come.

The youth knew it too. He was looking for a turning which might allow him to rejoin the coast road by following a rough square. His mind raced ahead to where he could then go if he was successful. Not back to his own place, obviously. He began to evolve a vague, crazy plan to take the Lotus back to its owner and ask for his protection against the persecution of the law.

Disaster on the roads often comes from the most unexpected quarter. The traffic police were aware of that. They looked upon old ladies in Morris Minors with different eyes from other men. Perhaps they would have been just marginally more prepared for the actions of this one than the youth. She came out of the drive of a big house on his right, hidden by high privet hedges until she was almost on the road. And when she approached that road, she looked only briefly to her right, towards the centre of the town, where she was used to seeing vehicles. Not at all to her left, where the youth and his police pursuers were bearing down upon her at a speed she had never approached in her life. Slowly, inexorably, she pulled across the road and into the path of the Lotus.

The police driver was still a hundred yards

behind the black coupé when these events began to unfold in apparent slow motion before him. Unusually in modern policemen under thirty, he was a regular churchgoer, but he snarled an involuntary 'Jesus Christ!' as he drove his right foot on to the brake pedal.

The youth had just spotted a turning he thought might offer possibilities when the wall of light green metal moved into his vision on his right. The Lotus had brakes befitting a car of its performance, and his reaction could not have been faster. But there was no question of his stopping in the distance between the two cars. He stood on the brakes, felt his weight thrown fully on to that desperate right foot as the car responded instantly and his body continued forward, even had time as he went into the skid to regret that he had never had the chance to fasten his safety-belt.

Still the small green car came on, and still the tiny white-haired figure did not look at the car hurtling towards her. The youth, gripping the steering-wheel with a strength he had not known he possessed, turned the car automatically into the skid as the tyres screamed agonizingly and the tired old eyes, turning belatedly upon him, seemed to widen until they filled the whole face. The Lotus slid up to the green metal wall, like a ship coming too rapidly to berth. Then, miraculously, as the Morris straightened on to its appointed path along the road, the black coupé, wheels still locked, responded to the efforts of the man at the wheel and swung away, up on to the deserted pavement, passing between the old green Morris and a low garden wall with three inches to spare on each side, as if it were an arrow shot from a bow instead of a car that was still not under control.

As the elderly driver of the Morris slewed her car sideways into an appropriately geriatric emergency stop, the Lotus rocked crazily between its front bumper and a concrete lamp standard and was back on the road. In almost the same instant, the police Rover passed the green Morris more conventionally on the right and dropped in behind its quarry.

The youth turned left, and the sergeant in the passenger seat of the Rover shouted 'Gotcha, mate!' through lips that were still dry. For the driver of the Lotus, still bringing his crazily bucking charge under control, had had no chance to see the red bar that denoted a cul-de-sac on the sign above him.

It would in truth have made little difference if he had. For the youth, with mind reeling from the carnage that should have been, was in no condition to elude them now. He was too good a driver to deceive himself that skill alone had saved him and the woman he might have killed; he knew that luck had been heavily on his side. And the knowledge shook him. He drove down the lane watching his own hands trembling on the wheel. When he came to the great slab of the factory wall and found that there was no way out, it was almost a relief.

When the traffic policemen opened the driver's door of the Lotus and ordered him out, he found that his legs would hardly support him. They spread him against the side of the Rover, with his arms splayed thinly across the roof, to search him: he had, after all, fled from the police, and they did not know why he was required by the CID of a neighbouring force. He might just have a weapon, or drugs. And the adrenalin was high in them too, from the chase and the crash that had seemed inevitable.

When they found nothing in the pockets of the tight, thin jeans, the sergeant said, 'Right lad, you're nicked. Get into the back of the car.' He did not speak too roughly, for he was still full of the relief of the accident avoided and the skill this boy had shown at the wheel. And their quarry no longer held any threat; he was going to go quietly, in the phrase they heard so often since the advent of TV cops.

The sergeant, who had seen far too much drama and tragedy on the roads, knew as the youth did not that it was a normal enough reaction to shock. As they took Andrew Lewis back past the Morris Minor he so nearly hit, he was silently weeping.

CHAPTER 11

For a woman who had recently inherited four hundred thousand pounds, Angela Harrison lived in modest circumstances.

The semi-detached 'thirties house was too close to its neighbour to have a garage; a parking-space had been paved in front of its cream front door. There was more privacy at the back of the house; it had a narrow rear garden which ran down to a disused canal that was covered in emerald weed. Hook surveyed this garden from the living-room window, estimating with an expert's eye the lines of Brussels sprouts and spring cabbage which dominated the vegetable plot in this winter season. It occupied over half of the land behind the house: the Sergeant approved this evidence of husbandry in an age he found frivolous in its preference for the herbaceous border.

It was a quiet place in the late morning, with children at school and many of the houses shut against the world. After the lofty remoteness of Edmund Craven's Edwardian mansion and the confident comfort of Walter Miller's older village house, this was a meaner place, with its cramped hall and through lounge. Yet a comfortable enough place a better spot than most people could choose to settle, even in England, Hook reminded himself automatically. Such thoughts came unprompted to a man who had been a Barnardo's boy, who still congratulated himself each night upon the privacy and independence afforded him by his own modest modern house. To Bert, his mortgage was not the millstone that he heard his neighbours talk about, but a talisman of his success in a world where these things had to be won.

Lambert would not have recognized Craven's daughter from the photographs of her in childhood and adolescence which they had seen at Tall Timbers. The records which Hook and the team in the murder room at CID had begun to compile for him told him that she was thirty-six: he would have taken her for a year or two older than that. Her face had the strong, regular bone-structure which recalled the handsome young woman of those aging photographs. And with the thought came the knowledge of why he had probed Walter Miller about Edmund Craven's relationship with his grandchildren: nowhere in Craven's house had he seen a picture which included those children, or even his daughter after she became a mother. Unusual, curious even, though his detective's mind made the reservation that such things might always have been removed by some other, unknown hand after the old man's death.

Angela Harrison had unusual grey-green eyes; her face was framed by dark brown hair. Lambert thought inconsequentially that she must once have been as blond as his own daughter, and he saw for an instant the happy laughter of early childhood and lost innocence upon the sober features before him. The vertical lines which ran between her eyes and down from the corners of her mouth were etched a little more deeply than they should have been. But the face was vigorous, not defeated; if it held a certain wary vigilance, Lambert could see her in a different context from this as a striking woman, dominating the company. Striking, not beautiful, just as in her youth she had been handsome rather than pretty; did the words represent anything more than a male presumption, and an individual one at that?

'"There's no art to find the mind's construction in the face,"' he said to Bert Hook as his Sergeant contemplated the vegetable plot; Angela Harrison had gone into the hall to answer a phone call before they could even begin.

'No, sir?' said Bert. He wondered what Shakespeare would have made of photofit pictures: he had never seen anyone but the blackest villains in those. 'Well, beauty is in the eye of the beholder.' He did not know that his cliché was a quotation, or he might have avoided it. The only quotation he really approved was the one embracing detection's codewords of observation and deduction, and that only because Holmes had been immortalized for him by his boyhood reading in the Barnardo's library. Even the derision of the CID for fictional amateurs had not been able to eliminate the watch-words of the old junkie for his loyal adherent; were they not the very *raison d'être* of the CID?

So Bert and his chief looked round now at the room hastily tidied for their visit, noting the children's books in the corner, the old typewriter upon the scratched oak table, the sideboard with its crowded collection of family photographs, the tiled fireplace which might be in demand for its rarity if its 'thirties design of three blending shades of green could be preserved for a few more years. John Lambert, looking at the paraphernalia of a busy, unexceptional life that was everywhere revealed, thought how little the poor, which these days included the struggling genteel, could conceal of themselves.

There was little trace here of the man of this house: he wondered whether he had one of the small bedrooms upstairs to stow the materials of his life, or whether he kept them at his place of work. He recalled Walter Miller's speculation that the struggling professional artist might have been envious of old Craven's spacious studio facilities. For the rest, much of the life of this small family was on show here, as it would not have been in a larger house where they had room to spread themselves and conceal the evidence from curious eyes like his.

Bert Hook looked at the swimming certificates, the cut-down golf clubs, the books on birds and football, the old mongrel dog with its chin obstinately in his hand, and thought that there could be happiness in a place like this. Not *more* than in a place like Tall Timbers; Bert, who had endured a superfluity of such sentiments from a series of well-meaning house-mothers in two homes, was sturdily resistant to such Victorian platitudes, which he saw as designed to keep upwardly mobile individuals like him in his place. He had only learned two days ago that that was what he was; he was waiting for the moment of maximum effect to visit the phrase upon his chief, in the secure knowledge that the Superintendent would be duly appalled by it.

'I'm sorry about that. Do sit down.' Angela Harrison was back with them, tall and slim, with a natural poise which made her dominate the narrow room, striving to seem at her ease in a situation where it would hardly be natural for her to be so. She had dressed to receive them in a formal grey suit which was beautifully pressed, but sufficiently out of fashion for even a Superintendent with the sketchiest knowledge of such things to realize that it must be some years old. She sat opposite them on the suite with its fading loose covers, skirt pulled demurely over the knees of her long legs. 'I know now about my father. It seems incredible, but I have to accept it.' She looked at him unblinkingly, a small smile fixed upon the wide lips. Her expression made Lambert think for a reason he could not define that this still-young face had seen much suffering, and came through it. He wondered how much pain her father's death and its present ramifications had brought to her.

'You understand, then, that we have to be interested initially in those people who had regular access to your father during the last six months or so of his life.'

'Yes. Five of us.' He thought wryly that he should have come to her first: she would not have allowed him to overlook Andrew Lewis. He was still embarrassed about that. 'I know all of them quite well. I have to face the fact that one of them killed my father.'

Not 'one of us', Lambert noticed: there was nothing odd about the reaction in a daughter, but she had carefully picked out the words which excluded herself from suspicion. He said, 'I presume you know how?'

She nodded. 'I can't think who would have been cruel enough to poison Dad systematically over the weeks like that.' So she knew the details and wasn't going to shirk them now. She had talked to someone he had already seen, plainly. Not Walter Miller, unless by telephone: he had come almost straight from there, after he had set in motion the machinery to trace Andrew Lewis. In that case, either Margaret Lewis or David Craven had been in contact with her; he had no idea at this moment which was the more likely. It was inevitable during murder investigations that people should exchange notes about the direction of his inquiries; he had long accepted the fact. But it was often interesting to know who had been talking to whom. He dismissed the alternative speculation that Angela Craven had conferred with no one, but given herself away by her knowledge: murderers who planned as carefully as this one did not make such elementary errors. She added with sudden vehemence, 'I hope you get the person who did it.'

'We shall, Mrs Harrison. I can promise you that.' The Chief Constable would have been proud of him. It was one of that luminary's dictums that his officers should always exude confidence to the public. 'May I ask who gave you the detail of your father's murder, Mrs Harrison?'

She looked down at the old dog, poking him affectionately with her foot as he threatened to investigate areas polite dogs leave untouched in public. Then she said, 'It was David who told me that Father had been killed by means of arsenic given in several doses to secure a cumulative effect.' It was a clinical enough description for him to be reminded for an instant of Burgess in his pathology lab. It was strange to hear a daughter speaking thus about the death of a father; but murder and the shock it brought affected the innocent as well as the guilty in a multitude of different ways, which were rarely easy to forecast. Even more than with all the others, he wished he had seen this cool, enigmatic woman immediately after the death rather than thirteen months later. She said, 'Beyond that, I know nothing of what you call the detail of the murder. Perhaps you can enlighten me.'

Lambert wondered if the smile with which he tried to ease the atmosphere was in bad taste; probably. *Touché*, Mrs Harrison. As yet, we have no more knowledge of the murder than the method you have outlined, and you are right to underline the fact that that gives us depressingly little detail. We do not know yet whether the arsenic was administered through your father's food or by other means. We do not know exactly when the fatal dosages were given. I have to tell you that until someone tells us such things, we are not likely to discover them for ourselves at this distance in time.'

'And do you think someone will conveniently volunteer this information to you?' She was mocking him now; whether humorously or bitterly, he could not be sure. Irony twinkled in the grey-green eyes, bringing a new attractiveness to the long face, with its lines of dignified suffering.

'"Volunteer" would not be the right word, Mrs Harrison. But I expect us to assemble most of these facts in due course. Sometimes we only get the full picture after we have made an arrest, of course.' It sounded like a threat, and he knew he was a little nettled. But a threat could be the right tactic, even to a grieving daughter. He must bear in mind always that she was a murder suspect: no sin for a man to labour in his vocation.

'You will understand that I have to be interested in the relationship of all the people in any sort of contact with your father, both with him and with each other.'

'With each other?' Her surprise was so sharp that he wondered what she had to conceal here.

'There is a strong incidence of collusion in cases like this. That opens up not only the possibility of a killing by one of the five in immediate contact with the deceased, but of a murder planned by someone outside that group, who used one of them to gain access to his victim.'

'I see.' Her eyes caught the daylight and were green for a moment as she looked past, gazing through the window to the rectangle of grey winter sky and the world of speculation. Her fingers drummed silently on the broad arm of her low chair while she weighed the idea and found she had to accept it. 'I loved my father very much, Superintendent Lambert. I think anyone you question will confirm that.'

'Indeed, they already have. I have been told, for instance, of your solicitude for him in the last months of his decline.'

She looked at him sharply, searching for any trace of irony or menace in the words. Although he was sure she was aware of the notion, she had scorned to arrange things so that they faced the light while she sat with her back to it. Lambert, remaining impassive, could see each move of those strong features; he recognized an opponent worthy of respect in this macabre game they had begun. Or an ally: only time would tell him that. She said, 'I went regularly to Tall Timbers during the weeks of Dad's decline, yes. I was concerned about him. With good reason, it now seems.'

He nodded. 'You may in the process have seen things which could be helpful to us now. Things which assume importance only now that we know a murder was committed.'

'I've been thinking about that already. But it's a long time ago.'

'And the memory plays tricks, for all of us. It will be difficult, for instance, for you to place events in their correct time sequence.'

She smiled grimly. 'In books, someone often keeps a diary, which turns out to be very convenient for people like you.'

'We've got a scene of crime team going carefully through Tall Timbers. I'm afraid they won't come up with anything as useful as that.'

'Or anything else at this distance in time, surely?' She had voiced his own thoughts; but the due processes had to be observed. He was pleased that she was behaving as though they were on the same side in this.

'You know that arsenic was used?'

'Yes. Margaret Lewis told me.'

'Can you recall anyone trying to obtain arsenic, or any behaviour which would now strike you as suspicious in that respect?'

'No. Whoever used it might have had it for years, of course. It doesn't deteriorate much. And it is present in some relatively innocent things; several garden insecticides contained it, before we all went green.' She must have caught the look of speculation on Bert Hook's face, for she said, 'I used to work in a pharmacy many years ago, before I was married. I never qualified formally – Dad didn't approve of education for women.' This time her smile was bitter.

Lambert said gently, 'And you didn't defy him?'

She took his surprise as a compliment, as he had hoped. 'I was a dutiful daughter, and my mum was already ill with cancer. Dad wouldn't make up any grant that I got, and his income was such that it was financially impossible for me to do the course without his cooperation. I promised myself I'd do it later, and of course never got round to it. I've regretted it these last few years when money has been so tight. I do the odd locum for a dispensing chemist, but as I'm not formally qualified I'm paid accordingly.'

They were on the very ground Lambert wanted to explore, and she had led them there herself. He thought it was by accident rather than deliberately, but she was so direct in her responses to his questions that he could not be sure who was controlling the direction the discourse took. He thought that she was probably the rare sort of woman who had no small talk; and with the thought, he warmed to her as a kindred spirit. He said, 'Your husband is a shadowy figure for us at this point–'

'That is because he had no connection with my father.'

For the first time, she was defensive. 'That in itself has to be of interest to us, Mrs Harrison. You must see that.'

Perhaps because he had credited her with the intelligence not to need longer explanations, she relaxed a little and did not argue. 'My father loved me, Superintendent, despite what I have just told you of my education. And I loved him.' It was her second use that morning of a declaration he felt she did not use very often to strangers; she bit her lip gently before she continued. 'That does not mean that he did not have his faults. They included a blind prejudice where religion was concerned. Bigotry seems to have gone out of fashion nowadays, except in Northern Ireland. Dad's was very un-English. Sometimes I thought he was using it merely as a stick to beat a man he would never have taken to anyway.'

'The man being your husband, Michael?'

She seemed surprised that he knew the name: that was the effect he had intended. The impression that the police were omniscient often made people reveal what they would have kept back from others. 'Yes. He couldn't win from the start so far as Dad was concerned. Michael was three years younger than me, and that wasn't going to be right for someone as conventional as Dad. I was twenty-four at the time and Mum had just died: I think Dad had presumed without thinking about it that I would stay at home with him. That made him more bitter when someone carried me off. Especially when that someone was an unsuccessful artist, not a knight in shining armour.'

'And you say your husband's religion became a bone of contention?'

'It was from the beginning. Michael is a Roman Catholic. A shifty papist, as Father called it. My dad was what he described as "an Anglican of the old school". I've never been sure what he meant by that – sometimes I felt he wasn't sure himself. Anyway, it gave him the grounds he was looking for to hate Michael.'

Lambert was surprised to hear that the shadowy Michael Harrison was anything as mundane as a Catholic: he had half-expected one of the minority religions that milked its flock of large sums for dubious purposes. He had himself been brought up as a Catholic, but apart from a few school-boy skirmishes and a sardonic inspector twenty years ago, he had met little in the way of prejudice. Perhaps his doubt showed as he said, 'And this was the major cause of the estrangement between your father and your husband?'

'It became so. I married in a Catholic church and pledged myself to bring up any children as Catholics. I don't think Dad thought that would actually happen until they came along. He blamed Michael for all of it. It was difficult to have a rational argument with him. He already had his heart trouble by then: perhaps it affected his judgements as well.'

'I wanted to ask you about your father's relationship with his grandchildren.'

She looked at him for a moment as if she were speculating about who had spoken to him about her offspring. He sensed that this woman, coolly elegant even in poverty, could become a dragon in defence of her children. Again he found himself applauding the quality: policemen saw too many examples of the dire results of parental neglect. 'Dad was delighted at first, with both of them. He called James the heir of all the Cravens.' She stopped for a moment, her face clouded by some unhappy recollection. 'When Paula was born, he swore she was the image of me. In fact, she's just like Michael, but my father couldn't see that.' Her face softened, lit by the pure pleasure of her mental image of her husband and her daughter together.

'But your father's affection for his grandchildren didn't last?'

She shook her shoulders a little, bringing herself back to present realities. 'No. At least, I don't think he ever ceased to care for them, but he deliberately cut himself off. I think he was punishing me for marrying Michael and bringing them up as Catholics. It was his own loss, of course.' She looked affectionately at the happy, posed photograph of a boy of about six with his arm protectively about the shoulders of his young sister. Seeing that their eyes had followed hers, she said, 'That was Paula's first day at school.'

'That would be about the time when your father began to see them less?'

'Yes. When it came home to him that they were to be brought up as Catholics. The climax came a little later when they made their first communions.' She gestured at another of the photographs. They looked together at the open, happy faces of the children and mused upon the foolishness of their elders.

It was Bert Hook, speaking as if he wished to remind her that he was taking notes upon her private sorrows, who said rather clumsily over his notebook, 'We heard from Mr Arkwright that your father made no reference to them in his will.

'No. He left money to me, though, so they were not forgotten.' Her face had set suddenly into a proud mask. Perhaps it was remembered suffering that caused the effect; perhaps an eagerness to conceal the shame she felt in this area for a father she had loved; perhaps even a triumph that the children he had neglected would enjoy his riches in the end. It was impossible to tell, for the face was as unmoving as a stone Pharaoh's.

Lambert said, 'Your husband never managed to repair his relationship with your father?'

'No. That was not his fault.'

'You say he's an artist?'

'He was. That is to say, for a number of years he tried to make his living from his work. He got a certain number of commissions for portraits, and sold quite a lot of his landscapes, which are his real love. But it isn't easy to make a living. Especially when the time comes for you to support a family.' He could see her anxious face pleading the cause to an unsympathetic parent. 'Michael eventually accepted the inevitable and took up teaching.'

The old Shavian cliché came automatically into Lambert's mind. Those who can, do; those who can't, teach. But perhaps it was only those who couldn't meet the current fashions in art who had to teach nowadays. The oil over the mantelpiece that he took to be an example of Michael Harrison's work had an air of menace that played curiously against its conventional Cotswold content of river and trees. Probably she had followed his thoughts, for she said defiantly, 'He's pretty good at teaching, actually. The local further education college wants him to go full-time.' She had that strange glow which comes to a woman who would never think of boasting, except when she speaks with pride of her own family.

Lambert said, 'I understand your husband commented adversely on your father's paintings.'

Her face registered surprise, speculation and anger in quick succession. 'Who told you that?'

'I'm sure you will understand that I cannot disclose that.'

'No.' He could see her conjecturing about his informant before she sighed and said, 'Well, it's true enough. Dad used the old coach-house at the back of the garden as a studio: he used to be quite a keen amateur, though in my view never as talented as Mum.' For a moment, there was another, older love in those unusual eyes. 'Dad asked my husband for an opinion when relationships between them were already strained, and Michael was foolish enough to be honest. As a matter of fact, he doesn't really know how to be anything else.' Pride in the notion shone clearly on the strong features, and they saw something of what had attracted this dominant, desirable woman to the younger man.

Lambert wondered how many relationships had been ruined by honesty as uncompromising as Michael Harrison's. It would not have cost even a dedicated artist so much to be ambivalent with the old man, surely. Perhaps Walter Miller's conjecture that the impoverished professional had been jealous of the studio facilities enjoyed by the ungifted amateur was a shrewd one. The intelligent Mr Miller knew this family well and must not be underrated as a suspect.

Lambert looked at the picture of Michael Harrison with his wife, and saw a pleasant, slightly-built man with shrewd brown eyes. He was tidily dressed in casual clothes, with none of the bohemian extravagance of dress the public expects of its artists. He did not even have the almost obligatory beard. Two of the pictures caught him looking at his wife with something near adulation.

Lambert watched Bert Hook until he finished writing. Then he said, 'You know that your father was planning a new will?' She nodded, as though she did not trust herself to speak; for the first time, she was clearly anxious. Perhaps she thought he knew more about this than he did. To conceal his ignorance, he kept his question as general as possible. 'Have you any idea of what the contents of the new will would have been?'

'No.' She looked at the carpet between them; he was sure now that she was worried about the extent of his knowledge. 'Dad didn't talk to me about it.'

Her expression made him think that he probably had. 'But no doubt you have some idea of what he intended.'

She searched his face, found it uninformative, and switched her attention to Bert Hook; the Sergeant adopted what he hoped was an oriental inscrutability. Accepting eventually that she would have to speak, she said reluctantly, 'I presume Dad meant to cut David out. He wasn't pleased when he found David was going to sell the house.'

Lambert nodded slowly. 'I know this can't be easy for you, Mrs Harrison. But of course you must not withhold information in a case like this: I'm sure you appreciate that. I must ask you now whether you know, rather than merely suspect, that your brother would have been the chief sufferer in any re-writing of your father's will.'

'No. I should have told you if I had.'

'And you had no reason to think your father might intend to cut out you or your children from his provisions?'

'No.' She must have been aware that they were on to her own motive now, but she gave them no more than the monosyllable. For a moment, he wondered quite how sane this calm, quiet woman was where her family was involved. Her face had set again, with the intense, unbalanced concentration of a child. Or an old person: Lambert saw for a moment in the strong face the woman she might become in old age, obstinately shutting out the world, pretending that for her it did not exist. He was sure she knew more about this: it was extremely unlikely that Edmund Craven would have made changes without consulting or informing this daughter who had been so concerned for him in his last weeks. But he was equally convinced that he would get no more from her at this stage.

'Do you know of anyone else who might have suffered in a new will?'

She looked at him with wide eyes, as if she did not at first understand, like one coming out of a dream. Perhaps she had not expected him to desist from the line of questioning about her brother so quickly. Her forehead furrowed, as if she were now having to give attention to some smaller question. He could detect the relief in her voice as she said, 'I suppose Margaret Lewis could have lost the house in Burnham-on-Sea. She was the other main beneficiary.'

He noticed how she ignored herself in this; perhaps that was natural enough. 'Indeed. Did you see anything in your father's manner or behaviour which might have indicated such a move?'

She hesitated. 'He had no resentment against Margaret herself. Rather the reverse. But he certainly took against her son. And with good reason.'

Lambert wished he had a better picture of the elusive Andrew Lewis; he must remedy the deficiency as soon as he could. At present, he could only say rather lamely, 'You will need to explain that to me, I'm afraid.'

Perhaps she was relieved to have attention diverted for a while from herself and her brother, for she said with some relish, 'Andrew Lewis was what is charitably called a problem child. He crashed motor-bikes. He drove without insurance. He was involved in a brawl where someone was knifed. Eventually he went to prison for a few months. His mother couldn't see him as the young lout he was. Perhaps I can understand that. But Dad took a thorough dislike to Andrew Lewis.'

'Not surprisingly, perhaps. But does that have any bearing on your father's death?'

She paused a long time before she replied; he felt that she was choosing her words carefully before she spoke. 'Dad was old and ill, don't forget. And he was prone to hold the sins of the children against the parents.' She gave a bitter smile at her inversion of the usual sentiment, so that he thought she was thinking again of her own children, blameless as they were. She stared unseeingly at Bert Hook's notebook, giving the illusion for a moment that she was mesmerized by his writing hand, as though it were a hypnotist's watch.

'You mean that he might have planned to cut Margaret Lewis out of his will because of her son's transgressions?'

She came abruptly out of her trance and stared at him aggressively. 'I mean it's a possibility, no more. You invited me to speculate about the new will.'

'Indeed I did. Because of the nature of this particular investigation, I have to encourage speculation among all those closely concerned at this stage. I need a picture of your father's household at that time, a feeling of the atmosphere, which in this case I can only get at second hand.' He wondered if she would pick up the implication he had intended: that he would be asking other people to speculate about her part in all his. He would have been interested in her reaction to that thought. But she seemed intent only upon developing the thesis upon which she had embarked.

'I may be quite wrong. I'm only offering it as a possibility. I didn't even consider it at the time. If I had, I'd have talked to Dad on Margaret's behalf. She couldn't afford to lose that house.'

Lambert said very quietly, 'In the light of

that, do you think she could have been tempted to kill your father? From what we know of the method so far, you must realize that she had the best opportunity.'

She gasped at the directness of that. She had remained physically very still throughout the interview even when she had been under stress. Now for the first time her hands clasped together and she could not prevent the fingers from kneading each other. He wondered if she were being tempted to try to divert his attention away from her brother. But her reply when it came was not quite what he had expected. 'I can't see Margaret Lewis murdering my father. But her son had been involved in one violent crime already. And whatever faults Andrew Lewis has, he's very fond of Margaret. If he thought his mother was being robbed of what she had been promised, he might well have done anything to put things right.'

The grey-green eyes flashed wildly at him as she tossed her brown hair back, in a gesture which seemed curiously adolescent. Not many members of the public are invited to accuse someone of murder, and it was not surprising that the moment brought a febrile excitement even to a woman with her degree of control.

Lambert was left thinking of Walter Miller's more tangible evidence, of the picture he had given of Andrew Lewis standing aghast when he was surprised with Edmund Craven's medicine.

CHAPTER 12

Bert Hook was in many respects a caricature of the village bobby of popular
imagination. He was rubicund of countenance, deliberate of movement, slightly
overweight now in his early forties.

It was easy to see him in the mind's eye
riding a heavy black police bike around the
Cotswold hamlets of the 'fifties, controlling
the high-spirited youth of an earlier era with
snippets of well-chosen advice. It took only
a slightly greater leap of the imagination to
see him directing fouler-mouthed contemporary adolescents with equal facility.

Facts as well as fancy were available to
support this image of community pillar and
servant. The off-duty Hook had dominated
the village greens of Gloucestershire and
Herefordshire on many summer afternoons,
as fearsome opening bowler, sturdy hitter
and surprisingly nimble mid-wicket. Never
claiming to be more than a brisk military
medium, Bert had made the best batsmen
in the area hurry their shots. The days of the
squire might be long gone, but many a
stockbroker and estate agent returned to the
office on Monday morning moving carefully

with the tenderness of the weekend bruises.

Hook enjoyed the idea of himself as honest yeoman. When it suited him, he would add a deliberate gravity to his bearing, becoming ponderous in speech as well as manner. The public's notion of what is usual being normally a generation behind the reality, Bert Hook was in the public view a thoroughly conventional, even reassuring, representative of the law. It was a quality that John Lambert, who had good reason to hold a very different view of the speed of thought and judgement of his subordinate, found useful on numerous occasions. There is nothing a criminal can do which will so quickly undermine his liberty as to underestimate a CID man. Most of them know it and are careful to avoid the error, but Bert Hook fooled them more often than anyone the Superintendent had ever come across.

And in one respect Bert Hook was rare among sergeants. He was prone to give the underdog the benefit of the doubt. Most policemen think that underdogs deserve to be exactly that; and it has to be said that the evidence they come across overwhelmingly supports their view. It was the only area where Bert was occasionally unpopular with his peers, whose experience of the seamier side of human nature convinced them in their more jaundiced moments that Bert should have been a social worker rather than a detective-sergeant.

When therefore Lambert discussed Andrew Lewis with him as they journeyed to interview him in Bristol, Hook was reluctant to accept the verdict of others without his own assessment of the youth. 'If everyone with a history of teenage motoring offences was locked up, the prisons would be even more overcrowded than at the moment,' he said.

'He already has a conviction for GBH,' Lambert pointed out.

'As an accessory, so far as I can see,' said Hook.

Lambert grinned. He wondered how much Hook's attitude was a reaction to Detective-Inspector Rushton, who had produced the police computer information on Margaret Lewis's son like a magician triumphantly brandishing his final rabbit. 'Apparently he fled in a stolen car when the local uniformed men tried to bring him in for us to question.'

Bert Hook considered this carefully, while the russet foliage flowed past the window of the Vauxhall in a steady stream. Finally he said, 'It's a long step from stealing cars to planning and executing a murder like this.'

'That's true enough, certainly. But we know he was around at the time, and that his mother thought it prudent to conceal that presence from us.'

'Mothers tend to be over-protective when it's not always necessary. Don't forget she's the only parent he has.'

Lambert, who knew that that was one more than Bert had been able to count on, did not take up that. He said, 'Angela Harrison said he was very attached to that one parent. In her view, he might well have killed for her if her interests were being threatened.'

'Purely hypothetical, you'd say to me, if I offered you anything like that!' said his Sergeant indignantly.

'Indeed I would. Interesting, though; Mrs Harrison didn't try to implicate anyone else.'

'Considering two of the other possibilities were herself and her own brother, that's not very surprising,' said Hook, with something as near to sarcasm as he thought it polite for a sergeant to risk with a superintendent.

Lambert braked to let in a driver who had been determined to overtake them even as the road narrowed, using an expression his wife had spent years eliminating from his vocabulary. 'According to Walter Miller, he was caught with his hand in Edmund Craven's medicine cabinet five days before the old man's death.'

Hook paused over his reply to this. Lambert as usual had got it right from memory: Bert had checked his notes to be sure of Miller's wording during the first stages of their journey. Eventually he said rather lamely, 'There may be a perfectly innocent explanation of that.'

Lambert smiled, acknowledging his small victory in the argument. 'There may be indeed, Bert. If there is, young Andrew apparently was not prepared to volunteer it to Mr Miller or anyone else at the time.'

Bert thought of saying that they didn't yet know how he had been asked, decided it sounded too much like that police *bête noire* the defence counsel, and elected to change the line of discussion. He said abruptly, 'My money's still on David Craven.'

'I thought it just might be. I could see him rubbing you up the wrong way – it's no good looking hurt, Bert, you're not yet as inscrutable as you would like to be. And long may it remain so, say I. If it cheers you up, I would have to agree that there are things which point very directly towards him as a murderer. From what we hear of his business dealings, from the bank and others as well as what he admits himself, he had been both unscrupulous and un-successful in the years before his father's death. That is often a fatal combination: it leads to desperation. And both of us know by now that desperation is the one common element in a whole range of different murders.'

There was silence as each reviewed in his mind's eye the desperation of the men and women they had seen driven to this darkest of crimes, from women and children driven to terminal violence by years of abuse, through the kaleidoscope of what the French dramatize as 'crimes of passion', to those killings where men have found themselves in the ultimate corner after playing for and losing big financial stakes. Was Edmund Craven's only son going to be one to place in this last category?

Hook said, 'It looks as though David Craven was to be the chief loser in the will that never was. He as much as admitted so himself.'

'Yes. That will worries me. No one is admitting to more than surmise about the way the old man planned to change things, but I'm sure at least one person knew something more definite; and maybe more than one.'

'David Craven?'

'Possibly. Especially if the chief changes concerned him. But according to what he and everyone else says, relationships between himself and his father were strained in those last months, after the old man found that his son planned to dispose of the house. From what we have been able to piece together about the atmosphere in Tall Timbers in the weeks during which old

Craven was poisoned, it seems more likely that he would discuss his plans with his daughter or Margaret Lewis.'

'Or even Walter Miller,' said Hook reluctantly: he did not really want to move away from his suspicions of David Craven. 'Edmund Craven had known him longer than anyone; he was the only contemporary he had to talk to. And sometimes there are advantages in having someone to talk to about a will who is not a significant beneficiary.'

'Detachment. Mmm. I wonder if Mr Miller was quite as detached as he gave us to believe.'

Lambert slowed the car and they watched three small rabbits starting away through the hedge on their right, wondering if they were old enough to survive the winter and its predators. Then Hook said firmly, 'I liked him.' He wondered if his chief's dislike of transatlantic intrusions upon the language extended to human representatives of the United States. 'He's been in this country for a long time now, you know,' he admonished, as if he were gently chiding the entrenched prejudice of the elderly.

'Yes. He seemed only too anxious to forget the past and dwell in the present. Unusual in one of his years. I wonder what he was hiding.' Hook recognized from experience this wilful tendency towards the arcane in his chief. He was quite clear what his re-action should be. Any tendency to play the fictional Great Detective should be actively discouraged in senior policemen – the disease was unknown below the rank of inspector.

Hook passed hastily on to a different subject. 'I liked both the women,' he said abruptly.

'Ah,' said his chief, '"Is this that haughty, gallant, gay Lothario?"'

The Sergeant decided to ignore such impenetrable flippancy. 'Everyone seems to think Margaret Lewis served the old boy well. That's not necessarily typical of housekeepers.'

'It's probably true that she was diligent in her service to old Craven. But you must allow that your views are probably coloured by the many descendants of Mrs Squeers you met in your distant youth.'

'Not so many. And not so distant,' returned the Sergeant steadily.

'Mrs Lewis is personable. And highly competent, I'm sure. And deceptive, when it suits her: she conveniently left out any mention of her son in our conversation. They're all qualities which would be useful to someone planning a murder like this. We shall have to talk to her again in due course.'

'Why do you think she concealed her son's presence in the house at the time of the murder? She must have known that some-one was sure to tell us about Andrew sooner or later.' Unconsciously, Hook already knew and used the boy's first name, as few CID men would have done in the case of a youth with a record.

They were on a straight stretch of road, so that Lambert could permit himself the small movement of the arms that had to do duty as a shoulder shrug. 'It would be interesting to know. Perhaps no more than the instinct of a mother to protect her suspect chicken. Perhaps the wish to warn him that we were pursuing a murder investigation. Perhaps, if they had planned the murder together, the chance to confer about their stories to make sure they tallied. Perhaps we'll have a better idea after we've seen her son.'

That thought seemed to close the file for the moment on Margaret Lewis. With the day almost over, the sun had made a belated appearance over the estuary of the Severn on their right. They watched it silvering the great reaches of wet sand that stretched for miles here at low tide. When the vista passed from them behind a drab green winter meadow, it was as though someone had turned off an electric bulb. Bert Hook felt his spirits falling with the light. He said unwillingly, 'What did you think of Angela Harrison?'

Lambert took so long to reply that his sergeant thought for a moment that he was going to be ignored. 'That she was the centre of a happy and united family. I suppose that if I think that without seeing either her husband or her children, she must be a pretty strong personality. All the signs are that she was also a good daughter to Edmund Craven in trying circumstances. Other people say so: that's always interesting when someone has inherited money, because that's when jealousy tends to take over and people find faults they never saw before.'

'You liked her too, then.' Hook made it a statement, not a question: he was still professionally sensitive about the way he had been picked up about his liking for the two women.

'Yes, I did. But she lied to us on at least one occasion. And I'm afraid she wouldn't be the first admirable person to commit murder. Certainly not the first likeable one: I think you and I would probably have quite liked Crippen and one or two others.'

They were running into the town now. The last two of a ragged crowd of schoolboys newly released from education scampered belatedly across the zebra crossing behind their fellows and offered a fleeting V-sign to the occupants of the aging Vauxhall. Hook, attempting a lofty indifference which was difficult from a level below the provocation, wished that his chief would at least occasionally use a police vehicle with the appropriate markings of authority. He said dolefully, 'I wish it wasn't all so long ago. I feel I can't be certain of anything about anyone yet. It's a murky pool.'

As they drove into the police station car park, Lambert was still toying with the conventional metaphor. 'A pool into which a murderer threw a stone. The ripples are still moving out from it, even at this stage. We've caught a few of them: we must trace them back to their centre.'

They went slowly into the big modern building to meet their fifth suspect.

CHAPTER 13

Interview rooms in police stations are not designed to please the eye. They are at best functional, at worst cold and ugly.

The one on the outskirts of Bristol to which Andrew Lewis was brought to confront the CID was about average. It was not cold: the four-year-old building enjoyed the benefits of a modern heating system. It did not have the gloss paint over bare brick which brought the air of the public lavatory to many city centre interview rooms. But it was not designed to reassure its non-police occupants, and in that respect the design succeeded admirably.

The room was very small; when it was occupied by two large policemen, and the man they had come eighty miles to see, it was quite claustrophobic. Perhaps because of its smallness, the primrose yellow with which some daring innovator had emulsioned the walls was marked in many places with the scuff-marks of chairs and clothing. The fluorescent light which was positioned in the exact centre of the ceiling was not particularly powerful, but in that tiny, windowless space its white glare seemed at first quite blinding, reinforcing the impression that this was a room where it would be futile to attempt to hide things.

Furniture, as one would expect in such a place, was cut to the irreducible minimum: a single chair on each side of the small square table which stood beneath the light. Here questioner and questioned could confront each other with their eyes no more than three feet apart and every change of feature mercilessly illumined by the shadowless light. Lambert called for an extra chair and positioned it so that neither he nor Hook should dominate their side of the table; the effect for the man who was now brought to sit opposite them was no doubt of an increase in the forces ranged against him rather than a diminution of the intensity. It was a situation designed to discourage truculence.

Andrew Lewis had no truculence. Still in his torn jeans and oil-stained shirt, with one lace broken in his trainers, he almost cringed as he was brought in and ordered to sit down. He had his mother's ash-blonde hair and blue eyes; the first was dishevelled, the second full of the unfocused fear of a child in a world of hostile adults. He had not asked for a wash, so that he had not been offered one: the uniformed branch did not see putting young tearaways at their ease as part of their brief.

Lewis was no tearaway. His thin, hunched shoulders trembled as he waited to be questioned. The grubby stains which ran in irregular smears beneath the eyes only emphasized the youth in the fresh, unlined face. At this moment, it was easy to see why Margaret Lewis might feel the need to defend this vulnerable creature with all the resources at her command. Biology was a powerful force. And Lambert had a sense of fair play that was increasingly old-fashioned: he felt an illogical annoyance against the men who had tried to help him by sending a suspect in like this. He called for the only alleviation the system had to offer. In three minutes, a constable brought in three steaming mugs of tea, setting the smallest one before Lewis with the fraction of a second's unconscious hesitation which was all his sense of discipline allowed to his resentment.

Lambert, who had lately given up all sweetening, tried not to watch Bert Hook's large hands struggling incongruously to drop sweeteners from his plastic dispenser into his tea. He said to the apprehensive man opposite to them, 'How old are you?' They knew the answer from the growing pile of material which was being assembled for them in the murder room at Oldford, but it was a neutral way of beginning with a subject who was full of distrust.

'Twenty-two.'

'Have you been in trouble with the police before?' He regretted that 'before' immediately, with its implication that Lewis was up against the system and all its resources.

'You people know all about that.' The young face stared at the table between them, face blank as a sheet of grubby notepaper. Like a child who has done wrong and knows it, he was lapsing into a trance-like sullenness, defying a reaction to an adult world seeking a sign of remorse.

Lambert, aware of his colleague beside him studying those tight-shut features, took a quick decision. Without a word, he motioned Hook to take on the questioning.

The Sergeant allowed himself a swift flash of surprise, no more. He took over the central role with the slightest nod of acceptance. Then he said nothing for what seemed a very long time. The seconds stretched out slowly, painfully, until the silence in that tiny, stifling room seemed like a tangible thing.

Eventually, as Hook knew must happen, the youth's eyes were drawn upwards, slowly, painfully, as if by some agency outside himself. The Sergeant gave him a small, slow smile; Lewis looked down again, but both of them knew now that there was a kind of contact, neither friendly nor hostile. Bert said, 'We'd rather hear it from you, lad.'

The youth lifted a hand to his hair, moving

it slowly back from where it hung over his left eye, stroking it over his scalp into a semblance of order. It was the first movement he had made since he had been ordered to sit on the chair. He said dully, as if speaking against his inclination, 'Where do you want me to begin?'

This time the silence was not a tactic. Hook was thinking furiously. 'Have the people here told you why you were brought in?'

'No. I ran away.' He sounded as though he were explaining why the people who had locked him in a cell were not at fault. Perhaps he thought that if there was any misunderstanding, he would be the ultimate sufferer.

'So I heard. Led them quite a dance. Naughty lad.' Perhaps Lewis caught a friendly rather than a threatening note in the words, for he glanced quickly up at Hook, then across at the impassive Lambert. Hook said formally, 'Your mother was housekeeper to a certain Mr Edmund Craven, who died just over a year ago. We now know that what was originally registered as a death from natural causes was in fact a murder. Did you know that?'

Lewis licked his lips. 'Yes.' Plainly he wondered what was coming next. Hook, indulging his natural inclination, took his time. And all the while he watched the young man opposite him.

'Do you know how?'

Lewis shook his head, as though he did not trust himself to speak. His interlocutors studied him, wondering whether his ignorance was genuine. This time his eyes did not twitch upwards to theirs. He did not see the affirmation Lambert gave to Hook before the Sergeant gave the detail. 'He was poisoned. In fact he was given several dosages of arsenic over a period of months. Someone planned this murder very carefully and carried it through very ruthlessly.'

Now Lewis did look at them. And the blue, revealing eyes were full of fear. Whether it was the horror which descends upon the innocent in face of the evidence of evil, or the alarm of the killer who sees that his methods are revealed, it was impossible to say. Presently he looked between them, towards the door of the room, not as if he expected any release from there, but rather as if he expected it to open new and even grimmer revelations. Perhaps he decided eventually that Hook was the nearest thing to a friend for him in this place. He said directly to the Sergeant, securing for the moment a brittle calm, 'That is horrible. But I didn't do it, and I don't know who did.'

'Maybe not, lad. But perhaps you know more than you realize. In any case, we need to clear you of suspicion. We think that from what we know of the murder, it was probably committed by someone who had regular access to the victim in the three months or so before he died.'

Andrew glanced sharply from one to the other. 'I was there then,' he said, through lips that were so nearly shut that even in that small room they could barely hear him.

'Exactly,' said Hook calmly. 'And that's why we're here now. We need to clear you if we can, and also find what you know about any of the other people involved.'

By putting the emphasis on clearing the young man rather than the seriousness of his position as a suspect, Hook kept him talking instead of lapsing back into the sullen panic where he had begun. Lewis said, 'I was there. I didn't see much. I kept out of Craven's way as much as I could.'

'Why was that?'

'He didn't like me. I didn't like him much. But I didn't know he was – dying.' The recollection of opportunities missed and things which would have been better left unsaid passed across his face. It was probably the first time this youth had felt the irrevocability of death; for the men opposite him, it was a look they had seen too often before.

'Had you given him reason to dislike you?'

Lewis sighed. He was relaxed enough now

180

to permit himself a tiny rueful smile, recognizing that he was going to volunteer the information he had been denying them at the beginning of the interview. 'Yes, I suppose so. He didn't like younger people much anyway – you should ask his daughter and her husband about that. Once I got in trouble with the police, he didn't even want me in the house.'

'That is not an unusual attitude. How did you get into trouble?'

A sour little smile again. 'My mother would tell you that I got into the wrong company. It's true, but it's too easy an excuse.' Andrew Lewis was more intelligent than the frightened weakling he had appeared to be at the beginning of the interview. Lambert's first, irritated reaction was that this did not necessarily make things less complicated: it might bring him back into focus as a possible murderer or accomplice. His thin lips were framing words carefully now, as he began the story he had thought to deny them. 'When I left school, I had six O-levels, but the area was in the grip of the 'eighties recession. Things are a lot better now for school-leavers. I got various small jobs in supermarkets, most of them temporary. Then I went to an engineering firm on a YTS scheme. I did quite well, but at the end of six months the employer got rid of me, at the point where he would have had to pay proper wages.'

'You found you were just cheap labour, and when you ceased to be cheap he dispensed with you and looked for another government trainee.' Hook sounded quite resentful himself, and it was not a response he simulated to encourage confidence in the man opposite him: he had seen too much abuse of the scheme to distrust what Andrew Lewis was telling him now.

'I'd always been quite good with engines, which had won me friends among older boys after I left school. After the YTS fiasco, I was feeling pretty bitter and I didn't even look for proper employment. I spent my time repairing motor-bikes and old cars for the lads I knew. I didn't always get paid what I had been promised.'

Hook nodded. It was the start of a pilgrim's progress of life's disillusionments. Perhaps the boy would have gone less far along this road if he had had a father to advise him: Bert liked him better for not offering the absence as a mitigation of his conduct. He said, 'And it was at this time that you first came before the courts?'

'It was stupid, really. After a Christmas party I gave someone a lift on the back of someone else's moped – I don't drink, you see, or scarcely, anyway. It was a week before I was due to take my test. Of course, the police caught me. Eventually, I was done not just for carrying an unauthorized pillion passenger but for taking a vehicle away without the owner's consent. I hadn't done that, but I think the bloke thought he'd get away with things more easily himself if he said I had.'

'You got a fine?'

'Two hundred quid. And a ban. And six penalty points on my licence.'

If Hook thought it harsh, he gave no sign. 'That was the beginning of your troubles.' He could understand young, keen constables wanting a conviction. No youngster ever beat the system, unless he had more money and influence than young Andrew Lewis. He did not at this moment agree with Angela Harrison's description of him, as 'a lout'.

Lewis was in more of a dilemma than he cared to show. 'Never trust a policeman' was a dictum that had been quoted to him often in his short life, and all his previous experience had confirmed it. Now, in what he had thought his greatest crisis, he had to decide how far to trust this equable, understanding man in plain clothes. He wanted to, and perhaps in truth he had not very much choice in the matter. He said, 'I suppose it was the real beginning of disaster for me, yes. I thought the magistrates had thrown the book at me, and all my friends encouraged me to be bitter. The case made the local papers: there had been cannabis at the party, though I wasn't involved in that. I couldn't get any permanent work, and I was too bitter to listen to the right people.'

'Like your mother,' said Hook quietly.

Lewis looked at him quickly, suspecting some attempt to trap him. But his confidence held. He gave a small shrug of his thin shoulders and said, 'Yes, Mum was about the only one giving sensible advice, but most boys of seventeen think they know more than their mothers. I was still repairing cars for the wrong people. And when I was asked, I drove one of those cars on the wrong occasion.'

He paused, and Hook said, 'Did you know where you were going?'

Lewis looked at him for several seconds before he replied, 'No. But perhaps I should have done. It was a Jaguar and I think I was so anxious to drive it that I didn't ask too many questions.' He said apologetically, 'I'm keen on cars, and I think I can drive a bit.' It was the first thing that he said that even approached a boast.

'So I hear,' said Hook rather grimly. 'I believe you can handle a Lotus when you're given the chance.'

It reminded Lewis of the trouble he was in. He looked cast down again. He was looking down at the table when he went on in a monotone, 'It turned out that my

184

companions were holding up a little general shop run by a Pakistani. They'd got me because I could handle the car for a quick getaway: I'd just tuned it up. I got out of the car to see what was going on and walked straight into a major incident. My passenger was threatening the shopkeeper with a knife. He'd never have used it, but–'

'No one intends to use a weapon when they take it with them, lad. Then things happen.'

'I suppose so. Anyway, the shopkeeper's wife had rung the police and we were caught in the shop.'

'And the jury didn't believe that you hadn't known what the whole thing was about until you got there.'

Lewis nodded miserably. Recollecting an incident he had been over a thousand times in his own mind was unpleasant therapy.

'Would you have believed your story, if you'd been in their position?'

'I suppose not.'

'Of course you wouldn't. There are times when if you behave badly, you just have to live with the consequences; you've learned that the hard way. At least I hope you have.'

Lewis did not respond to that: perhaps he was thinking of his drive in the Lotus. Eventually he said, 'I don't suppose you believe me either.'

Hook sighed. 'For what it's worth, I think

I do. If it wasn't true, I'd have expected a bright lad like you to come up with a more convincing story by now. But it doesn't matter a damn now whether I believe you or not.'

Andrew Lewis said nothing to that. He was not going to explain what he hardly recognized himself, that it had suddenly become important to him that this bluff man who was questioning him should accept that what he said was reliable. He reverted to matters of indisputable fact. 'The chap with the knife went to prison. I was sent to a Borstal for four months: it was still a week to my eighteenth birthday at the time of the crime.'

'You went back to Tall Timbers when you were released?'

'Yes. I managed after a while to get quite a lot of work servicing and repairing people's vehicles, but Mr Craven stopped me getting a permanent mechanic's job in the area. Every time I was being considered, he rang up and asked them if they really wanted to employ a jailbird. He knew all the local garage-owners – he'd lived in the area all his life.'

Hook was silent for a moment, considering the picture of the household at Tall Timbers indicated by this. He decided that he did not much like the late Edmund Craven: such positive malevolence went beyond what he would allow to the natural prejudice of old age against youth. Beside him, Lambert was thinking of Walter Miller's view that young Lewis had 'shown he could be violent' and 'hated Ed'. The second at least seemed to be justified, whatever the provocation. It made this man a more convincing murder suspect; he was capable of acting impulsively, as he had shown even today in his flight. Whether he was capable of the planning and nerve to conduct a murder over several weeks remained to be investigated; in alliance with some other person, it was certainly a possibility.

Hook said, 'You obviously had no love for the late Mr Craven.'

Lewis had the air now of a man determined to clear the air. It was a reaction they met often enough among people who were not confirmed criminals; sometimes there was a kind of therapy involved. It was also a syndrome which some offenders were expert in simulating, a fact which could make life difficult for persevering detectives. 'No. For the most part I kept out of his way, because I didn't want to make things difficult for Mum. He'd been quite good to her, and I knew he planned to leave her the house in Burnham. I was frightened to death she might lose that through me.'

Lambert spoke now, for the first time

187

since the beginning of the interview. 'Did you think he was the kind of man who might have punished an innocent parent for what he didn't like in her offspring?'

If Lewis thought that the phrasing gave a wider context to the question than his own problems, he gave no sign of it. He said, 'I do, yes. He more or less threatened me with that, on one occasion.'

Hook said, 'We'd better know that occasion, Andrew. Other people will probably recall it as well as you.'

'I'd been repairing a window that was jammed in Mr Craven's bedroom. He accused me of taking some money that had been on the dressing-table and ordered me out of the house. I knew I hadn't taken anything, and I'm afraid I shouted back at him. My mother eventually arrived to calm him down and get me off the scene. It was she who eventually found the money intact, in the top drawer of the dressing-table.'

It was a little scene which opened up possibilities, where the CID men wanted only certainties. Hook said a little wearily, 'Did anyone else know of this?'

Lewis nodded. 'Angela Harrison was in the house at the time. She heard the row between us and arrived with Mum to find out what it was all about. I think she believed her father – only natural, I suppose. It was only later that Mum found the money.'

'When was this? Can you remember?'

'About two months before Mr Craven died. I'd been saving up to move out, and the row made me even more determined.'

'So you left more or less immediately?'

'No. But I began looking for a place in earnest. I moved out just after he died.' Perhaps he caught the sinister overtones of this timing, for he shrugged helplessly. 'I looked for a place in Burnham because I knew Mum would be moving to the house there. Eventually.'

The last word sounded like a belated attempt to extricate himself from a damning statement. Hook said, 'In those last months of Edmund Craven's life, you were probably in the house more often than anyone except your mother. Did you see anything which strikes you as suspicious conduct, now that you know that a murder was being executed at the time?'

'No.' His negative was so prompt that he thought it needed explanation. 'I've thought about it, you see, since Mum told me it was murder.'

Hook nodded, looked at Lambert for instructions, received a slight shake of the head. He said, 'Well, keep on thinking, there's a good lad. And if you think of anything at all – any unusual food or drink brought into the house, for instance – let us know right away, it won't get anyone into trouble if it was innocent. Remember that this was a very nasty crime indeed.'

Again, Hook looked at Lambert interrogatively, and found him now as uncommunicative as a sphinx: he was able to divine his chief's secret amusement only because he had worked with him now for many years. He turned back to their suspect. 'Why did you try to evade questioning today?'

Lewis gave them a perfunctory account of the young constable's approach to him as he finished servicing the Lotus. It was enough for experienced men to deduce the full picture. He concluded dolefully, 'Once I was in the car, I panicked. When the traffic patrol gave chase, I just put my foot down. I – I nearly had a bad crash in the end.' Beneath the dirt, his soiled, too-young features were ashen with the recollection.

'So I believe,' said Hook drily. 'I heard that if you hadn't been a proper little Stirling Moss, there would have been a right pile-up.'

Andrew Lewis looked puzzled: Stirling Moss was a legend from an age before he was born; he was not sure whether he was being complimented or admonished.

Lambert spoke now, as Hook had been willing him to do. 'It isn't on our patch, and I've no jurisdiction over traffic police. But we'll see what we can do to make sure no charges are preferred. I understand there was no damage to either the police vehicle or the Lotus you road-tested so thoroughly. Next time, try to assist us with our inquiries without so dramatic a prelude, please.'

Lambert disappeared to make the first lenient police arrangements which Andrew Lewis had ever experienced. It was Hook who took the call which came through from the murder room in Oldford. DI Rushton was urgent with news, but he was not going to waste it on a mere sergeant. 'Is the Superintendent coming into CID today?' he asked brusquely.

'I understand he intends to come straight to the murder room from here for a report. We're just about to leave,' Hook said stiffly.

'Good. I'll save it until you get here, then. Just tell the Super that the scene of crime team has come up with something extremely interesting at Tall Timbers.'

CHAPTER 14

'You didn't tell them?'

'No. Perhaps I should have done.' Walter Miller gave a smile that was meant to relieve his anxious wife. It was so fleeting that she felt even more uncertain.

She said, 'But it had nothing to do with Ed's death.'

'No. But they might not see it like that.'

'I don't see how they can find out.' What she had meant as a statement emerged almost as a question: she was looking for reassurance.

'They're trying to piece together Ed's habits and movements over his last year. They're talking to everyone who was close to him. God knows what they'll tell him about me.'

'But they can't know what happened all those years ago.'

He smiled. It was a grim, mirthless recognition of her naïvety. 'You can't be certain of that. I think Ed's children do know, from their attitude, though obviously I've never discussed it with them.'

'Obviously.' Even after forty years, Dorothy Miller could not reconcile the contrast of his relaxed, transatlantic drawl with the terse import of the statements he was making. She felt that they were heading for the row she had never intended.

'It may be that Margaret Lewis knows too,' he said.

She felt a cold, hopeless annoyance that she could not be rid of this thing after all these years. 'Are you sure you're not imagining this? Giving a deliberate importance to something that will never be raised?'

He looked down into her white, angry face. 'In their eyes, it gives me a motive, Dorothy. That's all.'

He walked abruptly away from her into his study and shut the door. She heard him speaking on the phone to someone, and wondered whether it was one of those other suspects he had mentioned. A little while later he went out, without another word to her. She cursed the way the death of Ed Craven had come between them like this, reviving bitternesses she had thought safely buried. Then, staring bleak and unseeing through the window, she began to contemplate the nightmare she had refused to countenance: the possibility that the husband whose bed she shared was a murderer....

Walter Miller drove out towards the Malvern hills. There, on a path where Elgar had walked and composed his most English of music while Miller was an infant, the elderly American began to climb away from the road and civilization. In his tweed plus-twos and jacket, he looked more English than most of the natives who came here now.

There was a well-worn track at first, for he trod upon an ancient way where men had gone before him for over a thousand years. When he turned through a five-barred gate marked 'Private' and passed almost immediately by a smaller notice which allowed 'No shooting without permit', he was on a quieter, less distinct path, which ran through sporadic woodland. It was well into the afternoon of the short winter day, and one would not have expected his walk to be disturbed by any other human presence in that place, at that hour.

Yet one would have been wrong in that. Not more than five minutes after Miller, another man walked the same well-marked public path. At the point where the elderly American had moved from the public track on to private land, he turned to survey the ground behind him and the hill above, as if checking to see that he was not observed. If that was his purpose, he must have been satisfied, for there was no evidence of any other being over an area of several square miles.

David Craven looked at his watch. It was

almost four: there could be scarcely half an hour of twilight left. He turned on to the faint track that Miller had followed, lengthening his stride as he moved through the intermittent patches of scrub to the thicker wood beyond.

Craven was not dressed like an English country gentleman, as his predecessor had been, for he had come here with minimal notice. He had merely thrown a short car coat over his city suit, and he took care in his light shoes to avoid the dark patches where surface moisture turned into mud.

He carried, however, one accoutrement which might have been expected in someone moving here. Whether it was adopted merely so that his journey here might not excite comment, or whether he proposed any actual use of it, would be clear only with the passage of time.

Casually draped across his left arm, he carried a double-barrelled shotgun.

CHAPTER 15

Like an old dog going back to its bed, Lambert was glad to re-enter the familiar environment of the CID headquarters at Oldford. No doubt the modern station where they had interviewed Andrew Lewis was more efficient in many respects, but he felt a cosy comfort now in the nineteenth-century stone building, which had been a school until its falling rolls and made available in the 'eighties for the growth industry of crime prevention.

He felt so amiably disposed that he handed over the initial section of the conference in the murder room to Detective-Inspector Rushton. The course on 'Resource Management' which Lambert had recently attended at the police training school advised such moves where possible, and Rushton certainly appeared gratified by the role it accorded him.

'Perhaps if I give us a quick overview of what is ongoing, we can then get down to the nitty gritty,' he said briskly.

Lambert winced inwardly, then smiled a sickly smile as he caught Hook's delighted glance. It was the kind of thing the Sergeant might have concocted to bait him deliberately: he feared that Rushton's Americanisms were quite unconscious. He braced himself not to groan if 'parameters' should rear their Cerberus-like heads in the ensuing development. Of the rest, only Dr Burgess, drawn here from his pathology lab by what he sensed was an invitation from Rushton to involve himself in the machinery of a police murder investigation, seemed to notice anything unusual in Rushton's language. The three detective-constables merely bent forward in dutiful attention, the very embodiment, they hoped, of the razor-sharp awareness Rushton encouraged as the appropriate attitude in his team.

Rushton went on, 'There have been one or two interesting things turned up by the scene of crime team. Perhaps we could come to those in a few minutes.' Lambert already half-regretted his decision to hand over the conduct of the meeting. Rushton was stage managing it to make the maximum impact with his own news, but he could hardly be deprived of control at this stage. The Inspector said, 'Perhaps we could pick Dr Burgess's brains first, because I'm not sure how long he can stay.'

'Wild horses would remove me only with difficulty,' said Burgess graciously. 'How can I be of assistance?'

'Only, I think, in confirming and perhaps

filling out the details of the poisoning. We know it was arsenic; can you give us any more details of how it was administered?'

Burgess leaned back and pressed the tips of his fingers together; they looked for a moment as though his immaculate dark blue worsted suit had been devised specifically as a background for their manicured perfection. 'You will have read the official PM report by now. It does not do a lot more than make official what I told Superintendent Lambert in the early stages. Death was from arsenic poisoning, in what looks like three stages, from analysis of hair samples taken from the corpse.'

'Can you tell us any more about the method of administration?'

Burgess might well have thought he had given them quite a lot from a corpse thirteen months old, but he was as enthusiastic as a schoolboy to be brought into that police preserve, the murder room. 'No doubt arsenic was ingested in food or drink. One of its advantages for a poisoner is that the unfortunate recipient cannot detect the sorts of quantities which were probable here if they are placed in the right foodstuffs. Arsenic is soluble: one of the favourite methods back in the 'thirties and 'forties was to put it in chocolate or sweetmeats, but any strong-flavoured food or drink would do. If you mix it with sugar, you could cheerfully sprinkle it upon your cornflakes or muesli without detecting it.' He beamed round the company of detectives, happy that he need not here disguise his normal robust curiosity in the face of violent death.

'How easy is it to obtain?' said Rushton, like a counsel carefully avoiding leading his witness.

'Nowadays, quite difficult. It used to be in a lot of cosmetics; it's still in quite a few, but generally in quite minute quantities. It also used to be used in quite lethal dosages in some garden insecticides. They have been withdrawn from sale to the public, but of course it's quite possible that there would have been bottles in the garden shed at Tall Timbers which have been around for years. In the good old days of value for money, the quantities used in spraying were so small that, except in the largest gardens, bottles of insecticides normally lasted for years. I suppose in the hands of some more abstemious members of the fair sex, the same could be said for cosmetics. The snag for a poisoner with both cosmetics and insecticides is that arsenic is used with chemicals which are often nauseous: it might be more difficult to disguise its use from the victim. But there are ways: it would depend upon the skill of the murderer,' he ended gnomically.

'How long does arsenic keep?' said Rushton.

Burgess settled back again, obviously delighted to be quizzed. 'Virtually indefinitely. Arsenic has been found in bodies which have lain in the grave for as long as twenty-two years.'

'If, therefore, someone had somehow obtained arsenic, it could have been kept, at Tall Timbers or elsewhere, for a number of years before this crime was committed?' Rushton gave the impression of being very pleased with himself.

'It could indeed. I have no doubt that there are lethal quantities of this highly useful substance lying in the dressing-table drawers of innocent-seeming ladies all over the country.' He grinned around the guardians of the law at this happy thought.

'Dr Burgess has an imagination bred on the more sensational branches of detective fiction,' said Lambert, as his constables wondered what to make of this. 'Most members of the public are, in his book, "mad, bad and dangerous to know".'

Burgess's smile was that of a man who sees he is winning the game. 'You make my point for me, Superintendent. Poor, gentle Caroline Lamb would obviously have been tempted to poison the philandering Byron, if she had had the means available and he had remained in one place for long enough.'

Lambert was aware of the five assembled heads turning back towards him in unison, like those of tennis spectators. But it was Rushton who said severely, 'Would you think, Dr Burgess, that someone administered pure arsenic in this way, rather than using some apparently innocent compound which contained arsenic?'

Burgess looked at him distastefully for a moment, unwilling to be recalled from the beguiling track of his exchanges with Lambert. Then a new thought enchanted him, so thoroughly that his relish for it became in the end positively beatific. 'That would be my guess, Inspector. But only that: it couldn't even be dignified as an opinion. I should have to say it was a guess in court. It's no more, in fact, than a hunch.' He rubbed his hands together enthusiastically. 'I've always wanted to play a hunch.' He ignored the blank faces of the constables to beam seraphically at Lambert.

The Superintendent said sternly, 'But even if you are right, any one of the people who frequented the house in the last three months of Craven's life could have made use of the stuff.'

'Oh, indubitably,' said Burgess happily. 'It must be considerations like that that make your job of detection so absorbing and entertaining.'

Rushton felt he was in danger of losing control of this. He said hastily, 'Perhaps we could consider what we know for certain, and our views on what I suppose might be called the inner ring of suspects.' He looked uncertainly at Lambert. 'I suppose we should ask Dr Burgess to withdraw for this part of our meeting.'

Lambert looked at the pathologist's eyes, which were pleading with a childish intensity not to be excluded from the adults' conversation; he was aware that Burgess was doing what Rushton would no doubt call 'sending himself up'. He said drily, 'I'm sure it would be useful for Dr Burgess to stay – if he can manage the time, of course. He might be able to offer us useful guidance on the possibilities of various speculations we might make. I'm anxious to encourage speculation, behind our own doors, in the absence of more tangible evidence.'

DI Rushton, who thought he had some tangible evidence, held his peace with difficulty. If his chief chose not to play things by the book and allow non-police personnel into an exchange of views of this kind, it had better be on his own head, even if it meant that control of this particular crime seminar was returned to him.

Lambert watched the DI for a moment, assessing his silence, before he said, 'There appear to be five people in what Inspector Rushton calls our "inner ring" of suspects. Or can anyone add to or reduce that number?' Heads shook glumly around him;

202

the constables looked at Rushton, but he said nothing. Lambert said with a sigh, 'Perhaps in due course some will appear more suspect than others. Can we begin with Edmund Craven's two children? As we all know, a domestic murder by a near relative is statistically the strongest possibility.'

The only one who seemed prepared to speak was Bert Hook, who said at a nod from his chief, 'If we're asked to speculate, David Craven has got to be the favourite. He's a pretty shady operator; we know now that five years ago he was trying to bribe local councillors who were members of the Planning Committee, though of course it never came to court. We know from his sister and Margaret Lewis that he had had a serious quarrel with his father about the future of Tall Timbers; indeed, he admitted as much himself when we saw him. He doesn't like Margaret Lewis–'

'Which could yet be in his favour,' said Rushton unexpectedly. He was cutting down the Sergeant in the midst of his rather ponderous stride. With a spurt of irritation, Lambert realized that these two did not like each other at all; if this was going to get in the way of their work, he would need to sort it out. Everyone looked at Rushton to enlarge upon his enigmatic interruption, but he said tersely, 'Carry on, please.' Only his antipathy to Hook had drawn him into words he now regretted.

Bert said magisterially, 'He doesn't like Margaret Lewis, and she plainly has no great love for him. Indeed, no one except his sister appears concerned to defend him. We haven't so far pinned down the exact details of the new will which his father planned, but every indication is that David Craven would have been the loser. He seems to think so himself. He already had planning permission confirmed for the site of Tall Timbers and he stood to make a packet when he inherited. Two further points: his property company was in a pretty desperate state, so that he couldn't afford to wait too long to get his hands on the site; and he came regularly to the house in those last weeks of his father's life, as he had not been doing earlier.'

Lambert said, 'Plenty of motive, I agree. And quite a bit of circumstantial support for your choice, Bert. Nothing that would get us a conviction yet – unless anyone else can add to the picture?'

As he looked round hopefully, DC Green, the youngest of the men on the case, said diffidently, 'He always *looks* so guilty when he's around the site. We saw him there several times when we were gathering the scene of crime material. We felt he might be looking for something in the house, but we never caught him searching. Of course, he's every right to be in what is his own house, even if he isn't living there.'

Rushton was prepared to discourage such rambling thought, but Lambert said cheerfully, 'Keep your eye on him, though, as far as you can. Do you think he's found what he's been looking for?'

'I doubt it, sir. He still seems to be watching us over his shoulder: almost skulking about on his own patch, if you know what I mean.'

Lambert thought this quite a vivid description from a lad – which was how he thought of twenty-three-year-olds nowadays – on his first CID assignment. It was Rushton, not noted for a psychological approach to crime, who now said, 'Has David Craven the nerve to carry through a murder like this? Watching an old man – a parent in his case – die a protracted death, which he could presumably have called off at any stage?'

Lambert said immediately, 'That's certainly a point to bear in mind.' He was glad to have something to praise from his immediate subordinate, for he felt he was becoming less than objective about Rushton. 'I agree it doesn't seem his kind of murder, but there are two things we should remember. First there are plenty of instances of men in desperate situations behaving out of character when driven into a corner of some kind. Secondly, this kind of killing often turns out to be a matter of collusion between two or more of the parties involved; if that were the case, I certainly wouldn't rule out David Craven.'

Dr Burgess, who had kept quiet for what was for him an inordinately long time in deference to his dubious status in the meeting, said, 'Oh, I'm so glad. If it has to be one of your five, I'm with Sergeant Hook: I do hope it's David Craven.' If Lambert's look of high disdain was meant to abash him, it was totally ineffective.

Lambert made a single note about David Craven before he said, 'What did you all make of Angela Harrison?'

This time no one seemed prepared to begin. It was Rushton who eventually said, striving to deal with the facts he had known this infuriating Superintendent to insist upon in the past, 'She had ample opportunity, certainly. She was in and out of the house almost every day in those last weeks; she often took in her father's food, and she seems to have been keener than any one that he should not miss the medicine he was taking for his heart condition. But according to what she and everyone else says, she had a great affection for the old man.'

'*Odi et amo?*' said Dr Burgess. His rather old–fashioned reading tastes led him to expect that the Great Detective would welcome a quotation from Catullus at about this stage. He was quite cast down by the blank silence which greeted his contribution.

Lambert, passing through the state education system a generation behind Burgess, had dropped Latin early in life, thus ensuring his first great flaw as a master investigator in the doctor's assessment. He struggled for a moment before he was able to say to his colleagues, 'I think Dr Burgess is putting the view that love and hate, the supreme passions, are never very far apart. Racine in my view puts it more cogently, but the idea is the important thing for us.'

Burgess, far from being put down, had his faith in detection restored by Lambert's indulgence in referring to the French classicist. He said soberly, 'I've known Angela Craven – Angela Harrison as she is now – for many years. I can certainly confirm that she was very close to her father. Edmund upset her when she was a child by his harsh treatment of her mother. He was very difficult over her husband, whom he dismissed as a ne'er-do-well, and even over her children, but it never seemed to stop Angela from loving him. She's a very forthright lady, who's always gone her own way. Great sportswoman in her youth: county tennis and badminton player. She was on the way to becoming a great golfer, but she hardly seems to play at all now.' He stared glumly towards the high window and the great outdoors, sad at this great talent going to waste in a game he struggled ineffectively to master.

Hook thought of the picture of un-complaining poverty he had absorbed at Angela Harrison's rather shabby home. He was glad she had not rushed into con-spicuous display of her newly inherited wealth, just as he was glad she had not hastened back into that toffee-nosed game which he fancied had become too expensive for her. He said, 'She's fiercely devoted to her husband and her children, I think. It must have been hard for her with her father getting more and more difficult about them as he aged, but as Dr Burgess says, she seems never to have lost her affection for him.'

Rushton had never seen Angela Harrison. With the objectivity of the outsider, he said, 'If Craven had changed his will to cut her and his grandchildren out, it would give her every reason to remove from the scene both the draft of the new will and the father who proposed to make it.' Burgess bridled a little at such a suggestion about a champion golfer, but he found it difficult to under-mine its logic.

'This revised will worries me,' said Lambert. 'It's too elusive. I can accept, perhaps, that it was never made: that is probably why Craven was killed when he was. But it seems strange that the old man didn't discuss it with anyone. I think at least one person would have been taken into his confidence. From everything we hear, including what Dr Burgess has just told us to confirm our own impressions, Angela Harrison would seem the most likely recipient of his thoughts. Would you agree with that, Dr Burgess? You're the only one present who knew both father and daughter over a lengthy period.'

'Certainly I would. And I wouldn't rule out David Craven also as a confidant: his father had a soft spot for the prodigal son, even after all their disagreements. But it's not impossible that Edmund was planning a new will without consultation. Old people can be very secretive about these things as they become mistrustful of those around them. And often they feel the control of their estate is the only real power left to them.'

Lambert nodded. 'It's also quite possible that Craven would ask for views on his new will from someone not directly concerned. He obviously came to rely more and more on Margaret Lewis as he became weaker; and he had known Walter Miller for so many years that he might have thought it appropriate to consult an old friend, who could be detached because he was not heavily involved in either the old or the new wills. I just have the feeling as I question people that one person, and perhaps more than one, knows the dispositions in the new will that was never made.'

Rushton was becoming worried about concealing his information. He had expected they would turn to the person he thought it concerned long before this. He said rather desperately, 'What about Mrs Lewis, sir?'

Lambert shrugged. 'In the context of our murder investigation, she remains a puzzle. She seems to have cared very conscientiously, indeed to have had a real affection, for the dead man, even when he became tetchy and difficult.' He looked interrogatively at Burgess, who confirmed this with a nod. 'She also had the best and most continuous access of all to the victim. And her son told me this afternoon that she was threatened by Craven with the withdrawal of the house at Burnham-on-Sea on the new will, as a result of his conduct. So she may well have had a strong motive: even the possibility of the withdrawal of the house would be a tremendous blow to someone like her. It would mean the loss of the independence afforded to a woman in her position by having her own roof over her head. I think Margaret Lewis is a woman to whom independence is important.'

Rushton said, 'She has a nursing background, which could be significant in this case, in the light of what Dr Burgess said earlier about the acquisition and administration of arsenic.'

Bert Hook spoke up as though he were having a tooth drawn. He did not wish to denigrate the buxom Mrs Lewis, who had appealed inordinately to his staid but vulnerable heart. 'She did conceal from us the presence in the house at the time which matters of her son, Andrew. That might be no more than foolishness: not many people are very balanced when their children are concerned.' He thought for a moment of his own children, still both below the age of ten, and the things he might do to protect them.

'With a son with his record, perhaps it was only to be expected,' said Rushton harshly. He pressed on before Hook could marshal any defence of Andrew Lewis, for he had more urgent things to say. He addressed himself directly to Lambert. 'The scene of crime team has been most meticulous, sir. Most of the materials they have come up with have been merely routine findings: mainly hairs and clothing fibres which confirm the presence in the house of the five people I called our inner ring of suspects. But they discovered two things which are bound to be significant.'

Rushton was not a man with a strong sense of theatre, but now he paused automatically, preparing the way for his revelation as stagily as that old ham Burgess might have done. The small white jar he held up, already inside its plastic bag in preparation for its role in court as Exhibit A, looked unremarkable enough. Instead of explaining its importance, Rushton took a second bagged exhibit from the drawer of the filing cabinet whence he had produced the bottle. For policemen, who in these days see much of drugs and their consequences, it had more sinister associations than the jar. It was a hypodermic syringe, its needle glinting brightly as it caught the light.

Rushton, suddenly aware of the silence in the room, was embarrassed now by the theatricality he had contrived almost by accident. He said, 'The significance of these two objects is that, while they appear empty, they both contain residues of pure arsenic.'

Even for the experienced men there, there was a sense of melodrama as they gazed at the containers. By this time Lambert was feeling, as Rushton had feared, that these findings should have been revealed much earlier. Controlling himself in front of the constables, he said, 'I presume there were no prints, or you would have told us.'

'No, sir,' said Rushton. He wondered for an instant why Lambert should presume that, but he was given no time to dwell upon it.

The Superintendent said heavily, 'And where were they found?'

Rushton was eager again now; even if he had mistimed this, his information must surely be central to the case. 'The syringe was in the bathroom cabinet adjacent to Edmund Craven's bedroom, where the medicines for his heart and blood pressure were kept. According to both Mrs Lewis and Mrs Harrison, that bathroom has been scarcely used since Craven's death.'

'And the bottle?'

'The jar was found in the room adjacent to the kitchen used by Margaret Lewis.'

CHAPTER 16

Hook took the wheel of the Vauxhall as he was bidden. It was usually a sign that his chief was deep in thought.

As though in deference to this, the Sergeant eased the car through the quiet streets in a careful silence. In fact, he was doing some thinking himself. It was a full five minutes before he said, rather reluctantly, 'That bottle and syringe have got to be significant.' He received a grunt of assent, no more. They went another half-mile before he ventured, 'Surprising, too, after all these months.'

He thought that this time he was not getting a reply at all. It was a full minute before Lambert said gnomically, 'Perhaps the significance may be in that surprise.'

The leaves that had given a transient autumn glory to the wide, unpaved avenue where Edmund Craven had lived were now mostly fallen. Small flakes of snow were etching the skeletons of the great trees with a different kind of beauty, more remote, less friendly to the world of men. The ivy which climbed over the Edwardian walls of Tall Timbers had caught the snow which barely covered the ground, so that the fall looked greater here than anywhere else around, as though the elements themselves were closing in upon the house whose owner had been murdered, in full knowledge that his son had no use for it.

As if to echo that fanciful thought, a strip proclaiming 'Sold, Subject to Contract' had been set at an angle across the estate agent's sale board by the gate. Where on their previous visit there had been trim order around the long approach to the house, rotting leaves now lay in drifts across the lawns, taking on strange, surreal shapes as the snow began to disguise them. There was no point now in gardeners working here: soon the bulldozers would take over.

Sheltered by its canopy at the top of its three stone steps, the wide oak front door still looked polished and cared for. It opened almost as soon as they rang. Margaret Lewis this time looked white and strained. She had on a grey two-piece suit; to Hook, still troubled by the revelations of the conference in the Murder Room on the previous evening, she seemed dressed to give an impression of respectability in the dock. She nodded a curt response to Lambert's greeting and led them silently to a dining-room they had not seen before. Hook had not told her what they wished to speak to her about when he made the appointment. But she knew: she had seen the jar and the syringe taken away by the scene of crime officer.

Lambert asked her about them without preamble, and she answered him mostly in monosyllables. He watched her closely as he told her that both bottle and syringe had been found to contain traces of arsenic: this had to be the first time she had been told of the laboratory findings. The blue eyes seemed to darken a little as they widened in horror; they caught a quick intake of breath before the lips shut tight and thin, as if closing down on this sign of weakness. They permitted her a single, almost soundless 'Oh!' but that was all. She stared bleakly over the polished oak dining table and the rush-seated chairs to the small segment of leaden sky and back garden which was all she could see from this room. The small, slender fingers of her right hand played abstractedly with the single silver bracelet on her left wrist. It was clear that her mind was active; they would have given a good deal to know the subject of her thoughts.

Lambert was forced to say, 'Mrs Lewis, I have to ask you what you know about these items.'

She looked at him bleakly, wondering if she had any chance of being believed. 'Nothing.' The ash-blond hair, so neat and attractive on their previous visit, was sufficiently out of place to show her dismay; Lambert wondered whether so attractive a woman would deliberately contrive such an effect.

'Did either of them belong to you?'

'The jar might have.'

'It is a jar which once contained a well-known make of cold cream. I understand a similar jar was found on your dressing-table.'

'Yes.' She spoke almost before he had concluded his question. Then she looked into his face and struggled to qualify the admission; it was perhaps the first moment when she thought there was any real prospect that she might be believed. 'I use that brand regularly; so do thousands of other women. Ask your wife.'

He already had. 'Had you seen that particular jar before?'

'Who knows?' There was a little contempt for the question he had had to ask. 'It could be one of mine. In case you should think it worth asking, I certainly didn't use it to store arsenic.'

'What about the hypodermic?'

'I used to be a nurse, so I've seen thousands of hypodermics – I must have handled hundreds of that type myself at one time. I suppose it's just possible that I've seen that very one at some time in the past. But never here; and certainly never where it was

217

found, Superintendent.' Suddenly, after her zombie-like reception of them into the house, she was anxious to convince.

Lambert looked at her closely; now that there was again some sort of exchange between them, she might reveal more than she knew. The brooch at the centre of the white silk blouse beneath the grey jacket gleamed brightly in the prevailing dullness of the high, north-facing room. The nylons and the maroon leather shoes beneath the grey skirt were still and demure, as if reinforcing the calmness she had dressed to convey. The contrast with her bearing on their first visit came from her hands, which twisted and untwisted despite herself, fingers moving from the bracelet to the rings on her left hand and back again. But the dark blue eyes looked at him steadily enough; he could not tell from them whether her nervousness derived from guilt or from a situation she could not understand. He said to her, 'Will you show us exactly where they were found, please?'

She rose almost eagerly, as if even to be asked was a suggestion that their minds were still open. In the slight stiffness of her first steps, there was a glimpse of the middle age that none can escape, a reminder of her forty-six years. In this house so redolent of the tastes of a bygone age, with the hand of its dead master everywhere apparent, they had tended to think of this trim, chic representative of the modern era as being younger than her years. And her unconscious concession to a different view was but momentary: she moved thereafter as gracefully as ever as she led them through the spacious hall and up the wide staircase. Plodding behind her, Bert Hook appreciated the rounded calves and tried not to compute that he was younger than Craven's elegant housekeeper.

The Edwardians were prodigal of space, in an era that had less need to be cost-conscious. A long landing with a strip of Persian carpet at its centre ran the full length of the house on the first floor. She led them to the first of two adjacent doors at the end of this and opened it without hesitation. The bathroom within was like the rest of the house; there was ample floor space between the gleaming porcelain of bath, lavatory and washbasin, and a wide panelled door beside the last of these. 'Does that lead to Mr Craven's bedroom?' asked Lambert. It was the first murder he had ever investigated where he had not even bothered to visit the place of the death, preferring after the lapse of all this time to leave the routine stuff to the scene of crime team. Now, it seemed, he was proved wrong.

She nodded and quietly opened the door. They looked through at a double bed which was now stripped and draped with a dust cover. The inlaid mahogany of the massive bedroom suite and the heavy curtains were here more than ever suggestive of the man who had breathed his last in this room well over a year ago. As if to echo the thought, Margaret Lewis said behind them, 'Mr Craven hardly left the room in those last months'. Occasionally in their work they went into those sad rooms preserved by grieving parents as a sort of shrine to deceased offspring, often those who had died suddenly in road accidents. This reminded Hook of one of those rooms, with almost nothing changed from the moment its occupant died. But the reason here was only that no one had any more use for the place; soon it would crash in rubble amid the rest of these solidly built walls; Hook felt an illogical resentment against the man he still obstinately hoped was the perpetrator of this death, David Craven.

Margaret Lewis recalled him abruptly to the present as she said, 'This is where the hypodermic was found.' She had opened the mirrored door on a white wooden medicine cabinet which was fastened to the wall above the washbasin. It was an unexceptional enough place, with bottles and packets laid out neatly on two shelves. Lambert contrasted this order with the profuse untidiness of his own smaller cabinet at home, where medicaments threatened to spill forth each time the door was opened. But probably the doors of this cabinet were never opened.

He said, 'Presumably this bathroom has been scarcely used since Mr Craven died?'

'Not at all. So far as I am aware.' She added the rider with a sudden abhorrence, aware that if she was to be believed, some other presence had been here. A malign one.

'So that the syringe could have been there since the time of Mr Craven's death?'

'No. I cleaned the whole of the bedroom and this bathroom myself on the day after the funeral.' They could see her doing it, the last act of obeisance to the master she had served so well. Or the last rites in the successful dispatch of her victim.

'That included this cabinet?'

'Yes.' She spoke as if she resented the implication that she could be so slipshod a housekeeper. 'I cleared out all the medicaments that were no longer of any use: mostly Mr Craven's heart drugs. The ones you see there are the proprietary general ones for various minor ailments which might still be of use to others.' She paused while their eyes roamed automatically over the shelves, confirming that this was in fact the case. Then she said, with unexpected contempt, 'Do you really think that if I were

221

a murderer I should be stupid enough to leave a hypodermic with traces of arsenic here?'

There was a long pause, in which the only discernible sound was Margaret Lewis's agitated breathing. Hook thought for a moment that his chief was not going to reply to what he might dismiss as a rhetorical question; he could not know that his mind was running on to an entirely different issue. Eventually Lambert said, 'No, Mrs Lewis, since you ask me, I can hardly believe that you would. But the implication of the find is that if not you, then someone else was indeed very stupid, or very careless. Yet everything else about this killing points to someone both far-seeing and well organized. If we accept for the moment that the syringe was not here when you cleared the cabinet after Edmund Craven's funeral, we have to get some idea when it might have been put there. Are we to assume that this cupboard has not been used since the murder?'

'I suppose so. I haven't cleaned this area at all since then. Mrs Gordon, who comes in to clean, has vacuumed and dusted the bedroom and cleaned this bathroom from time to time, but she would have no need to open the medicine cabinet. You could check with her, but I doubt whether she has even opened the doors.'

'One of our team will check that in due course, Mrs Lewis. In the meantime, can we assume that, as far as you know, that syringe could have been put into this cabinet at any time in the last thirteen months?'

'Yes. At any rate–' Her head jerked up, not more than three feet from the face of the man who was questioning her. It was too close for her to conceal the fear which started suddenly into her pupils. At that moment, neither he nor she was certain whether he had led her here directly or not. In the spotless, old-fashioned bathroom, Hook was aware of a moment of crisis in a setting that seemed hardly appropriate.

Lambert said, 'The syringe and the jar are evidence, Mrs Lewis. For what it is worth, they may still prove significant evidence, though perhaps not in the way that might at first have been indicated. But it is our duty to consider all evidence. On our first visit here, you saw fit to conceal one important piece of evidence from us: the fact of your son's presence here at the time of the murder.'

They watched the firm shoulders sag beneath the smooth grey wool of her jacket. Her head dropped forward, nodding twice in acknowledgement. Hook, wishing that the human mind could be more easily disciplined, noted inconsequentially that there were no darker roots to the ash-blond hair.

'How long was it after the murder before your son moved out?' said Lambert quietly.

'About two months.' Her eyes were fixed so unblinkingly on Bert Hook's shoes that he wanted to explain that they had been soiled only by the journey up that long, snow-covered path.

'So this cabinet was no doubt in use for at least as long as that,' said Lambert, looking again at the contents in a gesture which made his words a statement rather than a question.

In this dim room, where the frosted glass filtered what light entered through the small window, her blue eyes looked almost black. They were wide with fear, for he had come unexpectedly to the area where she was most susceptible. Her low voice broke for an instant as she said uncertainly, 'I suppose it would have been.'

Lambert did not look back at her. He said, 'I said just now that we have to consider all evidence that is put before us. I have to tell you that we have been told that your son was seen with his hand in this cabinet a week before Edmund Craven's death.'

Hook thought she was going to fall. She staggered a little with the shock, almost lost her balance. Then she half-recovered and sat on the edge of the bath. Bert was glad she had not ended the moment sitting on the lid of the lavatory, removing what dignity remained from the little cameo. Lambert studied her intently in her distress; Hook, watching him in profile, realized just how ruthlessly single-minded this man could be. It was akin to those instants where wives see something new and hateworthy in husbands they thought they had explored and accepted. Then the moment passed and the Superintendent said gruffly, 'Perhaps we could go somewhere where we could all sit down.'

If she was grateful for the relief, she did not show it. Like one in shock, she led them out on to the landing and back towards the top of the stairs. After a few yards, she stopped so suddenly that they would have walked into her if they had been closer. Perhaps she felt too weak to descend the stairs. She half-turned towards Lambert with a tiny, mirthless smile, then opened a door to her right and led them into what they quickly perceived to be her own bed-room. She motioned them towards an elegant mahogany dual seat by the window, on which they deposited their large forms in gingerly unison; with its slender walnut legs and arms and its delicate tapestry seat, it hardly seemed designed for substantial police posteriors. Perched thus, they must have made an incongruous sight, but Margaret Lewis seemed not to notice it as she composed herself more naturally in the wicker chair by the wardrobe. Hook tried not to let his eyes dwell too obviously upon the big double bed behind her, with its duvet and soft blue pillow-slips; they were almost the first modern things they had registered in the house.

She had not uttered a word since the Superintendent's revelation about her son and the medicine cabinet. Hook wondered if the hypodermic was connected with him: he had not taken him for one who gambled with drugs, but few policemen would not consider the possibility nowadays. He was startled when she said, 'Walter Miller must have told you that. He didn't like Andrew any more than Edmund did.' It was the first time that day that they had heard her refer to her former employer by his first name. Even now, it might be no more than the association in her mind of the two old friends. She had recovered at least a measure of control; her voice was cold and even.

Lambert was cool enough himself as he replied, 'It is the duty of everyone to help the police in any way he can, Mrs Lewis. Mr Miller was doing no more than stating what he had seen. If you had not attempted to conceal your son's presence from us, Mr Miller's statement might have appeared less sensational.' He was less interested in rebuking her than making sure that she was perfectly honest now.

She said, 'No one round here had much time for Andrew. He did one or two foolish things when he was younger, but he was never vicious. Now he's trying desperately to pull things round and make his way in the world, but no one will give him a chance.' Suddenly she was weeping, almost silently, her eyes fixed on the carpet between them, her shoulders racked with the emotion.

Lambert studied her clinically. He left her to cry for a full minute, waiting to see if the extremes of emotion would produce any further revelation. He had seen men as well as women weep under interrogation more often than the public would suppose, so that the sight affected him less than it would have done at one time. Like a surgeon exploring a symptom, he said, 'Either you or he are going to tell us what Andrew was doing at that medicine cabinet, Mrs Lewis.'

When she looked up, Hook was shocked by her ravaged face. He realized yet again how the most raw and vulnerable area for almost all of humanity is its children. Her voice was still unsteady with tears as she said aghast, 'I can't tell you that, Superintendent. Andrew would never forgive me.'

Lambert said gently, 'I think he would, Mrs Lewis, in these circumstances. There is little alternative. You must see that unless we get another convincing explanation, the one

Mr Miller was suggesting is going to seem the obvious one.' He should not have acknowledged the source of the story, but she had guessed it so quickly that it could scarcely matter now.

She said, 'Will you let me explain to Andrew before you see him again?' Lambert nodded to Hook, preferring that his sergeant should offer the reassurance.

Hook said, 'There is nothing to stop you contacting him as soon as we leave here. No doubt he has told you of our interview with him at the police station near his home.'

She looked up, gratitude shining now through her exhaustion. 'Yes. He said you were kind to him.' Her surprise at the notion came through in her tone, and she gave a little, quickly suppressed giggle which showed how near she was to hysteria. She wiped her face with a now sodden handkerchief, studied it for a second, and said, 'Women's handkerchiefs are not designed to cope with their emotions!' The little joke was an acknowledgement that she was going to talk; all three of them relaxed a little.

'Andrew used that cabinet for his own medicine, Superintendent. Until the last days of Mr Craven's illness, when other people were around rather more, only I went there to get Edmund's medicine. On the odd day when I wasn't there, I left his medicine ready by his bed. So it was a safe place for Andrew to keep his own prescriptions.'

Lambert tried not to sound too eager as he brought her back to the core of the matter. 'But why should Andrew wish to keep his treatment a secret?'

She gave him a bitter smile. 'Andrew has not had too many good breaks from life. He had no father, and he was physically a bit of a weakling as a youngster. He had a bad time at school, and when he left he got in with the wrong set for a time – I think you've heard something about that from him. He was almost twenty when he was diagnosed as epileptic. It was a great shock to both of us. The treatment has been effective, thought – I can't think he was doing anything very wrong in trying to conceal it.' Her inflection made it an appeal.

Hook said, 'But why try to conceal it? Epilepsy isn't pleasant to contend with, I know, but it doesn't carry the social stigma it used to...' For a moment he was back in the home thirty years ago, sharing the distress of the boy who had had frequent fits, frightened that he would swallow his tongue before anyone could come.

Margaret Lewis looked at him almost affectionately. 'It wasn't the stigma, Sergeant Hook.' As previously in this investigation, Bert was absurdly pleased to hear his name remembered: the women at least in the case seemed highly civilized. 'You may have gathered that Andrew is rather keen on cars. As a matter of fact, he's very good with them.' For an instant, her pride in him shone through. Then she went on soberly, 'It seemed to be the only thing he had going for him. He was doing quite well in Burnham before all this blew up. He moved there partly because it was easier to conceal his affliction in a new place.'

Hook said, 'Was it really so important to hide it?'

She looked at him impatiently: she was near the end of her personal resources now. 'If you want to work with cars you need a driving licence. Epilepsy is one of the things that can deprive you of that. Andrew was in danger of losing the one thing in his life that he cared about; the one thing in which he could make a living. Do you wonder that he was anxious to conceal his illness?'

She was too occupied with her son and the unfairness of life even to study their re-actions in the silence which followed. They weighed her explanation of Andrew Lewis's presence in Edmund Craven's bathroom a week before the old man's death. It made sense of an incident that had previously admitted only a sinister explanation, though of course it did not mean the young man could not have committed the murder. He had had a better opportunity than most, and Craven's hatred of him and the threat to his mother's inheritance gave him motive enough.

Lambert eventually said, 'And where do you keep your supply of cold cream, Mrs Lewis?'

In a more aggressive tone, it would have made her feel that the screw was being turned even more tightly upon her. As it was, she took it that her explanation of her son's actions had been accepted. She gave them a tight little smile, acknowledging that she had known that they must come to this. She walked over to the small dressing-table; they could see her face composing itself in the single wide, bevelled mirror. Then she bent to the lowest of the three drawers on the right of its central recess. When she opened it, they saw a jewellery case, two small bottles of perfume, an unopened packet of lace-edged linen handkerchiefs, lipsticks, blusher, eyeshadow. And a jar identical to the one which lay in its plastic bag in the murder room at CID. She picked it up and gazed at it for a moment, then put it carefully back in its allotted place. The drawer was as neat as everything else about the room and its occupier.

Lambert studied the contents with her for a moment, then said, 'How often do you use this drawer?'

'Not very often. I keep the jewellery and

the perfume for special occasions. There don't seem to be many of those nowadays.' Her smile began by being bitter, then in a second transformed itself into an expression half happy and half embarrassed. 'I keep my presents from Andrew in that drawer.' Then her face resumed again the strain and fatigue they had seen earlier, as she thought about the discovery of that other jar. 'I feel – violated,' she said.

It was a sentiment they both heard often enough after houses had been burgled. Ironically, this time something had been added, rather than removed, from one of the secret places of a woman's life – assuming that the woman could be believed. Lambert said, 'We understand that. Tell me, would it not be more usual for a woman to keep her cold cream on top of the dressing-table?' He gestured vaguely at the surface beneath the mirror, where they could see every reaction on a face that looked more lined than they had ever seen it before.

That face now registered surprise, even the beginnings of alarm as she thought her word was being questioned. 'Probably it would. I got used to putting everything away when I shared a room with other nurses years ago. I suppose I've kept the habit; it never occurred to me before. Perhaps it's something to do with never having a home of my own. One learns that it is necessary to

232

be tidy.' There was a trace even through her fatigue of an irony which was curiously attractive. Then the dark eyes studied them as she said wearily, 'Does it matter?'

'I rather think it does.' It meant that her choice of brands was not observable by a casual observer whenever her door was ajar. That made it more likely that the jar which had been found was actually hers. Or that it had been planted by someone with intimate knowledge of her habits. 'How long is it since you last used anything else in that drawer?'

She thought. 'A week. I got some perfume out last Wednesday morning–' She stopped abruptly: it was the morning of their first visit to Tall Timbers after the exhumation. So she had prepared herself carefully to receive the representatives of the law: Lambert remembered how she had known about the exhumation and presumed that it meant there had been foul play.

He gave no sign that he had made the connection. 'Thank you. If you are correct in your supposition that both the jar and the syringe were placed in the house, they were almost certainly deposited together. Which would mean that they have been planted in the last week. More precisely, in the thirty-six hours between Wednesday morning and their discovery by the scene of crime team.'

She was not sure whether he was

accepting her story or pointing out how unlikely it was that such things could have happened in so short a time. In truth, he was thinking aloud, happy to pin down definite facts in a case that had so often denied them to him. He said hopefully, 'Were you in the house throughout those thirty-six hours?'

The pale brow furrowed in concentration. Then, unwillingly, she said, 'I went out about four o'clock on that Wednesday afternoon; I didn't get back until almost midnight, I'm afraid.'

Damn! thought both men in the room together. But Lambert's voice was professionally even as he said, 'The scene of crime boys would be there until about six.' This time, there had seemed no particular urgency about their work, so that they had been permitted to resume the next morning: another irony. 'May I ask where you were during the evening, Mrs Lewis?'

Hook wondered as he watched the emotions flashing across the mobile features if they were about to discover a liaison she had wished to conceal: surely this woman was too attractive not to have a companion waiting ardently for her somewhere? But she said in a low voice, 'I went to see Andrew. I wanted to discuss things with him, but I didn't want him coming here.'

'You have your own car?'

'Yes. David gave it to me when he took his father's big car away.' An unexpected thoughtfulness and generosity from a man of whom they had heard little that was creditable. Or an obligation which had to be met? Their calling and experience encouraged the cynical questioning of generosity.

Lambert sighed; he thought he knew the answer he was going to get now. 'Who to your knowledge has a key to Tall Timbers, apart from yourself?'

She did not need to think long. She was an efficient housekeeper, and it was the kind of question a woman living alone for the last year in a house of this size had automatically considered. 'Both Mr Craven's children, of course. I expect Walter Miller still has one, though I don't think he's been here since Mr Craven died. He certainly had one, because he often used to come to see Edmund on my day off. And of course the estate agents who have been handling the sale of the site have two keys–'

'And no doubt your son also has one,' said Lambert quietly.

'Yes,' she said; she thought of trying to make a little joke of it, but she was not sure that she could trust her voice so far. The idea of a son coming at dead of night to plant evidence which might incriminate his mother had a tinge of black farce, but they did not rule it out: they had seen stranger and crueller things than that. And the mind which had planned and executed the murder of a defenceless elderly man over a period of many weeks might take up any subterfuge when it felt the strands of the police net beginning to close...

Margaret Lewis was very near to exhaustion now. The smart grey suit and white blouse seemed to emphasize the paleness of the face above. There was little colour even in the lips, and they were still not relaxed. Lambert, watching the small white teeth pulling nervously at the lower one, realized that she had more to tell them yet. He prompted gently, 'I asked you when last we met to think of anything that might possibly bear on Mr Craven's death. Have you come up with anything?'

She nodded, bringing herself to speak. 'Walter Miller,' she said abruptly at last. 'It's probably nothing.' It was the qualification nearly everyone made when giving what they thought was incriminating information: it was surprising how many still talked of 'putting the noose round somebody's neck', even though they must know that was now thirty years out of date.

'Probably not. But you'd much better let us be the judge of that.' Sometimes you had to counter one cliché with another to offer comfort; Lambert gave her an encouraging smile.

'You said that the easiest way to give arsenic was by means of strongly flavoured food or drink. Would that include chocolate?' She did not need his nod of confirmation: it was merely to convince herself that she should be saying this that she asked. 'Mr Craven had a sweet tooth. I never touch chocolate, so it was rarely in the house. Mr Miller took to bringing Edmund a small box of chocolates each week when he came to play chess.'

'When did this begin to happen?'

'I think Walter had brought them just occasionally – probably on special occasions – for years. But he began to do it every week when Edmund became virtually housebound: I couldn't be precise, but say about a year ago.'

'Did they eat them together?'

'No. Walter Miller doesn't eat chocolates either. At least he says he doesn't: sometimes I used to think he was just being kind and leaving them all for Edmund when he was lonely.' She stopped then, aghast at the macabre interpretation that could now be put upon simple actions.

'So the chocolates were usually in Mr Craven's room for the best part of a week?'

'No. Much less than that. I should say they were normally gone within a day. Edmund meant to make them last, but he had too sweet a tooth for that.' Her face was suddenly lit by a wave of affection as she remembered the old man and his small weakness.

'So that anyone who administered poison by means of the chocolates would be pretty certain that no one else would be affected?'

She nodded. 'Edmund kept them in his bedside cabinet. They were the little treat he permitted himself in the long hours when he was alone. But you're making me say that Walter–'

'I'm doing nothing more than establishing the facts,' said Lambert hastily, trying to forestall another round of clichés. 'As you were acute enough to notice, those chocolates are a possible medium for poison, and I'm exploring the possibilities. I should perhaps point out that these include the opportunity for people other than Mr Miller to doctor the chocolates, once they were in the room.'

There was silence while Margaret Lewis digested the idea and found it unwelcome. All three of them were thinking now of the syringe found in the adjoining bathroom, the ideal method of injecting poison into chocolates without detection; perhaps after all it had more bearing than they had allowed.

Then the extension phone by the bed rang, startling in the silence of the high-ceilinged room. Margaret Lewis picked it up reluctantly, then passed it across in relief to Lambert. It was a woman's voice, one that at first he could not recognize. 'Super-intendent Lambert? Inspector Rushton told me I might get you on this number.' Lambert wondered at the determination she must have shown to get past the diligent Inspector. 'This is Mrs Miller: we met just briefly when you came to see Walter.'

'I remember. What can I do for you?'

'I need to speak to you. Can you come here now? My husband is out. It – it's about Ed Craven.'

CHAPTER 17

The killer of Edmund Craven had always had a cool brain. The planning of the murder had given that brain an intellectual pleasure, which was quite detached from any considerations of morality. As it planned the detail, the brain was not at all sure whether the murder would ever be carried out, for such things depended on qualities of will and determination which were wholly divorced from the cerebral activity which had thrown up the possibility of the killing.

Qualities which had not been previously explored in the murderer; this extension of self-knowledge had been wholly intriguing. The execution of the murder, with its meticulously planned stages, its careful observation of those around the victim to note any evidence in them of suspicion, had brought both excitement and satisfaction. The killing had been so smoothly achieved, so little suspected by those who might have been expected to be most on guard, that it had added immeasurably to the confidence of the executioner.

For that surely is what the killer was: an

agent of justice more sublime and more secure than the clumsy and unreliable processes of mortal laws. A justice which demanded the death of Edmund Craven so clearly that there was not that crisis of conscience which the killer had feared might cloud resolution as the successive crises of Craven's death by stages approached and passed. There was in the end no moral dilemma about this murder, none of the interference of emotion with judgement which had at the outset appeared a problem. There had been nothing more than a mounting excitement, an increasing awareness of a superior will and force, a satisfaction in the achievement which set a successful murderer apart from other men.

It had sometimes been difficult to savour the success in silence: that was one thing the killer had not anticipated. As the days after the funeral had become weeks, and the weeks had stretched into months, it had seemed at times almost impossible not to speak, to reveal to someone close the delicious completeness of the deception, the daring and capacity of one who could manipulate even that fell sergeant Death to serve a particular purpose. When the months had stretched beyond a year, the murderer had sometimes had to sit in a room alone, arms clasped across the chest in the security of isolation, rocking in silent glee with the clever completeness of it all.

The news of the exhumation had been a shock, but it had brought with it initially a sort of pleasure that at last the ingenuity, the wonderful ruthlessness of the despatch of the old man, could be revealed and appreciated. There was, too, a revival of that sense of danger, in which it seemed almost impossible to distinguish fear from pleasure, which the killer had felt during the slow execution which had been the lot of Edmund Craven: almost like the exultation that came from driving a fast car beyond the limits of normal safety, and coming through. One's reflexes had to be faster and quicker than those of ordinary men, and how exultant one became when it proved that they were. At first, the revelation of the death as a murder brought with it a sick excitement which was almost wholly pleasurable; here were a new set of problems, a new set of people to be outwitted by a killer whose vision was so superior to theirs.

That feeling had not lasted long. The people now involved were professionals. For a few moments only, the killer had enjoyed the contest of wits with the Superintendent who probed so quietly and the assistant who was so much less bovine than he at first appeared. Then reality had taken hold: these professional men were dangerous, totally unlike the amateurs that had been so easy to deceive because they found murder inconceivable. These men accepted it because they had seen so much of it. They were like physicians conducting exploratory operations, expecting to find the worst wherever they looked, prepared to cut out evil as dispassionately as surgeons.

The killer became watchful and realistic. Calm decisions and incisive actions are perfectly possible even after the borders of sanity have been crossed.

Murder was now established. Two alternatives, then: either its perpetrator must remain undiscovered, or someone else must seem to be the killer. A murderer must be both vigilant and opportunist, using whatever advantages remained open as the police net drew tight around the inner circle of suspects. Suspicion brought its effects; the people involved in the interviews became more of a group. It was easy to follow the course of the police investigation by discreet conversations with those involved after they had been interviewed. The murderer took the pulse of the inquiry through the reactions to Lambert's probings of those involved.

It was difficult to be certain when one had no means of comparison, but the killer's own interview seemed to go well, with suspicion pleasingly diverted to the areas previously planned. The signs were that police suspicion was centring where the murderer thought it should. But it was irritatingly difficult to be sure. And that Superintendent Lambert was an enigmatic figure to contend with. Latterly, he seemed to be asking questions which indicated that the killer was not yet clear of suspicion.

No one else suspected: the murderer was sure of that. It might yet be necessary to do something about Superintendent Lambert.

CHAPTER 18

A crisp winter morning should bring a lightening of the spirits. For David Craven, there was no such relief.

Solitude brought its own problems, as the police probed ever more deeply into the circumstances in which his father had died. After a night when he seemed scarcely to have slept at all, it was a relief to come in to his office and surround himself with people who were not directly involved with the investigation. His secretary had even time to be concerned about his gaunt looks, without speculating about the reasons for them – openly at least. He sipped the coffee she brought him and stared at the landscape print above the marble statue on the half-empty bookcase. It was an alpine scene; at the moment he was prepared to give his attention to anything far removed from Oldford and the Cotswolds.

This interlude of uneasy escapism did not last long for him. There was a sound of raised voices beyond the frosted glass: an angry male one and his secretary's, shrill with annoyance as the instinct to protect her employer from unauthorized disturbance was ignored. 'What next?' he muttered wearily to himself as he swivelled his chair towards the source of this disturbance.

The door burst open as he turned. The young, tousled head which dominated the entrance was alive with venom. The secretary's appalled face seemed even whiter beneath her carefully cut dark hair. 'I told him you were engaged and couldn't see him,' she said. Then, as she saw how patently un-engaged he was, she added, 'The police will be here for your nine-thirty appointment in a few minutes–'

'Engaged, is he?' said the young man. He looked with triumphant contempt at the deserted office and the empty desk. 'Well, I'm sure he isn't too busy to see me!' Andrew Lewis flung himself into the expensive armchair beside the desk in a movement which managed to retain aggression even as he subsided. He said to the secretary, 'You can go now. Mr Craven won't wish to have our discussion overhead.' He had been carried into the inner sanctum of Craven's office on the tide of his fury; like many men who nerve themselves to action which is not natural to them, he was now in danger of carrying his attitude into caricature.

David Craven nodded at her. He said quietly, 'All right, June,' and tried to draw support from his calmness. He had spent most of the small hours of this day convincing himself that Andrew Lewis was the most likely murderer of his father: this arrival just before the scheduled appointment with the police seemed suddenly providential.

The logic of his reasoning in the darkest hour before the dawn had seemed impeccable. Despite his antipathy to her, he could not really see Margaret Lewis as ruthless enough to kill off the man she had served so faithfully. His sister was even more unthinkable. She had remained close to her father even through his harsh treatment of the husband she loved and his shameful cutting-off of his grandchildren. And when she could have thrown suspicion on to her brother, she had withheld from the police the knowledge she had revealed to him of her father's revision of his will to disinherit his son. And Angela was keeping in touch with him, advising him of developments, when all the others involved seemed to have concluded that he was guilty: no murderess would spurn the ready chance of a scapegoat.

Walter Miller he had considered seriously as a suspect for some time; it would have been the least of possible evils to have as killer someone less closely involved with his father by ties of blood or physical proximity. Perhaps, too, the American was for him an alien presence even after all these years, and thus psychologically more acceptable as a suspect than others for that reason alone. But of all those close to his father, Walter Miller had had least to gain by the death. There was that old, half-remembered tension between his mother and the Millers which he had never understood at the time, but that could surely not survive for all those years after his mother's death.

No, the obvious candidate must be the unstable young man with a history of violence and a deep, possessive attachment to his mother and her interests. At four in the morning he had been certain of it. Now, when the man he had selected as murderer was quivering with anger in his office, conviction drained away.

Andrew Lewis watched the slim form of Craven's secretary dimming behind the frosted glass until he could no longer see it. Then he whirled on Craven and snarled. 'Why the hell don't you own up and have done with it?'

'Why the hell should I?' Craven was shaken by the young man's boldness.

'God knows I'd no reason to love your father, but I wouldn't have wished him dead. Now you've tried to implicate my mother and I won't have it.' His anger gave a kind of gravity to an assertion which might have been merely ridiculous.

'So you've heard about the jar and the syringe the police found at Tall Timbers.' Angela had told Craven of the confrontation between Margaret Lewis and the police over these things; he had foolishly forgotten that Margaret might have spoken to her son.

'Of course I've heard. The CID have been there and practically accused my mother of the murder.'

'And can you blame them?'

He regretted the easy riposte as soon as he had made it, for the young man shot out of his chair so violently that he was sure he was coming straight across the desk at him. He stopped, with his face quivering with rage, no more than eighteen inches from Craven's. The older man stared into eyes which were the exact blue of those eyes of Margaret Lewis which he had found such critical observers of his actions in his father's house. The mother's pupils had gleamed with a sardonic stillness; the son's now were full of hatred. The eyes of a man capable of murder.

Lewis said through clenched teeth, 'I can blame *you,* when I know you planted those things!'

'But I didn't.'

'Come off it. You killed your father because he had seen through you at last. And you almost got away with it. Well, I'm glad you're going to be caught. We'll see how you like being banged up in a cell night after night.'

Craven sneered, 'You'd be something of an authority on that, wouldn't you?'

Andrew Lewis might have hit him then. His breathing lurched into a wild gasp and his fists clenched. He told himself to keep control. He must not have one of his attacks: not now, of all times. Then, as though he recognized weakness in the other's desperation, he sank back into his chair and said quietly, 'I was never in prison, much as it pleased you and your father to say so.'

David Craven had actually pleaded for the young man in the face of his father's bitterness in those months after the boy's release from the young offenders' institution, but it seemed useless to say so now. And indeed, preoccupied as he had been with his own deepening financial problems, his protests had been feeble. His whole life seemed in his miserable retrospects of it to be a story of efforts made too little and too late. Lewis in his mention of the prison cell had hit upon the very nightmare which beset him when his confidence seeped away during the long hours of the night. He said hopelessly, 'I didn't turn him against you. Perhaps I could have helped a little more, but–'

'You stopped me getting jobs when I most

needed them. You even told your father to stop me using the old studio at the back of the house to repair motor-cycles. Now you're trying to frame me for murder. Why else plant a syringe? The pigs were bound to think of drugs, and people of my age...' In his anger, he fell back on the language his mother had persuaded him it was politic to abandon. The tirade of hate poured out, threatening in its release to engulf a man who had not even been aware of it before. Lewis was careless now of the danger of his illness, driven beyond the bounds of prudence by his wrath.

Craven had spent most of his life trying to avoid the well-merited consequences of dubious actions: to find himself now accused of things he had not done was a new and disturbing experience for the spoilt child who had never matured far enough to accept responsibility for his own deeds. He reeled before the onslaught, wanting to protest but unable to, clinging to the idea that at least this wild fury confirmed this shouting maniac as a murderer. He wondered when the words would stop; Lewis was relentless, scarcely needing to pause for breath. Now he was saying, 'If you knew I used that medicine cupboard for my medicines, why didn't you say something at the time? Instead of storing it up and waiting to tell the pigs—'

'But he didn't, you see.' The cool voice from the doorway had the effect of a bucket of cold water upon fighting dogs. The two white faces which had been facing each other with such concentration across Craven's desk turned dazedly towards the source of the interruption.

Lambert stood assessing them for a moment before he came unhurriedly into the room. He gestured to them to sit down. Obedient as children, they drew apart and sank back into their chairs. The two men who had been interrupted were wondering how long the CID men had been there, how much they had overheard, and Lambert read the thought as clearly as if it had been written for him. He gave them a mirthless smile in recognition of the fact; he had no intention of enlightening them. He sat and looked at them for a moment and said to the panting Andrew Lewis, 'Did Mr Craven not tell you that the pigs were due to arrive at any time?'

Lewis's wan cheeks gave a small wince of pain. He said sullenly, 'I didn't believe him.' Then, with the swift naïvety which went with his youth, his face brightened and he said, 'Have you come to arrest him?'

Lambert did not smile. It was Hook who said, 'Were you expecting us to?'

Lewis said, 'Yes. He did it. It's obvious.' The terse statements were stubbornly delivered, but he felt faint now as his confidence dropped away. These large, impassive men reminded him by their mere arrival that he was an amateur in the presence of professionals. He said, 'I came here to make him confess.' It sounded ridiculous; yet he had been sure when he burst in here that he would wring the admissions he wanted from the man opposite him.

Craven saw his discomfiture, watched the conviction which had been invested in him by his burning anger pass as abruptly as that fury. He said, 'This is your murderer, Superintendent, as I've no doubt you know. He was threatening more violence when you arrived.' His voice sounded peevish and empty, his assertions as weightless as those of the younger man who had accused him.

Lambert looked from one to the other, not troubling now to disguise his distaste. The language might be adult, but the attitudes were those of boys separated in the playground. He said, 'Have either of you anything to add to the statements you have already signed?'

The two men looked automatically at each other, like actors anxious not to be upstaged. Then they shook their heads together like comic clones, their first and last action in unison that morning. Lambert said to Lewis, 'I suggest you do not make contact of this kind again with anyone else involved in this murder inquiry. Indeed, I forbid it. Any suspicions or observations you entertain should be relayed to us.' Lewis looked thoroughly cowed as he stood to go. Lambert let him get half way to the door before he said, 'Incidentally, it was not Mr Craven who told us about your use of that medicine cabinet. I have no intention, of course, of telling you who did. Your accusation of Mr Craven merely illustrates the sort of difficulties you bring upon yourself by actions like those you took this morning. You have the number of the CID room: ring it if you feel you have anything useful to contribute to our work. Please do not leave the area without informing us of your intentions.'

It was patently a dismissal, and Andrew Lewis was only too ready now to get away. He went quietly through the outer office, passing without a glance the secretary he had so recently overwhelmed. Lambert did not trouble to watch him go; he had transferred his attention to the man behind the big desk before Lewis had moved three yards.

Because he felt the weak man's compulsion to fill the silence, David Craven said nervously, 'That's your murderer, in my view. But I suppose you need the evidence.'

Lambert did not bother to respond. He let the silence stretch until Craven felt compelled to lift his eyes from the desk to the faces of the men who studied him. Then he said, 'We arranged to see you this morning because of one or two queries relating to your conduct in the months before your father's death.'

They saw fear now in that tortured face; fear so clear that Hook wondered for the first time if this man had really the nerve for murder. But as long as the death had been presumed to stem from natural causes, there had been little need for nerve once the killing had been achieved. Craven asked from a dry throat, 'Oh yes? How can I help you?'

Lambert said, 'The chief area of difficulty for us is that of the new will your father proposed to make. No draft of it has ever been found: either none ever existed, or it has been destroyed. We have had views from various people as to what the new will would have contained: in my view, one person at least knew your father's intentions, but perhaps I shall never be able to prove that.'

Perhaps Craven thought he was being invited to fill the pause, for he said defensively, 'I didn't destroy any draft. I never even saw one.'

Hook extracted his photocopy of Craven's statement from his document case, though he knew the words he had originally written down himself clearly enough. He said, 'Yet when we interviewed you after the exhumation, you indicated clearly that you thought your father intended to cut you out of the new will.'

'I–I thought he did. Are you picking me up now for being honest?' Craven's tone was a mixture of puzzlement and apprehension.

Lambert said quickly. 'We should simply like to be absolutely clear. Did you or did you not know the contents of this will that everyone claims not to have seen?'

'Yes. Well, I think so.' He shook his head hopelessly and said, 'It's so long ago now. I had a blazing row with Dad when he found that I proposed to dispose of Tall Timbers after his death. He threatened to disinherit me there and then. When I heard he was making a new will, I suppose I assumed that was the purpose. Angela was closer to him than anyone, and she certainly thought that was to be the change, after he had talked to her. Margaret Lewis was so damned smug that I thought she knew as well...'

Lambert listened very carefully to Craven's rather disjointed recall of the events of some seventeen months ago. When he was sure it was finished, he said, 'Briefly, then: your father threatened during your quarrel to disinherit you. When you heard of a revised will, you assumed, reasonably enough, that the major change would be to cut you out. This seemed to be confirmed by the views of your sister and Mrs Lewis, who may have known more details of the new draft than ever came to your notice. Is that a fair summary?'

'Yes. Does this alter anything?'

'It's possible it might. There is one other thing we wanted to check with you. It relates to the same period – the months before your father's death. In fact, we can date this one quite precisely: we are interested in your reaction to a letter sent to you by the Manager of the Oldford branch of the National Westminster Bank on 27th August last year.'

'Six weeks before my father's death.' Craven was as acutely aware of the significance of the date as the men questioning him; he looked as if he was genuinely puzzled about what was coming next. 'I had many letters about credit at that time. My company was in difficulties. Fortunately for both of us, George Taylor at NatWest was persuaded to wait a little longer.' Craven's attempt at urbanity tailed away as he realized these men were investigating the very death which had brought about the revival of his fortunes.

Hook produced another of his documents, with a flourish worthy of Rushton. 'This is a copy of the letter sent to you by Mr Taylor. It draws attention to your failure to respond to the Bank's ultimatum about meeting at least the interest on your loans, and asks you to arrange an appointment urgently to see Mr Taylor.'

Craven was unabashed: he had obviously been used in the dark days to such summonses, but they were a thing of the past, his attitude proclaimed. He managed a semblance of relaxation as he said, 'It was a near thing for me financially at that time, I admit. But it's all water under the bridge now, Sergeant, and I can't see how this connects with my father's death.'

'Then I shall enlighten you,' said Lambert unsmilingly. As always, suspects were ordinary citizens unless and until they were proved guilty: that did not mean you had to like them. 'We wish to check Mr Taylor's recall of the subsequent interview against your own, to see if the two recollections tally.'

Perhaps Craven caught now at least an intimation of what was coming. He said cautiously, 'It was an anxious time for me. I had a lot of meetings of this kind. I'm not sure I can–'

'Mr Taylor is quite clear about the exchanges. He says you used an argument he had not heard from you before.'

'That's quite possible. Frankly, I was at my wits' end to stave off the institutions for a little longer, and any argument was welcome–'

'But you told Mr Taylor that there would

not be long to wait for a dramatic improvement in your circumstances. Because your father was dying. Because he would be dead, in your phrase, "within weeks".'

Craven was wide-eyed with shock. His eyes were fixed on Lambert's watchful, inscrutable features, as though held by some primitive spell. Eventually he faltered, 'I was in all kinds of difficulty at the time – prepared to use any argument...'

'Are you saying that Mr Taylor's account of what you said is substantially true?'

'It may be... Yes, I suppose it is.' He nodded miserably, as if admitting for the first time to himself that he had used such an argument.

Lambert was sure the man had forgotten the details of the occasion until reminded of them at this moment. That did not diminish its significance. 'How did you know that your father was going to die, Mr Craven?'

The man seemed to have shrunk behind his own large desk. He stared at its surface now, as if to look elsewhere would shatter what degree of brittle control he retained. It took him a long time to say, 'I was desperate. People were closing in on me from all sides. I was facing the bankruptcy court and worse. I used any and every argument with those who were pressing me. Dad was ill, failing even, with what I thought at the time was heart disease. I know I argued with various people who were threatening me that he wouldn't last long and that his death would solve my financial problems. If George Taylor says I used that argument with him, I've no reason to doubt him.'

His broken delivery of this was a strain on all of them. When Lambert was sure this was all that would be volunteered, he said, 'You asserted within six weeks of your father's death that you knew he would be dead "within weeks". That has a precision of timing that must surely strike you as quite chilling, now that your father's death is established as murder.'

Craven said wretchedly, 'I'm not proud of using Dad's illness like that. Financially, I was existing from day to day. I said Dad would be dead in a few weeks because that was the maximum extension I could hope for – if I'd thought they'd give me a few months on the basis if my expectations from the estate, I'd have said that.'

Lambert studied him, weighing his arguments, trying to assess the possibilities of his unlikely account being true. He said, 'Had you any innocent reason to feel your father might be near death?'

Craven looked like a drowning man who had been thrown a lifeline but had lost the co-ordination to grasp it. He began to speak, stopped, and shook his head hopelessly. Finally, speaking very quietly, he managed to put together, 'Only the evidence of my own senses when I visited him. He looked terrible, and his voice was getting weaker. You notice these things when you only see someone once a week. But I'm sure Angela and Margaret Lewis, who were seeing him every day, thought the same thing; I know they were getting more and more anxious about Dad's condition.'

'What about Walter Miller and Andrew Lewis? Did they express the same concern?'

'I don't remember. I didn't see very much of them at that time. Miller's visits didn't coincide with my own. Lewis was in the house, but he made himself scarce when any of us was around.'

Lambert stood up. 'Sergeant Hook has made full notes on what you have said. We shall need you to sign a supplementary statement later.' Craven nodded a dejected acquiescence; he couldn't think this would read any better than it had sounded in his ears as he told it. 'I repeat to you what I said to Mr Lewis. Come to us with any suspicions you may have in this matter: don't approach the party concerned directly. And please do not leave the area without informing us.'

They left him then, sitting miserably at his empty desk, staring unseeingly across the room at the alpine scene that seemed a part of a different and cleaner world.

CHAPTER 19

On the two-mile journey to the Miller's house, John Lambert was unusually communicative. Hook did not flatter himself that this sprang from a desire to keep him in the picture. Experience told him that the Superintendent was clarifying his own thoughts, organizing his approach to the interview with Dorothy Miller which lay ahead of them.

'Did you notice any point in our previous interview when Walter Miller seemed disturbed?' said Lambert, as he guided the big Vauxhall cautiously round a sharp bend in the narrow lane.

They thought of the big, affable American, handsome even in his seventies, confident in his account of Edmund Craven as fighter pilot almost half a century ago, anxious apparently that his old friend's killer should be brought to justice. Hook said unhurriedly, 'He seemed to become a little uneasy when he talked of wives. He's not alone in that, of course.' Behind the tiny male joke there was a real point; they had discussed it earlier in the progress of this investigation. But there had been no time to come back to it. After the victim had lain in his grave for thirteen months, this murder investigation seemed to the Sergeant to be proceeding at a headlong pace, as if events teemed upon themselves in a belated effort to make preparations to the corpse.

That was an illusion, of course. A successful murder inquiry made things happen. It was when they were getting nowhere that the routine and the dead ends seemed endless. Those killings in which the only impulse was a distorted sexual drive could lead to hunts which lasted for many months, without any guarantee of success. The possibilities were too wide, the number of suspects almost as great as the male population of the area – always male, he thought, with a wry disgust in his own sex. In the present caste the scents might be cold, but the number of suspects was probably no more than five: it seemed almost certain now that their killer must come from those people who had been constantly around Edmund Craven in his last months. And Bert Hook saw suspicion gathering comfortingly around his choice for the crime.

He pulled his attention hastily back to the present topic, visualizing the notes of the interview with Miller in his carefully rounded longhand, which he had studied as they set out towards the village where the Millers lived. 'According to Miller's account of their weekly chess meetings, old Craven only came to the Miller's house when Dorothy Miller was out,' he said.

Lambert nodded, giving a wide berth to a child wobbling disconcertingly on a battered bicycle as she heard the sound of the car behind her. 'Walter Miller seemed quite pleased when old Craven's failing health meant he had to go each week to Tall Timbers instead of them alternating the venue.' It was true, but Hook recalled it only now: as usual he was astounded by his chief's recall of the nuances of an interview.

They fell silent for the remaining two minutes of the drive, each forming his own picture of a Walter Miller thirty years younger, virile and handsome, sweeping the Mrs Craven they had never seen into an affair whose repercussions were possibly still resounding all these years after her death.

Hook had his own image so vividly in his mind's eye that he was quite resentful on Dorothy Miller's behalf when she opened the door. She had a natural courtesy which made her smile a welcome to these two large men who arrived menacingly at her door, moving soundlessly over the thin coating of snow which had coated the long path. The mellow stone of the house looked warmer than ever against the snow. Behind the trees, the sun was a huge crimson ball in a perfect

Cotswold sunset, so that the front of the house looked almost orange in its low rays. But behind, the woman's quick, automatic smile there was anxiety, burning in her like a consumption, making the light brown eyes unnaturally bright against cheeks which seemed for a moment to have caught the whiteness of the snow.

Lambert turned down drinks, and for once his sergeant did not resent it. What the woman had to say to them must be said at once; any delay would be nothing less than a cruelty. The detectives sat together on the chintz settee, feeling overlarge for its cottage proportions; Dorothy Miller perched like an anxious sparrow on the very edge of the armchair opposite them. Hook wondered where her husband was. He had no doubt that there was no chance of his returning to interrupt them. Even in her distress, this woman was too well organized for that.

She was anxious to talk, but she needed the formal introduction of Lambert's 'You wanted to speak to us, Mrs Miller,' to ease her into speech.

'Yes. Thank you for coming so quickly when I rang. Superintendent, there is something my husband concealed from you when you came here a few days ago.'

Lambert felt the old, familiar surge of excitement at the prospect of new information. An unbidden flash of self-knowledge

265

told him that it would be time to retire if that surge ever failed. The woman looked so distraught at her husband's concealments that he said encouragingly, 'That is never a good policy, Mrs Miller. But people hold things back far more often than you might think. Anyway, we're here now for you to make amends.' He smiled as encouragingly as if she were a distraught child. And for a moment he wondered if she would think him patronizing. But this woman, who had struck them as so alert and in control during their previous brief contact with her, seemed to find only the reassurance he had intended in his words.

'Yes. It probably has nothing to do with the case – in fact I'm sure it hasn't, but you will need to be convinced of that, I suppose.' She stared miserably into the fire, whose cheerful flames danced in faint reflection across her pallid features. Then she plucked her soft woollen cardigan unnecessarily about her shoulders and transferred her gaze to the hearth. 'It happened a long time ago. It's just that I didn't like Walter concealing it from you.'

When she seemed to find it difficult to go on, Hook accepted Lambert's nod and said gently, 'We are anxious to find out all we could about old Mr Craven. The more one can find out about a murder victim, the clearer the possibilities become about the possible killer. It was especially difficult for us to get a picture of the victim in this case, where the crime was already thirteen months old. So we were pleased to be able to talk to Mr Miller about Edmund Craven's life when his wife was still alive.'

'Yes, I know. That is when he held something back.' She was tight-lipped and drawn, even after Hook's emollient contribution. On the low wall at the end of the garden a robin surveyed the white winter landscape and chirped briefly at the great red orb of the setting sun, as if posing for an early Christmas card. There would be a hard frost on this still, clear night. 'He was trying to protect me. He shouldn't have done. You see, what he tried to hide gives him a motive for murder.'

For a moment, Lambert's mind was unworthily preoccupied with the ramifications of the law and the implications of a wife's evidence against her spouse. Then he said, 'We can make no promise, but we are as discreet as we can be about old affairs of the heart.' It was curious how often clichés floated to the surface in situations like these; and strange how often they were effective. 'Unless they have a direct bearing on the case, there is rarely any need for these things to come out in court.' He thought sourly of how often nowadays the cheque-books of the tabloids bought forth lurid stories which had no such relevance, once a murderer had been convicted and acquired an abattoir glamour.

She nodded, without looking at him. Then, suddenly, the words tumbled out, almost without punctuation, as if an invisible check had been abruptly removed. 'Ed Craven and I had an affair, Superintendent. It was nearly thirty years ago now. It lasted almost a year. Then Walter found out.'

Lambert felt Hook stiffen slightly beside him. They were such old hands by now that neither of them betrayed anything in their faces. They had been caught out when their experience should have protected them. Picking up the significant facts, they had made the wrong deductions. Walter Miller had certainly been disturbed by the mention of wives, had ensured that Edmund Craven only came to the house when Dorothy was out, had been pleased when the infirmity of Craven ensured that they could meet only at Tall Timbers. They had been right to suspect a sexual liaison in those far-off days, but they had picked the wrong pair, discounting the possibilities of the man who had faded and died against those of the one who had been such a vigorous physical presence before them.

A curious phrase in the will of Edmund Craven came back to Lambert in Alfred

Arkwright's dry tones. Walter Miller, in being allocated Craven's war memorabilia, had been called 'my old friend of many years, with whom I have shared so much'. Including, it now seemed, a wife. Lambert heard himself saying rather foolishly, 'That's a long time ago now.' He felt as if he were offering comfort in the confessional rather than establishing the facts in a murder inquiry.

'Yes. I think Walter wanted to protect me as well as himself when he didn't tell you about it.' Now that she had made her revelation, her relief made her a little more relaxed.

Perhaps she had never talked about this before, even to a woman friend. Lambert thought for a moment of the company director he had interviewed a few days ago in a fraud investigation, who had said without a hint of embarrassment of a woman who was involved, 'We were lovers, of course, for a few months, but that was all over quite quickly,' as if emotional life could be terminated as cleanly as a set of accounts. He said quietly, 'Thank you for telling us this, Mrs Miller. Probably, as you say, it has no bearing on the case.'

'But you see, from your point of view, it might have.' Having finally brought herself to speak, she was determined that all should be made clear. 'Walter is a passionate man,

Superintendent.' A trace of perverse pride came through in the assertion, and they saw her for a moment as a young woman who could break hearts, perhaps even cause men to kill. 'He swore he would kill Ed for what he had done. At the time he meant it; he tormented me by saying that he would wait until the time was right, until the opportunity presented itself. I think he forgave me a long time ago. I'm not sure he ever forgave Ed. Ed Craven, like Walter, was quite a bit older than me, and that allowed Walter to throw the blame almost entirely on to him, as the years passed and the breach healed between the two of us. The fact that they had been friends for twenty years before it happened, had come through most of the war together as comrades, made it much worse for Walter.'

She turned her palms fractionally upwards, allowed her rigid shoulders the tiny shrug which was another stage in their relaxation, and said, 'I still don't understand the male code in such matters. Walter was good to Ed in those last years. They enjoyed each other's company and for most of the time their friendship seemed fully restored. But Walter seemed to have separated off his resentment. It was almost as though he had it locked in a box and took it out from time to time to treasure in private, like a miser with his money. Perhaps I was the only one who saw how that hatred still burned.'

She looked into the fire again. The flames were brighter now upon her face as the day died, and the brown eyes sunk deep enough in their sockets to be invisible. Though she had said her piece now, it was a visage grey with apprehension. What she feared was that her husband, that handsome, passionate man with his relaxed transatlantic drawl, who nowadays took such affectionate care of her, had carried out his threat after all these years and murdered his old friend. That for thirteen months and more she had shared her bed and her life with a murderer. And even now, when she had brought herself at last to speak, there was not the complete relief she had hoped for; she realized as clearly as the men sitting opposite her that they could offer her no real reassurance for the moment. No reassurance that is, which would be of any value when she lay awake in the long hours of darkness beside that soundly sleeping presence, fighting the doubts that had seemed so small by day.

Lambert guessed all this, but to offer her comfort at this stage would have run counter to the whole process of detection. He watched her in silence for a moment. Then, timing his question with a clinical efficiency which ruthlessly cut across his sympathy for the woman, he said, 'I understand that your husband took a box of chocolate each week on his visits to Tall Timbers?'

'Yes.' She looked at him blankly, failing at first to see any implication in his question.

'For how long before Mr Craven's death did he do this?'

She thought hard, still untroubled by any sinister implication, still genuinely anxious to be helpful. 'It's difficult to be certain. What began as an occasional treat became a regular thing over a few months. That was as Ed's health failed and he became almost housebound. I should think Walter began to take them every week about six months before Ed died.' Now, belatedly, she caught her breath and, looked at him in horror. 'You can't think–? Poisoned chocolates! Surely that's a bad joke from the nineteen-thirties?'

Lambert said, 'From much earlier than that. Christiana Edmunds was killing people with poisoned chocolates in Brighton as long ago as 1870.' Burgess would have been proud of him for that, he thought.

As an attempt to defuse an emotional situation, however, it was a notable failure. He saw her fear turning to outrage and said hastily, 'We don't think anything yet, Mrs miller. We're assembling facts. One of them is that Edmund Craven died as a result of ingesting arsenic, in several stages. A second one is that one of the best ways of disguising arsenic is to combine it with some strong, sweet taste: chocolate is obviously an ideal medium. A third is that we now find that chocolates were taken each week into the house where Craven was murdered. You will agree, I think, that this constitutes a line of inquiry which it is part of our duty to pursue.'

He had spoken as sternly as if addressing a recalcitrant child. It had the effect of checking any lurch towards hysteria. She said stiffly, knowing that her views could hardly carry much weight in this atmosphere of objectivity, 'I'm sure Walter had nothing but the best intentions.' She caught Lambert's eye, for the first time in many minutes, and they exchanged small smiles at the formality of her words.

He said drily, 'Very probably not. I have to ask you if you ever saw him open one of those boxes of chocolates before he took it to Tall Timbers.'

'Never,' she said quickly. 'I never even saw him take them out of their paper bags. I'm sure he never tampered with them. Does that leave him in the clear?'

'I'm sure that your husband is far too intelligent a man to let you see him doctoring chocolates, if that is what he intended to do. But we have to ask. Sergeant Hook will record the negative fact that you saw nothing suspicious, alongside the hundreds of other facts which he and the rest of our team are assembling. Sooner or later, the facts which are the significant ones will form themselves into some kind of pattern.' That at any rate was the way it was supposed to work. Even when it did, it was easier to see the process in retrospect than at the time.

She said naïvely, 'Does this make Walter your leading suspect, then? I didn't know about the chocolates, and I've now given you a motive for him.' She looked at him bleakly, and he realized she was doing little more than thinking aloud. She had brought them here to voice the suspicions about her husband that she could no longer contain. Now, when he seemed threatened, she would have died to save him. It was not unusual; marriage was a strange institution, particularly when it endured as long as this one had.

Lambert did not look at Hook, as he said, 'Every one of the five people who had access to Edmund Craven in the crucial period has a motive, Mrs Miller. If motive alone was enough to prompt a killing, half the spouses in Britain would be lying dead. That is why we have to assemble all the facts we can. If we had known this was murder at the time it occurred, the Home Office pathologist would no doubt have been able to confirm or eliminate those chocolates as an instrument of death. As it is, we have to take into account every possibility. One of those, of course, is that those chocolates could have been used by someone other than your husband to kill the victim.'

He was merely trying to be fair; perhaps, indeed, this time it was he who was thinking aloud. But she took it as a comfort, and gave him a look that was a request for enlargement and explanation. Feeling he was offering her a little hope in exchange for her revelations about her past, he said, 'For what it's worth, the scene of crime team found a hypodermic syringe in the bathroom adjoining the bedroom where Mr Craven spent his last months. It would have been the ideal instrument for anyone wishing to inject a solution of arsenic into the chocolates your husband took to him. Any of the other four suspects, as well as your husband, could have used it.'

As if she knew how far he had stepped outside the code by which they operated, she said softly, 'Thank you, Superintendent Lambert. That puts things into perspective for me.'

'There are also many methods other than chocolate by which arsenic could have been administered.' He stood up. 'Thank you for telling us about your relationship with the late Mr Craven. No doubt you will be in touch with us again if anything occurs to you which might seem of even marginal relevance.'

Because he knew he had said more than he should have done, in an attempt to offer her what reassurance he could, he was trying to conclude formally. She herself offered the final sentiment, the platitude to complete his little homily, as she showed them out. 'Yes. The sooner you make your arrest, the sooner the innocent will be able to resume their normal lives.'

She stood beneath the lamp on the stone porch, watching them go as politely as if they had been old friends. A long-haired black cat with a white front picked its way past them in the snow, dainty even in its distaste for the frost-sequined surface, then darted swiftly into the house before the door could shut upon this icy world. They waved a brief unaccustomed farewell from the gate, both hoping that for Dorothy Miller at least the nightmare would lift rather than close in.

CHAPTER 20

There were not many people about in the CID section at the station. The digital clock over the door of the murder room showed 18.37. It took Lambert a few moments to remember that this was Friday: when the working days got beyond twelve hours, he found now that he rather lost count of their passing.

Even in the police force, the British weekend claimed its obeisance. The routine office work was put away; he realized now why there were fewer policemen and fewer lighted offices than he had been expecting. He dismissed Bert Hook to set up his Christmas tree with the nine-year-old twins who were eagerly awaiting him. Then he sat for a few moments at his quiet desk, briefly indulging himself with nostalgia, remembering the wide-eyed girls who had once helped him to decorate his own trees, but were now grown up and gone. Then he reflected on how strong a presence children were in this case. That only son whom Edmund Craven had foolishly indulged over the years, who had been so anxious to get his hands on the lucrative site of his father's house; that daughter who had resented the dead man's treatment of her mother and her own children; Margaret Lewis and her son, each passionately defensive of the other's interests.

These musings prompted him to ring his wife, to tell her that he would be home within the hour. As he reached for the phone, his eyes roamed over the various notes upon a desk he had not seen for two days, and the impulse was forgotten.

Rushton had reluctantly taken a day off, assured by his chief that this case was unlikely to reach its resolution in his absence. Lambert found as usual that it was easier to appreciate the DI's efficiency without his presence. The notes of their conference in the murder room earlier in the week were neatly typed in a folder, the follow-up inquiries they had agreed upon had been pursued and were neatly summarized, with Rushton's own intelligent comments added where appropriate.

The other notes on his desk emphasized negatively how well organized, how much in bureaucratic control of his team, DI Rushton was. Compared with his briefings, the rest were thoughtless, even occasionally imprecise. It was the last of them which was the only one of any importance. It was scrawled as if the writer had been anxious to resume some other duty; as if he had failed to appreciate the significance it might have in a murder investigation. '16.23 hours. Message from Mr David Craven's secretary. He would like to see Superintendent Lambert. No one else will do. He suggests 19.30 hours at Tall Timbers. Tried to contact you, sir, to pass on the message, but there was no reply from your car phone.'

It was signed by the young detective-sergeant who had been added to the team to take part in his first murder investigation. For a moment, Lambert wondered unworthily if Rushton had chosen him merely to underline his own qualities of precision and persistence. Then he dismissed the thought: Rushton might not want competition, but he was secure enough not to be threatened by it. And he was too good a policeman to import sloppiness deliberately into his team.

The DS should have recognized the potential of Craven's request: it was almost always significant when a leading suspect in an inquiry actually asked to meet its leader. He should have made sure he got in touch with his chief, not left a note on his desk after a single unsuccessful effort to speak to him by phone. At 4.23 Lambert and Hook had been with Dorothy Miller, but at any time since then the car phone would have made contact. The station sergeant would have gone on trying the number, if only he had been asked. Lambert hoped wearily that this was not more evidence of the old divisions between the CID and the uniformed men which he had striven so hard to eliminate.

He looked back to Rushton's notes on each of the suspects and tried the number given for David Craven. As he had expected, there was no reply; presumably it was a work number. He studied the note again, as if the scrawled words could themselves give a clue to what David Craven wanted to say. None of the CID team was around, though he could have raised whoever he wanted quite quickly by the phone which dominated policemen's lives. He wanted Bert Hook, but the picture of the Sergeant with the boys who had come to him relatively late in life obtruded itself sentimentally upon his thoughts. Because he wanted no one else, he told himself obstinately that Craven's message suggested he would talk only to him, that a third party might impede communication.

He tried to ring Christine to tell her he would be home within the hour. The line rang engaged: probably Caroline was ringing her mother from Nottingham, as she often did on Fridays. No matter; the call had been motivated by no more than the tiny prickling of long-subdued conscience. He would be home soon for the meal that had no doubt been ready for some time, able to say now that he had tried to make contact and found the line engaged. He checked with the station sergeant on the way out that Detective-Sergeant Rogers had not asked that he should be contacted with the message from David Craven, went into the night wondering whether the bollocking should be a ritual one from Rushton or a more private word from himself.

Tall Timbers looked more massive and isolated in the freezing moonlight. With only the square black outline visible against the stars, its air of leisured Edwardian comfort was removed. The windows which gave the house its design as a place for human shelter were removed from the silhouette, so that the shape seemed to rear itself like a massive blind presence above him, menacing, anonymous, shutting out the stars, even the blue-black night itself, as he went towards it.

The illusion of a great beast, denied its sight and turning dangerous, was reinforced by the bulldozer which loomed suddenly against the skyline on his left, like some primæval monster which had lumbered from its cave to attack the house. Already, two of the massive oaks that gave this place its name had fallen victim to it: even on this frosty night, Lambert could catch the acrid smell of roots and soil exposed to the air for the first time in a hundred years. The tearing apart of the site and the house, so bitterly opposed by Edmund Craven, had been initiated now by his son. To his left reared the machine which was the violent instrument of change; to his right, the massive, helpless house, the dinosaur of the twentieth century.

As Lambert neared the first of the four wide stone steps which led up to the heavy oak door, he caught through the small leaded window beside it the dim amber of a single bulb at the back of the high Edwardian hall. He recognized the householder's ritual warning to criminals that the place might be occupied, and smiled grimly in the darkness. This light, if it were the only one in the house, would invite rather than deter any burglar who knew his trade. It might be comforting for a householder re-entering a lonely house at night after an absence, but that would be the limit of its usefulness.

He rang the bell because he had to, but he knew as he did so that no one would come to this door to answer. The sound echoed, distant, but clear and sonorous in the enveloping silence of the house. No David Craven, then. Had he merely assumed that Lambert could not make the meeting after he had failed to confirm the time? Had he failed to appear from some more sinister cause? Lambert looked away to either side.

There were other houses there, he knew, but he could neither see nor hear anything of them. They seemed like great ships that had changed their berths in the darkness; he had not thought the houses in the avenue were quite so far apart. No wonder this site had potential for a development of flats: he tested that mundane thought as if it could banish more sinister imaginings about this place and its absent owner.

He went around the side of the house to see if there were any lights at the back. There was a single outside light on the rear corner of the high brick house, but like the one at the front it was not switched on. The clear illumination of the ground around the house would have been a more powerful deterrent to any felon than that small gesture of indoor lighting. The thought made him wonder where Margaret Lewis was. Perhaps with her son? But she could be anywhere; with a friend or at a cinema. Her caretaker role in the house did not demand a twenty-four-hour presence; no doubt she would be back in due course. He admired her nerve in living alone here; in coming back to an empty house of this size late at night. As always, thoughts of admiration were tempered by the evil presence of murder unsolved: mettle of this sort would be admirable equipment for their killer.

There was no light in the rear rooms of the

house. But, blazing unnaturally bright through the frosty night, there was a rectangle of light from a building at the bottom of the long garden. It was sixty yards away, through darkness made more absolute by the trees which overhung the path to it. This was the place which Edmund Craven had used as a studio for his amateur paintings, where latterly Andrew Lewis had repaired motor-bikes and cars. Who could be there at this hour?

He called through the darkness towards the light. His uncertain 'Is anyone there?' brought back a memory of a poem he had learned at school, *The Listeners*. This silence, like De La Mare's, stole softly back around him. He wondered whether to call again, and louder. Though he told himself he did not wish to intrude unannounced upon someone's privacy, in reality he was back in his childhood, with the city child's irrational fear of country darkness, which as a boy he could never admit. Then the thought of the neighbourhood watch schemes he knew operated in the area stilled his tongue; it would never do for a CID Superintendent to have to explain his presence here to staunch civilian guardians of the laws. For an Englishman, embarrassment can be a more potent force even than fear.

As he set off down the frozen path, the thought that had been no more than a vague presentiment formed itself into words, with the irritating timing characteristic of such notions: he wished Bert Hook was here with him; that he had ignored David Craven's instruction that he should come alone; that he had brought someone, anyone, with him here. Well, it was too late now: he thrust the instinct aside and stepped out resolutely into the darkness. It was the last of several wrong decisions.

Halfway down the narrow line of paving stones which led towards the light, there was a small garden hut, which made the blackness to his right even more absolute. As he picked his way with eyes cast down to the grey surface which was the only guide he had to his route, he never saw the figure which emerged softly behind him from this deepest of darkness.

Perhaps he caught the rustle of a movement, or the pressure which a neighbouring human presence seems to place upon the cool night air. Something at any rate made him half turn, so that he caught the full force of the blow above his right temple. The mind of an active man works so quickly in a crisis that he was aware in the instant before he was hit both of his foolishness in coming here alone at night, and of the fact that he had not told even Christine of where he was.

Then the blackness around him exploded

into a blinding white light and the pain crashed through a head that was surely too small to contain it. All sense had left him well before he hit the ground.

CHAPTER 21

The strident chords of *News at Ten* crashed into Christine Lambert's unwilling ears, insisting on what she would rather have ignored: that it was now ten o'clock on a freezing night and John was still not home.

There was nothing too unusual about that. But by now she would normally have heard from him; even his tardy sense of domestic responsibility normally prodded him to ring home before this time, especially now that his car had the phone that he had resisted as long as he could. Police wives are disciplined early to a routine of disappointed children and ruined meals. When John was in his twenties and still making his way in the force, it had been a severe blow to the status of a CID officer if his wife had the temerity to ring in to inquire about his whereabouts.

They had almost split up in those days over his allegiance to his work before his home. That seemed so long ago that the wife who had objected to his brusque dismissal of her feelings and her aspirations might have been a different woman. She realized as she watched the difficulties of other young wives that her situation had not been the uniquely bleak one it had seemed at the time, when her own career seemed discarded for ever and her conversation restricted to the vocabulary of her pre-school children. Only when she had got back into teaching a few years later had she discovered the perspective she needed for her marriage to prosper.

She was not sure in truth how much she had changed from that young mother whose shrill insistence upon her rights had met a blank wall of resistance in her husband; perhaps she had merely added something to her. She had no delusions that John had changed. Mellowed, yes, but that did not imply change so much as a willingness to disguise the sharper edges of his determination. The adaptations had been hers, she recognized ruefully; she had grown to love his consistency, his very obstinacy. Nowadays, he behaved in the way he did to be true to himself rather than to satisfy colleagues above and below him. But she suspected he always had. The demands of a career had been a convenient constriction, used to justify what he would have done in any case.

Essentially, he had changed only in appearance from the slim, determined man who looked so distinguished in their wedding photographs. But age had brought the vulnerability he concealed so resolutely from all but her; the stiffnesses as he rolled from beds or armchairs, the rheumatism in the shoulders when he stood for any length of time, the first mutterings of enlarging prostate. She thought of these things now, and they brought with them an access of protective love that sent her resolutely to the phone.

She tried his car phone, as she had done an hour earlier: he never minded that. She rang the number of his office at CID, and found herself connected with the station sergeant at Oldford. They exchanged brief words about the progress of Sergeant Johnson's daughter in higher education – Christine had taught her, years ago. Then she asked after the whereabouts of her husband.

There was a tiny pause while Johnson prepared his voice to conceal concern: he had expected Lambert to be home hours ago. Then he said, 'He went out some time ago to see one of the people involved in this exhumation case, Mrs Lambert.' He would not have given her the name of David Craven even if he had remembered it; as a uniformed sergeant, he was in any case too occupied with more mundane matters to follow the arcane proceedings of CID. He saw the clock on his left registering 22.19. Far too early for the regular influx of Friday night drunks; far too late for Superintendent Lambert. Danger bells rang in Johnson's experienced head.

But his tones were carefully modulated, even cheerful, as he said, 'I'll try to find out where he is and ring you back.' It was not his fault that he failed to deceive Christine Lambert, for she also was experienced in these matters. She stared at the phone for minutes after she had put it down. When the volume of the television set increased as always for the adverts, she sprang across the room and turned it off as brutally as if they were a personal affront.

It was Rushton who found Lambert. When Johnson rang, he questioned him tersely and without comment about the Superintendent's movements. He heard of DS Rogers's note to his chief, of Lambert's inquiry at the station sergeant's desk as he left. There was a pause, just long enough for Johnson to divine that Rogers would be well advised to have a good story on the morrow. Then Rushton said, 'You think the Super went to Tall Timbers alone?' and Johnson caught the edge of surprise on his voice.

Rushton did not make that mistake himself. He arranged for two burly PCs in a patrol car to meet him at the house. Even his brief snap at the wife who cast her eyes to heaven at this abrupt end of his day off did not delay him. He was waiting in the wide gateway of the house when the men arrived; already he had checked that Margaret Lewis's car was in the garage. She opened the door promptly when they rang, so that Rushton wondered whether she had been waiting for them.

He was terse to the point of rudeness in his questions, for they were asked on a rising tide of apprehension. No, she had not known of any arrangement for David Craven to meet Superintendent Lambert at Tall Timbers. No, she did not know of any reason why David should choose to meet him here. No, David had not rung her to tell her of the meeting. But she had been out of the house since three o'clock that afternoon, making preparations for her forthcoming move at her property in Burnham-on-Sea. No, as far as she knew, no one had seen her entering or leaving that house.

He left one of the PCs to search the house. He and the other constable took the two torches which were standard equipment for the patrol car and set about exploring the frozen grounds.

There was no light now in the empty studio at the end of the garden. They were almost upon the body when their torches threw up its awkward outline. Lambert lay upon his face with one arm folded unnaturally beneath him and the other extended as though in supplication towards the small wooden shed upon his left. The blood, which had covered the left side of his face and formed an ugly pool against his cheek, gleamed black as their torches played across it. Their beams picked out each detail in turn as brilliantly and dramatically as spotlights in a theatre; all else was black in the deep shade of the cypresses, which overhung this place as though it were a neglected cemetery.

Rushton was convinced that this was indeed a corpse. He was conscious of his companion's quick, uncontrolled breathing behind him as he knelt to feel for a pulse. The young constable must have attended worse scenes than this; but this had the sick excitement, the charnel house glamour, of a superintendent killed in the course of his duties. Rushton felt already the fury rising within him as he touched the icy skin of his chief's forearm. No doubt this would be the young man's first experience of that corporate anger that runs through a police force when a colleague is brutally killed.

Except that it might not. Not for the moment, anyway. Rushton's probing fingers found a faint, slow pulse. 'Ambulance. Fast! Then bring the blankets from the back of your car.' He heard relief and exultation in his voice, and was glad to find them there. Alone now in the freezing darkness with the chief he had resented, he muttered to the senseless heap below him, 'Hold on. Hold on, you old bugger, for God's sake!'

Rushton rang Christine Lambert as the tail-lights of the ambulance disappeared. He had never met her; he plunged quickly into his story, anxious to get it out and add the platitudes of consolation before she could interrupt him with hysterics. She said nothing at all. When she was sure he had finished, she said, like a mother speaking of a forgetful child, 'Did he have his overcoat? He so often leaves it in the car when he gets out, however cold it is.' It was shock, he supposed. But it was not, after all, as inconsequential an inquiry as it sounded: Lambert would probably have died of shock and exposure some time ago without that coat.

Rushton paused for a moment; then, reluctantly, he dialled Bert Hook's home number. Then he went grimly through the hall of the house to the high drawing-room, with its furniture labelled with lot numbers for the forthcoming auction. There was a damp, acrid smell from the bars of an electric fire which had not been used for some time; the room felt to him oppressively hot after the icy night he had left. He began to take a statement from a white-faced Margaret Lewis.

Whatever its deficiencies of manpower and administration, the National Health Service is still superb in cases of emergency. The private schemes, which suck out the powerful and articulate voices which might secure the resources it needs, cannot compete with it here.

Within two hours of the reception of Lambert's muffled form at the hospital, he had received three pints of blood, had his cranium surveyed from multiple angles in the scanner, been connected to drip feed and cardiac monitor. He had also been stripped, washed and wrapped in the ubiquitous hospital gown. The ugly wound above his temple had been stitched and dressed with a huge absorbent pad, which looked like some gross appendage to the inert form when it was returned to the room in the intensive care unit.

When Christine and Bert Hook were allowed eventually to come and sit in forced intimacy in the small space on the side of the bed which was not occupied by machinery, the overwhelming impression was of clinical whiteness. The still form beneath the immaculate sheets seemed to have no life beyond the bandages and machines. The hands which lay upon those sheets, the motionless face upon the pillow, seemed scarcely less white than their surroundings.

Christine Lambert watched the slow movement of the liquid in the central venous line to her husband's throat, listened despite herself to the hypnotically macabre breathing of the ventilator on her left, wondered whether she should be cheered or depressed by the tiny agitation of the elephant tubing leading to the grey lips. The bed and what was in it seemed wholly controlled by tubes and the machines to which they were attached. The thought grew and would not be rejected: what was in the bed was not a man but a form which existed in some temporary limbo between life and death, whose status would be quietly changed when the machines ceased to operate.

Bert Hook said for the fourth time in the last hour, 'I should have been with him. He should never have gone alone.'

Christine Lambert thought: He should be comforting me, not blaming himself. All that policemen are concerned with is self, self, self. And then she thought as she glanced at him across the bed: I am glad that he is concerned. His anguish should itself be my comfort. Better that he should be upset over John than offering me platitudes about him being in the best hands.

After a few minutes, Hook said, 'He was a good boss. The best.' He looked at the still hands upon the sheets, not at her. She noted the past tense without resenting it. Perhaps Hook was more shocked than she, who had always expected this. At least he had not said, 'He was a good policeman.'

When the sister in her blue uniform came briskly into the room, wearing the cheerful smile she had donned at the door, her very energy seemed a breach of taste. She looked at the little cameo around the bed and said, 'He's holding his own, you know. He's in the best hands, now.' She wondered why the wife smiled bleakly at the phrase, as if acknowledging a private joke.

She took her to see Mr Hall. Sitting on a hard chair in the surgeon's office, Christine looked at the pile of files on his desk and tried to resist the feeling that even at this moment she must not take too much of his time. She was unnaturally calm, anxious only that he should keep nothing from her. She was conscious that he was studying her carefully as he introduced himself and explained his function, as though she were being assessed for a job. Apparently she was successful: he plunged without preliminaries into explanation.

'Has anyone spoken to you about the extent of your husband's injuries?' She shook her head almost imperceptibly; she had the absurd suspicion that speech would make the damage more extensive. 'The only one that matters is the blow to the head.

We've X-rayed his wrist, because he fell upon it very awkwardly, but I'm almost certain there's nothing more than a sprain there. The head injury is serious, I'm afraid.'

She found her voice at last; it seemed he expected to be prompted. 'How serious?'

'Time will tell. I'm not being evasive: I don't have the full results of all our tests yet. He has rude health and a thick skull on his side.' He was glad that he had tried the tough little joke. He only ventured it with those who looked strong; he was rewarded on this occasion by a tiny, acknowledging smile. 'Blows to the head are far more serious than is generally supposed. I blame Hollywood. People in Western saloons get up and fight on after cracks on the head that would often prove fatal. The biggest danger is a sub-dural hæmorrhage inside the skull, but he seems to have avoided that.'

She nodded, aware that this was the core of his news, wondering if he was preparing her for the worst. 'They affect the brain, don't they?' For a moment, she had a vivid image of John at a party months ago, pontificating about old age, asserting that the only thing he really feared was paralysis, demanding that if ever that happened the life-support machine was to be switched off...

'Yes. Let me say at once that everything we are running on your husband seems positive at the moment. There is nothing which indicates that brain functions are affected. He was hit very hard, with what at the moment I can only call the traditional blunt instrument. Had it been a couple of inches lower, it would have hit the temple and I don't think I'd have been talking to you now.'

She let the full sense of his comment sink into her mind. Then she said stupidly, 'There seem to be an awful lot of – tubes and machines.'

He smiled, happy to be able to offer some genuine reassurance. 'Yes. We tend to forget how frightening they are to people who don't know their functions. Most of them are merely precautionary. His system has had a severe shock, apart from the actual injury. We're trying to help it along for a bit. If all seems to be going well in the morning, we'll take him off the ventilator and the venous line. If he progresses as I hope, the catheter will come out later in the day.'

For the first time she felt he was going to survive this. 'Thank you. When will you be sure of the extent of the damage?'

He stood up; only now did her senses allow her to register how tired he looked. 'Our monitors tell us quite a lot. But we can't be certain about the extent of con-cussion, or the possibility of cerebral œdema. I won't be completely happy until he recovers consciousness. I'm afraid it's not easy to predict just when that might happen.'

The sister met her at the door of the room where her husband fought so quietly for his life. 'There's nothing more you can do here, Mrs Lambert. You should go home and get some sleep. We'll be in contact as soon as there is any news.'

She nodded, docile now that she knew there was no more news to be had. 'Thank you, I should speak to Sergeant Hook before I go, though.'

'The Sergeant left whilst you were with Mr Hall, Mrs Lambert. He asked me to tell you he was going in to CID, to start finding who did this.'

For the first time in her life she was comforted by what she had thought of as the male impulse to revenge. She insisted she was fit to drive, was surprised when she looked at her watch to find that it was after five. She stopped at the door to thank the sister for what they were doing for John.

The sister smiled, glad to be able to resume her medical duties without lay presence, but full of tenderness for the woman going back to an empty house. 'Remember, he's in the best hands now!' she said.

CHAPTER 22

Rushton came in to CID before eight. He had already been in charge of the case for eight hours. GBH on a policeman cuts swiftly through red tape. It also unites a police force. The Chief Constable when he had been awoken with the news had been as angry as the humblest copper on the beat.

The Detective-Inspector was looking forward to disposing his forces and preparing his strategy in peace in a quiet CID section. He had made the effort to get in at this hour after being up until three, so that he had the right to expect that. One obstinate presence was there before him. Had been there, in fact, since five, two hours before the cold December dawn. Grey with worry, looking old enough to be pensioned off, exuding the bitter determination that would imbue the section until the bludgeoner was brought to book. Bert Hook, fists clenched at his side, looking for a physical outlet for his frustration.

Rushton's first reaction was that he could have done without this. He said, 'John Lambert is holding his own.'

'I know. I came here from there.' Hook

made it sound like a reproof, as if Rushton had been remiss in his duties not to present himself at the stricken man's bedside. The fact that Hook intended no such effect could hardly be expected to register with the younger man.

'I've been too busy trying to arrest his assailant to go there.' Rushton's voice was ominously aggressive.

Hook was too anxious for news to notice. 'Have you got him?'

'No. He didn't go to his own house last night. We'll get him when he goes in to work.'

'If he goes in, you mean. The bastard could be miles away by now!'

Rushton felt again an unspoken condemnation of his weakness. But he was curiously reassured to find Hook automatically assuming that this was their man. He had never spoken to David Craven himself, though he had read the transcripts of the various interviews with him. He said, 'He could also be in some woman's bed. We'll wait to see if he turns up at his office before we put out a general alert.' It was time to assert himself.

'If I get my hands on the bastard–'

'Don't be stupid, Bert!' Rushton cut in crisply with the official line: Hook had played into his hands. 'You're too old in the tooth for that kind of talk. I'll take you off the case unless you can guarantee to control yourself.'

'You can't do that!' Hook's outrage outran logic. He was looking for a target for his frustration and anger.

It was the sort of situation Rushton was good at. He said coolly, 'I can and I will if you make it necessary. You know that perfectly well. Whether you like it or not, I'm your superior officer. If you go on talking like a raw young copper with a hot head, you won't touch this case again.'

Hook looked at him hard. The red veining in his eyes was accentuated by the darkness all around them. Thirty-six hours without sleep have more effect on a man over forty; he looked like a meths drinker sliding downwards. He said, 'All right. I know the rules.'

Rushton relaxed a little. 'I suppose you're confident it *was* David Craven?' No one now was talking of the murder of Edmund Craven: the battering and possible murder of a superintendent had funnelled all police energy on to that violent moment in the darkness.

Hook started to reply, then stopped and took a long breath. He had been warned once, and rightly, about being headstrong; he did not intend to offer the younger man any further opportunity to assert his rank. He said, 'As confident as I can be. I think he killed his father to get his hands on his inheritance, because he knew he was about to be cut out of the new will. God knows why he tried to kill John Lambert. Presumably he knew we were getting close to him.'

'Well, at least he's played into our hands now. It shouldn't be too difficult to get the proof–'

'We'll get a confession – once he's brought in,' said Hook grimly. He made the fact that Craven wasn't in a cell at this minute sound like dereliction of duty for the Inspector.

'When we do, Bert, I shall interview him myself. Is that absolutely clear?' Rushton's tone was pure ice.

'Can I be present?'

'We'll decide that at the time. No promises.'

For the first time in years, Hook regretted turning down a decade ago the chance to move beyond sergeant's rank. He might have been taking over this case himself, instead of accepting orders from some jumped up... But he knew that Rushton was right. He must prove he was in control of himself before he could be entrusted with interviewing the man who had struck down his chief. Better start now. 'I've been looking on the Super's desk,' he said.

Rushton chose not to take this as a challenge to his authority. Especially now. The Inspector said carefully, 'And what did you find, Bert?' The smile he added emerged as rather artificial, but he meant it well.

'Not very much. I think he meant to interview David Craven again today, even before Craven asked to meet him last night. Presumably he felt we were getting near an arrest.'

'We're even nearer now,' said Rushton grimly.

'There was just one note in John's diary in relation to this case,' said Hook hesitantly. He had slipped into the first name again without noticing it; perhaps it was something to do with that lonely vigil at the bedside with Christine Lambert. He wondered if this byway was still worth exploring after last night's dramatic turn in events. 'He was planning to see the vicar of the parish church in Oldford.'

Rushton raised his eyebrows. 'Why?'

Hook did not like to admit the extent of his ignorance. He occasionally resented Lambert's tendency to keep his own counsel until he was sure of his ground: to say so now would sound like a betrayal. 'I don't know exactly. Old Craven fell out with his daughter over religion. Maybe the son too, for all we know. I presume John wanted to put some detail on that.' For a moment he found himself waiting for his chief's mock horror at the Amercianism. It made him feel both alone and inadequate.

Rushton stood up. Hook wasn't the only one looking desperately for action in this situation. 'I'd like you to follow that one up yourself, Bert. I'm going to be in Craven's office to receive him when he arrives.'

Hook was not sure whether he was being guided into a cul-de-sac while the Inspector took on the main action. He had a blind trust in Lambert which made him feel that this vicar might yet be important. It was action, anyway; and action of any sort must be better than waiting on events at the hospital.

As if he followed the thought, Rushton said as he made for the door, 'Call at the hospital on your way to the vicarage, Bert. Give me a ring on my car-phone to let me know how the Super is.'

They did not let him in to see John Lambert again. The day sister was young, brisk, impersonal, and very firm. But no doubt highly competent: her summary of the situation would have been a model for young police officers. 'He's still unconscious, I'm afraid. We've slowed down the ventilator, without ill effects. Mr Hall will be seeing him in ten minutes, and I'm pretty sure he'll take him off it altogether. Things are going as well as could be expected: perhaps rather better than that.'

Hook rang Rushton with the news. The

Inspector listened without comment. 'That's good,' he said. 'Perhaps he'll recover consciousness later today.' He sounded preoccupied, so that for a moment Hook thought he was doing no more than going through the motions of concern. Then he said, 'It seems you were right about David Craven. He's nowhere to be found. As far as we can tell, he seems to have left the area in a hurry last night.'

CHAPTER 23

The Reverend Aubrey Allcock was now retired. Bert Hook decided within two minutes that this could only help the reputation of his church.

The former vicar was short, portly, smooth-skinned and with the white hair that should have decked a man of his age and calling with venerability. Hook found instead an uncanny and disconcerting resemblance to a confidence trickster he had arrested four years earlier, who had wrought havoc among the savings of the elderly widows of Cheltenham.

'Yes, I knew Edmund Craven, Sergeant. Rather well at one time. He was quite a pillar of our church in his younger days.' His hands caressed the memory of his departed parishioner.

'So we were given to understand. But apparently he had some sort of disagreement with you a year or two before his death.'

The vicar looked pained. Hook, resolutely banishing his image of the elderly confidence trickster, found it disconcertingly replaced by Dickens's Mr Chadband: a quarter of a century earlier, Dickens had been one of the few authors universally approved in Barnardo's homes. Allcock said, with the air of one determined to be charitable to a hostile world, 'Disagreement would be too strong a word. Mr Craven found it difficult to be totally in sympathy with the modern ecumenical trend.' He lowered his voice and looked at the walls and windows of his comfortable lounge, as if the Inquisition might be surrounding his little bungalow. 'I sometimes feel there is something to be said for his point of view.'

Hook considered now that it might perhaps have been the personnel rather than the doctrine of the parish church that had driven old Craven away. He said, 'So he stopped coming to church because you were moving closer to other Christian communities?'

'That would be a gross over-simplification of the views of a man who is unfortunately no longer in the land of the living to defend himself. But as a summary, it would serve, I suppose.'

Hook was beginning to think that the Reverend Allcock might be the most appropriately named man he had ever met. He said roughly, 'In particular, he had about as much time for the Roman Catholics as Ian Paisley, I'm told.'

Allcock's half-smile suggested the weary

tolerance of a world which would have excited lesser men to condemnation. 'It is correct that he was not of the Papist persuasion.' His lips twitched, as if he intended to develop this thought into an anecdote; then he thought better of it.

Hook was wondering desperately what Lambert had hoped to get from this old humbug, and wishing more fervently with each passing moment that the Superintendent had been here to shoot down this strange bird himself. He said desperately, 'And no doubt you know Mr Craven's children as well.'

'Alas, not as intimately as I did at one time, Sergeant.' The adverb had inescapable *News of the World* connotations for a policeman, but Allcock's eyes were fixed in fond remembrance upon the ceiling, as if he saw pictures there which were invisible to less saintly eyes. 'Angela and David made the arrangements for the funeral; Angela mainly, as you would expect.' Hook had been waiting for this moment to press his questions about David Craven, but Allcock moved on, speaking for the first time with animation. 'Angela is much younger than her brother, of course. She was a wonderful sportswoman until she had the children. She had the build for it. Strong arms, strong legs; oh, a wonderfully – er – healthy girl, Sergeant.' He brought forth the adjective with such breathy sincerity that it might have come straight from the *Kama Sutra*.

'Yes. We saw some of her trophies when we interviewed her. Perhaps we could talk a little about her brother–'

'A wonderful figure of a woman. Junoesque, I believe they would have said when I was a young man.' He cast his eyes to the ceiling again in seraphic reminiscence; his expression suggested that what might have been lascivious recall in ordinary men was a remembrance imbued with Christian *charitas* in him.

Hook knew that Allcock's rather abrupt retirement from the ranks of the active clergy was rumoured to have had a priapic element. Fortunately, the girl had been well able to look after herself and there had been no charges: there was something to be said after all for the experience and robust approach of today's youth. The Sergeant worried with some desperation how he was to move Allcock on to David Craven without antagonizing him and make him uncooperative.

Help came from an unexpected quarter. Allcock's down-trodden sister arrived with the coffee he had offered his visitor with a lordly air when he arrived. 'Put it down over here, Celia,' he said, with an expansive sweep of the clerical arm towards the low table beside him. It was difficult to see another surface in the room which might have accommodated the tray, but the hunched figure did not seem resentful. She muttered a phrase about biscuits and disappeared to bring them; they could hear her opening tins in the invisible kitchen.

Her advent had the effect of moving Allcock on quite abruptly from Angela Harrison to her brother. He said hastily, as if trying to give the impression that this had been his theme when they were interrupted, 'We didn't see much of David Craven after he got married. I suppose he was busy with other things.' He sighed, as though treating with determined charity one who had sold out to Mammon. 'But he came to see me about his father's funeral. With Angela, of course.' He seemed about to be side-tracked into lubricious nostalgia once again, but the re-entrance of his sister with the biscuits recalled him to the duller paths of duty. 'They asked me to officiate at the interment, and I was happy to do so. David made a generous donation to the church just afterwards.'

When he came into his eagerly awaited inheritance, thought Hook grimly. But Allcock intoned, 'There is more joy in heaven over one sinner returned to the fold ... But no doubt you can complete the quotation for yourself, Sergeant?'

'Indeed I can,' said Hook, who had had a

succession of such tags thrown at him throughout his childhood years in the care of well-meaning housemothers. They had seemed then as they did now more appropriate for the needles of Victorian samplers than for a small boy full of largely innocent energy. 'There was no talk at the time of a cremation?'

'Oh no.' Allcock shuddered as though the suggestion was quite indecorous. 'Edward's children assured me that that is what he wanted.'

Hook noticed the small slip in the name with more resentment than he would have expected: he felt on the part of the dead man that it indicated that this old fraud was claiming a greater degree of friendship than had been the case. He said roughly, 'If he disliked everything Roman Catholic so much, I thought he might have considered a cremation.'

'Oh, you mustn't assume anything like that, Sergeant.' Allcock's patronizing smile indicated a serious flaw in detection here. 'Many of my brethren – I always thought of them like that – chose what we must still regard as the traditional method for the disposal of one's mortal remains. There are people who still believe literally in the resurrection of the dead when the eventual day of judgement comes. I was happy to find Angela and David quite insistent that

that is what their father would have wanted. And David, as I say, was quite generous after the funeral.'

I'll bet he was, thought Hook. Sheer relief that the old man was in the ground, no doubt. He wondered what the long-legged Angela Harrison, so preoccupied nowadays with her children, would think if she knew she featured in the hot imaginings of this dubious representative of the cloth; probably she would be balanced enough to laugh it off, he thought. He said, 'No doubt you have heard by now that Edmund Craven was murdered. What you probably don't know is that my senior colleague, Superintendent Lambert, was struck down last night and is at present fighting for his life in Oldford Hospital.'

Aubrey Allcock threw up his hands in slow motion. Bert Hook thought it the most insincere demonstration of regret he had ever seen, and prepared to interrupt the man if he came out with any sentiment to the effect that in the midst of life we are in death. When mercifully he cast his eyes mournfully to the carpet and said nothing, Hook said, 'Edmund Craven seems to have been estranged from his daughter by religion: her husband is a Roman Catholic. And from his son by a variety of things, the last and most serious of which was David's plan to demolish Tall Timbers and erect flats. Do you think either of them might have killed him?'

Allcock gasped at the monstrous indelicacy of the suggestion. 'I find it quite impossible even to speculate upon such a thing,' he said, as if the very question was a slur upon his integrity.

Yet Hook was sure he had given the question careful thought. 'And nothing took place at around the time of the funeral or since which you thought in any way odd?'

'No, Sergeant. I don't want to tell you your job, but I think you're on the wrong track here. David may have his faults, but I can't think either of the children would have killed a father such as they had.'

'Well, someone did!' said Hook harshly. For a moment he was tempted to shock this unctuous hypocrite with the details of David Craven's assignation with his chief and the subsequent brutalities, but discretion prevailed and he went on to ask him about the other suspects. Allcock knew them, but was unwilling to contemplate murder by any of them except Andrew Lewis. Even he, Allcock decided eventually, was probably 'too well brought up' to be capable of murder. Hook wondered wryly what this man would think of his own upbringing.

Wondering desperately why he was here at all, he said, 'Was Mrs Miller also a parishioner of yours?'

Allcock glanced at him warily. 'She was a very pretty woman in her prime. I regret to say that she was only an intermittent attender at my church in her later years.' He regarded his plump hands, which looked as though they had never undertaken an hour of manual work, as if considering mournfully whether these two facts might be related.

Hook wondered if Allcock knew about the affair between Edmund Craven and Dorothy Miller. He said casually, 'I don't suppose you heard of any scandal about her at that time?'

The effect of this on Allcock was surprising. He looked both startled and apprehensive. Eventually he said, 'Let he who is without sin cast the first stone, Sergeant.' Having cast his eyes so far towards his elusive heaven that their pupils disappeared, he remained thus, like a child who believes himself invisible because his head cannot be seen. His auditor was left wondering whether Allcock had his own pecadilloes to conceal in this area.

Hook said, 'The Millers were in close touch with Edmund Craven in the months before he died. Do you know of any reason why either of them should have killed him?'

Allcock came back to the same level as his interlocutor. As his eyes became visible once more, there was in them a look of consider-able relief. He thought for a moment and said, 'Walter Miller is an American, of course. I have to say that he is a man capable of considerable violence.' It was not clear whether he introduced the first fact as explanation or excuse for the second one. Perhaps it was merely to demonstrate again the immense charity of the speaker, who was determined to find mitigation even for aggression in a man who did not turn the other cheek: Hook found himself expecting that allusion at any moment. He had a suspicion the aggression might on this occasion have been directed at a randy clergyman, but he supposed it was useful to have confirmed what Dorothy Miller had already suggested: that her husband was capable of violence in the aftermath of jealousy.

He was suddenly anxious to be away from this man and this room, with its smells of stale tobacco smoke and air too long unchanged. He said a ritual, 'Please be sure to let us know if anything comes to mind. Anything at all that you may remember. Things may come back to you now that we've talked.'

As he drove back into the town, he thought: David Craven sealed your lips with his hefty donation, whether or not you had any thought about his guilt.

He wondered again just why Lambert had planned a visit to the Reverend Aubrey Allcock.

CHAPTER 24

Rushton caught up with David Craven in the detention room at Heathrow.

He had booked a ticked on a flight to Milan in his own name: he was not the kind of criminal to have the false passport at the ready which would enable him to assume an alias. The computer threw him up immediately as a wanted person. He made no difficulty about his detention, and Rushton was on his way down the M4 to collect him within the hour.

As he led his sergeant through the crowds to collect his man, the airport was full of people travelling to all parts of the globe for Christmas. The duty-free shop was packed; its bright yellow and red plastic bags dotted the huge lounge, brighter almost than the myriad Christmas packages which poked everywhere from the personal luggage bags. Planes for most destinations were taking off on time on the cold, clear day; passengers were unwontedly cheerful, bright with the anticipation of friends and homes re-visited. It seemed a strange place to arrest a man.

It was not, of course. It was the anniversary of Lockerbie, and the airport staff were

318

well aware of it, though under strict instructions not to recall it to their customers. The atmosphere in this large, bare room was very different from the cheerful bustle outside it. More evil men than simple murderers had been arrested here over the years: men who had despatched, or tried to despatch, into oblivion masses of people they had never seen.

The room seemed to retain a miasma of their distorted ethics. It must have been twenty metres long and half as broad. Yet it seemed claustrophobic. There were no windows here, save a single pane of one-way glass, through which the occupants might be observed by those who had set them there. The long, pale-blue walls had no pictures. The furniture was functional and well-maintained, far better than that of the public areas in most city police stations, but anonymous. The dark blue plastic of its coverings stared back impassively from a score and more of identical chairs: in an age of terrorism, the room had to be ready for large groups of detainees. It was a room that might have been designed by Kafka to depress and intimidate. David Craven had been there for almost three hours.

Rushton felt he was putting him out of his misery as he uttered the old formula: 'David Alexander Craven, you are charged with the murder of Edmund George Craven. You are not obliged to say anything, but anything you do say may be used in evidence.'

It was difficult to say whether Craven was stunned or resigned: perhaps it was both. He looked like a hunted animal which had so exhausted itself that capture came as a relief. He was haggard with loss of sleep. Though he had shaved, he had cut himself twice on the chin; the dark spots of dried blood looked like the beginning of some ugly and dangerous rash. The collar of his expensive car coat was half up and half down. One of his shoelaces trailed unnoticed on the floor. There was the smell of stale whisky upon his breath, but he had had no drink since he had been led to this room.

Rushton said, 'Where did you spend last night?' He was hoping for a confession; it seemed a neutral enough way to begin to build some sort of relationship with the man.

'At a hotel on the outskirts of Slough,' said Craven. Rushton would not have been surprised to hear him say he had spent it under a hedge. Perhaps Craven divined as much, for he said, 'I didn't sleep much,' making it sound like an apology.

'Why did you run?' said the Inspector after a pause.

Craven glanced up at him; his dark blue eyes looked as black as the shadows beneath them. He said hopelessly, 'You were going to arrest me.'

'And now we have.' Rushton didn't know what Lambert had planned: even what he had thought in those last hours before he was struck down. 'Running never does much good.'

'How is Superintendent Lambert?'

Rushton felt a surge of anger that his assailant should now express concern. 'He'll survive, they say now.' His latest information was that Lambert was conscious, but he was not inclined to discuss his condition here. 'You might at least avoid the charge of murdering a policeman, if that's what concerns you.' Detective-Sergeant Rogers, who had ridden here in chastened mood with the Detective-Inspector to make the arrest, made a careful note of Craven's question and did not look up. He was more relieved than anyone by Lambert's progress in the last thirty-six hours.

Craven said harshly, 'I didn't attack him. I heard about it on the radio in my hotel room.' His voice carried no conviction, even to himself.

'Who did, then?'

'How should I know?' Craven's haunted eyes looked round the bleak walls and found no relief there.

'You must have heard also on the radio that we wanted you.'

'To help with your inquiries, yes.' Craven

attempted sarcasm on the familiar blanket phrase, but he could not quite bring it off. 'Well, I'm here, aren't I?'

Rushton wondered whether to take him off to stew in the cells for a few hours at Oldford. It might be the best way to secure a confession: Craven did not look the kind of man who would be at his best in adversity. Rushton decided to try a little longer here first; that at least would give him two bites at the cherry. He said, 'It is in your own interest to be as helpful as you can to us.'

This time Craven's bitter laugh came naturally enough. 'Which means offering you a confession, tying myself up neatly and throwing myself on the mercy of the law. Well, that at least I'm not going to do; I've helped you far too much already.'

Rushton thought of Lambert in hospital, recovering from the blow that could so easily have killed him. He was obscurely aware that the Superintendent would have handled this better. That irritation was heaped on to the anger he had determined to control. 'You're in trouble, Craven. Running away was as good as a confession.' His contempt came out in the phrase, as though they were children discussing a boy's refusal to stand still and put up his fists in the playground. When confrontations with people in custody led nowhere, they often ended like this, with the police asserting the simple facts of their control. 'You're going to be banged up for a long time, sunshine.'

Craven said hopelessly, 'I didn't do it.' His face set sullenly, like a child's refusing the facts thrust at him by an adult.

'Then why run?'

The hunched shoulders twitched a little; it was too small a movement to be called a shrug. When he looked up and found the policemen still watching every reaction, he said, 'Margaret Lewis always tried to put the blame on me; so did her son. Well, I suppose that was predictable enough. But I met Walter Miller last week and it was obvious he wanted me to say that I'd killed my father. And I'd taken a gun with me because I thought I might be meeting a murderer in a lonely place!' He laughed bitterly at the irony of the thought. 'Perhaps I was, for all I know: I'm certain one of those three did it. But you won't believe that. Everyone seemed to know that Dad had been planning to cut me out of his new will.' Rushton noted with satisfaction this first definite admission of what they had all suspected. 'When eventually it because obvious that even my sister, who has always stood by me, was beginning to think I'd done it, I realized how little chance there was that anyone else would believe me.' He spoke in the even monotone of one both exhausted and defeated, as if his words were not of himself but of someone with whom he had no emotional connection.

Rushton was not impressed. There was an edge of contempt on his voice as he called, 'And why did you try to kill Superintendent Lambert? Because he was getting too close to you?'

'I didn't!' It was the first real vehemence Craven had shown: perhaps he felt the police net drawing tight now around him. 'I wouldn't have wanted him dead. He was the man I thought might get me out of this. He's a clever devil; I realized that.'

It was a defiant reversal for the quarry to pin his hopes on the hunter. But perhaps it did not sound convincing even to the speaker. He looked into the faces of the two CID men and found them only watching to see when he would break. There was silence as each side waited for a move from the other.

But the resolution of the taut little scene came unexpectedly from without. There was a brief knock at the distant door of the big room, a prelude to the almost simultaneous entry of a member of the airport police, who hurried across the dark carpet to the Detective-Inspector and said, 'This message just came through from Oldford for you, Mr Rushton.'

Rushton's face creased into a mirthless

smile as he read the two brief sentences on the fax paper. He looked with a kind of triumphant distaste at his prisoner. 'The scene of crime team have found the weapon which struck down Superintendent Lambert. A marble statue from your office. Ring that lawyer now if you like. He'd better be good.'

CHAPTER 25

After twenty-four hours, John Lambert had recovered consciousness and the various tubes were removed. After forty-eight hours, he was allowed to sit in a chair in his dressing-gown. After sixty hours, he had finished his grapes and was becoming a nuisance.

Christine refused to have any mention of work, and she held steadfastly to her decision. Her husband knew better now than to try to break that taboo, as he might have done twenty years earlier. His head might hurt a little still, but it was functioning adequately: he bided his time and waited for the visit of Bert Hook.

The Sergeant came tentatively into the ward where his recovering chief now lay, carrying a spray of freesias which looked absurdly out of place in his large hands. His relief was manifest when a nurse removed them from him with skilled dexterity and the practised bromide words about their beauty. He sat on the edge of the chair by Lambert's bed with his feet tucked back beneath it, looking for all the world as if he had come to take a statement. Visiting the sick was not one of his many strengths.

He asked the only question that would have concerned him in his chief's place 'How soon are you expecting to get out of here?'

'Within two days, they say. Possibly even tomorrow if I'm a good boy. They clear out everyone they can before Christmas. Christine has brought my clothes in already, but I think that was just to stop me bothering the staff.'

Hook nodded thoughtfully and subsided. Lambert, finding that he had to make the conversation, felt cheated of his invalid status. Yet with Hook it suited him well enough. They were old companions now, with no real need to hasten into the gaps inevitable in a dialogue in which neither side had any small talk. And it enabled him to arrive at the topic that interested him without any great difficulty.

'I saw the Reverend Allcock at his retirement bungalow,' said Hook. He wanted to ask why it had been necessary, but Lambert took him through a detailed account of the interview without commenting on its unremarkable content. 'He conducted the funeral of Edmund Craven as the family requested?'

'Yes. He liaised with Angela Harrison over it. I had difficulty in controlling his lascivious imaginings at the recollection: he's a randy old bugger!'

'I bow to your judgement as ever in such matters.'

They skirted carefully round DI Rushton's direction of the case before Lambert said, 'Have you arrested the killer of Edmund Craven yet, then?'

'We have indeed. He'll be in court to-morrow morning, charged with first degree murder. We'll be asking for a remand, I expect, pending further charges. He hasn't been charged with the assault on you yet. I suppose we had to wait to see if you'd survive.'

The black joke fell flat. Lambert stared wide-eyed at the Sergeant, so that Hook wondered if his recovery was going quite as smoothly as everyone seemed to think. Eventually he said, 'You've arrested whom?'

'David Craven, of course.'

'Was it you who charged him?'

'No. DI Rushton and DS Roger did the actual arrest. He was stopped at Heathrow when he was trying to leave the country.' Hook did not care to admit that he had been kept away from Craven because Rushton feared he might not control himself in the face of what the man had done to his chief. The idea seemed both unprofessional and embarrassingly sentimental.

Lambert nodded absently. 'Has he confessed?'

'Not yet, as far as I know. I haven't seen him myself. He's got the lawyers busy, of course. No doubt in due course he'll come up with the best brief.' The resentment against those able to buy themselves the privilege of the best defence burned strong in Bert Hook; most policemen of his age have learned to accept such things with the weary cynicism of those who know they cannot affect the system.

'No doubt he will, if it comes to it. Have you found the weapon with which this was done?' Lambert gestured towards the dressing on the side of his head.

'Yes. It was a marble figure from Craven's office. You may remember it from our visit. Forensic have confirmed it: there was enough Lambert hair and gore still adhering to make it easy for them.'

The Superintendent winced a little in the face of this robust approach, his hand straying for a second automatically towards his wound. Then he said grimly, 'And where was this so easily identifiable statue found?'

Hook thought his chief's tone did not show due respect for the diligence of the scene of crime team. 'Under the trees at the edge of the site. Near where the clearance work has begun for the flats development.'

Lambert nodded. 'Where it was certain to be found.' He looked past Hook, towards where girders were being hoisted into place for the extension to the hospital, watching for a moment the men in balaclavas guiding the steel carefully into position.

Hook said sturdily, 'It's evidence, anyway. Valuable evidence.' He wondered whether that fearful bang on the head was making his chief resentful of his colleagues' success in his absence. It would be quite untypical of Lambert, but he had heard before of personality changes following upon such injuries.

Lambert transferred his attention slowly back to his sergeant. 'That remains to be seen, Bert.'

'But it's quite certainly the thing you were hit with. And–'

'I'm sure it was the thing I was hit with. The question is, who hit me.' He stared at the fields rising in a gentle slope beyond the building works. The frost had disappeared during the day, but the leafless trees were still as sculptures. The sheep on the skyline looked larger than usual against the darkening blue of the afternoon sky. He tried to think of the invisible Severn flowing slowly through the next valley, but no clear picture would come before his mind's eye. It was surprising how quickly one became hospitalized; the world out there seemed remote from the warm cocoon of his existence here, where meals came on time and the day's landmarks were tablets and injections.

A resolution was forming in the Superintendent's mind, a determination which seemed to wax strong on the misapprehensions of others. He said, 'When does Craven go to court?'

'Tomorrow morning in Oldford. He'll be remanded to the Crown Court, of course.'

'He mustn't go. Drop the charges.' Lambert was looking past Hook, giving his orders without explanation, like a not very benevolent despot.

Hook was not offended. He realized now that recovery in this case was slower than had been thought at first. Lambert would be his equable self again in due course, but it would take more time than they had been anticipating. He said, 'That's out of my hands, sir.' It was the first time he could remember using the title in years, save on certain public occasions. He realized he was trying to make the denial of a sick person's whim more easy for himself; he wanted this to be the decision of a huge and impersonal machine rather than of the Sergeant who had followed this frail-looking figure so unquestioningly for so long. 'I don't think the Chief Constable would sanction us drawing back at this stage. Unless–'

'Unless we had someone else to charge. Someone who might even plead guilty.'

Lambert's tone made Hook look hard at him, wondering whether there might after

331

all be more in this than the effects of severe concussion upon an active mind. The very doubt was a tribute to what he had seen this unlikely figure in winceyette pyjamas achieve in the past. Lambert's head had been shaved around the wound, to allow the medication team free access to it. The flesh there looked curiously pink and naked, the blue veins now exposed more vulnerable without their cover. The elaborate dressing looked as though it should itself be protected, as if only this small assembly of lint and gauze stood between the brain itself and a world full of menace. Even Lambert's wrist, bandaged as a precaution to assist the sprain, made him look like a cripple in the bed. Hook thought he had never seen the chief look so old. Yet he did not look at all light-headed. And in the circumstances, that was depressing.

The idea that the eyes are mirrors of the soul is a romantic concept which should not be tested on policemen. By training and experience, they have learned to suppress such nebulous propositions; their enemies, indeed, would deny them souls. On the other hand, it is often possible to follow the workings of a policeman's brain through studying his eyes. Now, when Lambert's eyes looked carefully around the ward without any movement of his head, the Sergeant divined his thought processes immediately.

And the divination filled him with instant alarm.

Lambert looked thoughtfully at the curtains surrounding the bed at the end of the ward, where the nurses were working unseen on a patient recently returned from theatre. Then he eased his legs thoughtfully over the edge of the bed. 'Those curtains are an excellent idea, Bert. Just pull ours around us: my clothes are in the locker.'

Hook agreed as though under hypnosis. Lambert dressed gingerly, while his sergeant tried like one in a nightmare to speak words which would not come. He found his hands moving unbidden to fasten the Superintendent's shoelaces, while Lambert sat above him on the bed, holding his feet obediently forward like a sickly but determined child. By the time Hook stuttered into a half-formed protest, it was too late. Lambert, finger upon his lips to call for silence, poked his invalid head for a moment between the curtains to ascertain whether the coast was clear, then drew them back with a stage magician's elaborate gesture to reveal himself fully clothed to an uncaring ward.

There was a brief but embarrassing scene in sister's office at the end of the ward. While Lambert insisted calmly upon his right to discharge himself, the guardian of medical standards turned to vent her frustration upon the innocent Hook, as if he were the instigator rather than the victim of this outrageous breach of protocol.

Lambert affected not to notice the proffered arm as he walked unaided to the lift, wondering if the massive concentration this seemed to necessitate was obvious to observers. By the time he had covered the hundred and fifty yards of tarmac to Hook's car, he looked exhausted. He allowed the Sergeant to stow him carefully into the passenger seat like an octogenarian, even allowed himself the luxury of a few seconds with eyes closed as Hook went round the car to the driver's door.

But by the time Hook had started the Orion's engine and looked questioningly at him, he was able to speak with something near his old authority. He settled himself back into his seat and looked straight ahead through the windscreen at the winter afternoon, as if savouring the familiar professional mantle he had resumed so irregularly. After the warmth of the hospital, he shivered a little.

Then he said, 'Let's go to Angela Harrison's house.'

CHAPTER 26

It was snowing steadily on their way to the outskirts of the town where Angela Harrison lived. There might yet be a white Christmas, though there were still four days to go.

Hook felt the wheels slide a little as he turned on to the new snow which covered the surface of the cul-de-sac, with its rows of closely set houses. On this higher ground there were already two inches of snow, but the sun came through as they parked, and the flakes thinned to a slow descent of fine particles that was merely picturesque. Lambert sat for a full minute watching it through the windscreen, until Hook wondered whether his physical fragility was making him more than usually sensitive to the winter beauty which had descended even upon this suburban dullness. The events of the half-hour which followed made him realize how his chief had been gathering his depleted resources for the ordeal ahead.

The sound of children's voices seemed to break Lambert's trance. When they arrived at the house, they found Angela Harrison flushed and happy, organizing the building of a snowman in the rear garden. Her own two children, a boy and a girl of about six and seven, were left under the supervision of a slightly older neighbour's child while their mother came back indoors to talk to the detectives.

If Edmund Craven's daughter was at all disconcerted to find them at her door, she gave no sign of it. As she ushered them into the lounge at the back of the house, she seemed no more than a little surprised to be receiving them unannounced. The Christmas tree in the corner of the room had been decorated in the last hour: the last of the shiny baubles lay in the box beside it. Hook pictured how his own children also would be distracted by the magic of snow from even this Christmas task. There was a fire in the hearth today, as if to welcome the season; even with the wire of the fire-guard in front of it, Angela's golf and tennis cups on the sideboard glinted cheerfully with the reflected flames.

Lambert had been sufficiently disoriented by the hospital routine to forget that the schools would now be closed for Christmas; he had not reckoned on conducting this with children around. There was no sign of Michael Harrison, though they felt the husband's presence strongly in the house. The policemen sat on the edges of the comfortable, shabby armchairs; in retrospect, Hook thought he was probably the only one of the three who did not know what was about to happen.

He got an inkling from his chief's reaction to Angela Harrison's opening inquiry. She said politely, 'How is the head, Superintendent? I heard you'd been attacked.' The grey-green eyes seemed to belie the conventional inquiry after his health: they stared glassily at the huge dressing on the side of his head.

Lambert looked at her coldly and totally ignored the query. He said heavily, 'I suppose you know why we are here?'

Her disarming smile did not extend to her eyes as she said, 'I know my brother is in custody. Indeed, I have been to see him ... Superintendent Lambert, I hope you are not expecting me to give evidence against my brother.' She used his title sternly, like a teacher disciplining a child with his full name.

Lambert's answering smile was as without humour as hers had been. 'On the contrary, I expect that when we leave here we shall be in a position to release him immediately.' He turned his head to Hook, without taking his eyes off the woman opposite them. 'Sergeant, charge Mrs Harrison with the murder of her father, please.'

The pause was not long, though it seemed

337

agonizingly so to Hook. His brain worked more swiftly than he would have believed possible, weighing the possibilities of Lambert's mind being unbalanced by fever and medication, of the embarrassment that might be caused to all by the arrest of this smiling mother in front of her children. He cursed his chief for not warning him of this, for the sense of theatre which always seemed to beset him on such occasions. And with that curse came the blind faith in his man which made him know he was going to follow his instruction. The whole process was completed in two seconds.

'Angela Harrison, you are charged with the murder of Edmund George Craven. 'You are not obliged to say anything, but anything you do say will be taken down and may be used in evidence...' Hook could scarcely believe his own ears as he intoned the familiar words.

He thought he was prepared for any reaction from the handsome woman opposite: anger, outrage, contempt, even laughter. Anything, in fact, but for the quiet monotone in which she said, 'He always preferred David to me, even when we were children. However badly he behaved, Dad was always prepared to laugh it off. It was all right while Mother was alive.' She was staring into the fire, as though long-dead memories glowed there. She said in a tone of surprise, as though she were discovering the fact for the first time in herself, 'I loved him, but I never forgave him for the way he treated Mum.'

Lambert was aware of his head throbbing, but he felt no pain. The effect of adrenalin on a head still tender from the savage blow he had received was strange. As he watched his sergeant writing down the words of a murderess, he felt so thoroughly in control that he could time the exchanges to make sure Hook's record was accurate. He said, 'It was the will that drove you to kill, wasn't it?'

She did not even transfer her gaze from the fire. 'Yes. He showed me the draft he had made. It cut me and the children out entirely, and gave virtually everything to David. I couldn't forgive Dad for doing that to his grandchildren.'

Through the double-glazed window, Lambert could see but not hear the children, laughing excitedly as the three of them strove to roll even further the huge snowball that was to be the snowman's body. He hoped they would never realize that they had been the innocent provocation for murder; there would be horror enough for them without that. Their mother said, 'People made the assumption that it was David who was to be cut out of the new will. It was easy enough for me to foster that impression.' For the first time, they caught the contempt for the ordinary run of humanity characteristic of the psychopath.

Lambert said softly, 'We never found that draft.'

Still she looked into the fire, but now she smiled the knowing smile of the human being losing touch with her kind. 'I took it away on the night I gave my father the final dose of arsenic. I burned it in this very grate.' Then, for the first time since she had been charged, she looked at Lambert, almost as though she was surprised to find that it was he who was there. With the air of one delighting in her own acumen, she said slyly, 'What evidence have you got against me? All the evidence points to Margaret Lewis, or Andrew Lewis, or Walter Miller. Or at my precious brother, David – you've already arrested him.' She closed her arms across her breasts and hugged herself a little: even as she spoke of others she was preoccupied with herself, in the way of the severely disturbed.

Lambert thought she had given them all they needed in the past few minutes, but he said, 'That evidence was much too easy for us to come by, Angela.' The first name slipped out before he knew it: already he was addressing the criminal as a Broadmoor case. 'The cold cream jar in Margaret Lewis's scullery, the syringe in the bathroom: it was inconceivable that any murderer would have left such things there for over a year after the crime. It made the people you were trying to incriminate less likely suspects, in my mind. And there were no fingerprints on either of them: there should have been, particularly on the cold cream jar.'

Angela Harrison gave no signs of having heard or understood, though he knew she had. She rocked backwards and forwards a little on the edge of her chair, like a child preoccupied with her own thoughts. Her voice seemed to come from a long way off as she said, 'And what made you suspect me?'

'I didn't particularly, at first. But one files away certain facts as one proceeds. The killer had to have a supply of arsenic, though it need not have been acquired recently, since it keeps a long time without noticeable deterioration. So anyone might have taken the opportunity over the years. But you were the likeliest source, in view of the locum work you have done quite recently in pharmacies.'

She said, 'Dad would never let me train properly. He didn't believe in higher education for girls – David could waste as much time and money as he wanted, but not me. Well, I learned enough to kill him in the end.' She gave a small, horrid giggle of satisfaction at the neatness of the retribution.

Her face shone, almost luminous in the firelight. The lines and the years seemed to be dropping away now. Straight-backed and without care, she glowed with an impenetrable, old-master serenity, transcending the squalid values of the world she saw around her.

Lambert saw this effect, and pressed hastily on, 'You had better access to the victim in the crucial period than anyone else except Margaret Lewis, whom you more or less excluded by your clumsy attempt to implicate her with the cold cream jar. You were the one who fed your father each time Mrs Lewis had her weekly day off, which gave you the ideal opportunity.'

She nodded slowly, like one accepting a satisfactory solution to an intellectual puzzle. She stared again into the fire, as if that detached her from the reality of her situation in the quiet room. Outside, the snowman was having his head lifted carefully into position; the mongrel dog barked excitedly around the base, tail wagging furiously. She said, 'I thought for a year that I had succeeded. I had to improvise when you dug him up.' She was as brutal and direct with the phrase as a child. 'The cold cream jar was the obvious thing for Margaret Lewis. I put the hypodermic syringe in for that smug bastard Walter Miller, who did nothing about his wife when she wronged

Mum all those years ago with Dad.' So she had found out about that, though she could have been only a small child at the time: the catalogue of hate against the father everyone had thought she cherished had been building all the time.

Lambert, anxious to keep her talking, to wrap up the whole of this nightmare in one session, said, 'Sergeant Hook talked to the Reverend Allcock while I was in hospital.'

'Randy Roger we used to call him, in the old days at the tennis club.' Her voice was harsh, her giggle edged with hysteria. 'Backs to the walls and hands on ha'pennies, girls!' She held her hands aloft as she chanted the mock-slogan. Then, with the abrupt change of mood characteristic of her condition, she said, 'And what did he have to tell you about me?'

Hook was glad she ignored him and addressed her question to Lambert: he would not have trusted himself to give any coherent explanation. The Superintendent said, 'We talked to him about the funeral arrangements you made for your father.'

She smiled a smile of superior wisdom at the fire. '"Interment at Oldfield Parish Church at three p.m. No flowers, by request; donations to The British Heart Foundation." Nice touch, I thought.'

'I suppose you did. But I thought your father might have favoured a cremation,

343

especially in view of his feelings against the Roman Catholic Church. I'm well aware that Rome has now sanctioned cremation, but the overwhelming majority of Catholics are still buried rather than cremated, especially those of your father's generation. So I checked out the details of the funeral arrangements made for your late father. Walter Miller told me that you made all the arguments for the funeral. Then I found that all the arguments for a burial came from you, though you convinced other people that it was your father's wish.'

'"Daddy always wanted a burial. He was a great traditionalist."' She mimed a young girl's naïvety; the impersonation sat horribly upon her. 'That's what I told them, and they believed easily enough. It meant I only needed one doctor's signature for the death certificate. That was easy enough from old Dr Carroll. A cremation would have destroyed the evidence for ever, but it would have meant a confirmation of the cause of death from a second doctor, and I couldn't risk that. I had to insist quite strongly on the interment at the time, but memories blur easily, I find. I've almost convinced most people by now that it was David who insisted on a burial rather than a cremation.' She smiled her contentment at her cleverness; perhaps she had already forgotten her situation.

'Yes. Why did you go to so much trouble to implicate David in the last few days?'

The grey-green eyes flashed a sudden wild look at Lambert, as though she would at any moment spring at him. The effect was the more terrifying after her previous detachment. But her hatred was not of him, but of the brother he had brought relentlessly before her consciousness. 'David deserved all he got. Dad forgave everything he did, over thirty years and more. Whatever scrapes he got into, he was forgiven. He didn't give a damn about Dad or his wishes – he was even going to allow Tall Timbers to be pulled down. It was easy enough for me to convince David that the will change he never saw was designed to cut out him, not me. I told him you had indicated to me that he was your chief suspect, and he swallowed it all; I'd protected him for so many years from the worst of his silliness that he thought I was trying to help him now. He was never very bright.' She smiled into the fire at the thought, looking like a priggish schoolgirl asserting her superiority to a lumpish older brother.

Bert Hook might not have been in the room for what attention she had given him. He said now, 'Why did you try to kill Superintendent Lambert?'

Still she did not look at him. For a moment he thought she was going to ignore

345

his question completely, for she gazed at the family photographs to the right of the fire as though she had not even heard him. Then she said, 'He was the only one who was getting near to me. I heard from Margaret Lewis that he hadn't swallowed the evidence I planted in the house. And I knew David was going to run for it. I'd already told him before you even saw me that I'd worked out who'd killed Dad. I began to let him see that I thought it was him. I planted the idea in his head that he was about to be arrested after you'd seen him that morning with Andrew Lewis. It was easy enough to get him to go: he was always inclined to run away rather than face the consequences of anything.' She found her contempt for this pusillanimity in her brother very satisfying, as though it complemented all that had gone before and gave a convincing logic to her actions.

Lambert said quietly, 'You have a very strange idea of the way the CID operates. It would only have been a matter of time before you were arrested, even if you'd killed me.' Hook, head bent over his notebook, wondered if it would really have been as straightforward as that.

She stood up and walked across the room to open the window; they felt the sudden blast of air into the warm room like a cold douche of reality upon the unreal scene within it. She called to the children outside, 'That looks good. Tie a knot in the scarf round his neck, and put that old trilby on the side of his head.' For that moment, she was no more and no less than an affectionate mother, admiring and encouraging the efforts of her children.

Then she turned back to the two men and said, 'I took the statue of Aphrodite from David's office when I went to see him on the day before he fled. Didn't you find it at Tall Timbers?' She sounded as though she were inquiring about a lost handbag.

Lambert said, 'It was found all right, as you intended. Too easily found, like the other things you planted. If your brother had really used a weapon which could be traced so directly to him, he would hardly have disposed of it in the grounds of the very house where the assault took place.'

She looked at him with her head a little on one side for a moment, then nodded slowly, as if accepting his argument about some trivial conversational point. In the silent house, so much less solid than the one where she had murdered, they heard the Yale key turning in the lock of the front door quite clearly. At a nod from Lambert, Bert Hook went into the hall to intercept the husband they had never seen.

Lambert glanced automatically at the striking portrait of the murderess which dominated this room from its position over the fireplace. Perhaps Michael Harrison had suspected that his wife had done all this; perhaps he had even known it. For there was no noise of raised voices from the mean hall beyond the lounge door. Lambert kept his eyes carefully upon his captive through the muffled exchanges, but she had gone back to staring unblinkingly into the fire.

She said just one more thing as they prepared to take her away. 'Will Michael and the children lose the money now?'

Lambert and Hook exchanged startled glances. The Superintendent said, 'We're not lawyers, Mrs Harrison. If your brother chooses to leave things as they are, I think it likely your family might keep the money.' She nodded contentedly, as if that resolved her last concern in the world she was leaving. He did not want a violent scene in front of these young children; he wondered if that consideration had persuaded him to go further than he should have done.

They left Michael Harrison with a child on each side of him at the gate, a small hand held tightly in each of his larger ones. Angela gave them a smile and a brief wave, as if she were trying not to make too much of a weekend's absence. Lambert, sitting beside her in the back of the Orion, felt his head throbbing painfully as exhaustion approached. It did not make the tableau they had left in the snow-covered cul-de-sac any less painful.

That image remained imprinted upon his mind even after they had delivered his murderer to the cells. He let it stay there until he was delivered home and put to bed by a relieved Christine. It was better than the image of the Broadmoor room where Angela Harrison would spend the rest of her life.

The publishers hope that this book has given you enjoyable reading. Large Print Books are especially designed to be as easy to see and hold as possible. If you wish a complete list of our books please ask at your local library or write directly to:

Magna Large Print Books
Magna House, Long Preston,
Skipton, North Yorkshire.
BD23 4ND

This Large Print Book, for people
who cannot read normal print,
is published under the auspices of

THE ULVERSCROFT FOUNDATION